CRIMINAL INTENTIONS

SEASON ONE, EPISODE ONE

"THE CARDIGANS"

COLE MCCADE

[TABLE OF CONTENTS]

[CONTENT WARNING]

CONSIDERING THAT *CRIMINAL INTENTIONS* IS serialized in the form of episodic novels akin to a television series, I think it's safe to rate this using U.S. FCC television standards and mark it TV-MA. *Criminal Intentions* follows multiple homicide investigations and, at times, can graphically depict the act or aftermath of attempted or successful murder.

While it's a given that a series about homicide investigations will describe actual homicides, it may be wise to review content warnings regarding the specifics of cases depicted in each episode.

Content warnings for Season 1, Episode 1, "The Cardigans," include:

- Death by strangulation.
- Dismemberment.
- Grave desecration.
- Desecration of dead bodies.
- Blood, gore, and graphic depiction of post-mortem decay.
- Deaths of queer characters.

- Threats against other queer characters.
- Discussion of untreated mental illness.
- Obsessive thoughts and fixations.
- Use of the slur "fag hag."
- Alcohol consumption.
- Use of firearms.

Content warnings for the afterword include:
- Violent child abuse.
- Gaslighting.
- Discussion of cults.

Please read at your discretion, and make whatever decisions are best for you regarding content that may or may not be safe for you.

Take care of yourselves, loves.

–C

[READING NOTE]

THE CHARACTER SADE MARCUS USES the pronouns they/them/their as their preferred gender-neutral pronouns for a genderqueer and two-spirit person from the Lumbee nation.

[0: ANATOMY OF A CRIME SCENE]

DARIAN PARK DOESN'T YET KNOW he's dead.

He's high on the taste of sugar-candy lips, drunk on the thrill of body to body. His blood runs the color of flickering lights, glitter-hot in his veins, and when the music pounds through him he's a heartbeat in motion, twisting through the tangle of writhing flesh stretched from wall to wall in the packed club. Hands try to grasp him, draw him close, possess him, but he flirts and slides just out of reach.

He isn't for these men. He isn't for anyone.

Darian is wild, and after the shittiest breakup of his life he's not ready to let another man tie him down.

He's drugged on the power of his own body by the time the hot sweet burn of three strawberry sangria shots, downed all in a row, evaporates off his tongue and fizzles in his veins. He's sparks lit to gasoline, ready to make bad decisions—and though he tells himself to walk away before one of those bad decisions has a voice and a name and the touch of rough-knuckled hands over Darian's skin, he already knows the empty ache in the pit of his stomach won't let him leave all by himself.

He's fireworks shooting into the sky, and he doesn't want to burst alone.

One cigarette, he thinks. One cigarette to clear his head; then he'll decide. Eenie-meenie-mini-mo, this little piggy, that little piggy, one, two, *I choose you.* Someone's waiting to go home with him tonight, but first he needs to shake his buzz.

He steps out the side exit near the bar, escaping from the groin-deep pulse of bass into the quieter sounds of stop-and-start traffic. The alley smells like rain on pavement and the shades of smokers past, their haunts in the butts piled against the club's brick wall. He lights up, takes that deep drag of fire flowing fierce and warm down into his throat, and contemplates the memory of a man with close-cropped hair and deep hazel eyes who, as Darian flirted just out of his reach, had briefly let out a sweet and thrilling growl that licked its tongue down Darian's back to knot in the hollow of his spine.

Him, Darian decides, and taps the ash from his cigarette. Embers flicker, fall, die before they strike the pavement.

And a stinging band of pain snaps around his neck, cutting a line of scraping acid into his flesh.

He doesn't feel the cigarette falling from his fingers. The cigarette is already a moment past, gone, forgotten. All other moments have fled—everything before, everything after.

There is only now, the struggle to breathe, the ripping tumble of his heart, the confusion of his pulse. The way the street lights blur into watercolor streaks, melting across his vision. The sensation of something cold and slick beneath his grasping fingers, pressed too tight against his neck to pry free. It's squeezing, crushing, and every breath is a knot.

He's strangely aware that the choking cord wrapped around his neck grows warmer with every passing second, absorbing the heat of his body, stealing it away as if stealing his life.

He can smell someone, the musk of their body rushing in on each inhalation.

Everything is slow, so slow.

His thoughts.

His pulse.

His heart, fading away until it's as muted as the club's ongoing bass thrombosis filtered through insulating brick walls.

He is brick, heavy.

He wants to struggle, but can't. His limbs are wood, his feet anchored by their own weight.

It's quick, so quick.

He's dying, just like that. He knows the taste of his own fear, and it's yellow and vaguely sour and curdles the last remnants of strawberries left on his tongue.

And then he's gone.

His cigarette, forgotten, lies in a puddle, its cherry glow gone dark, its paper soaking up the last of the Baltimore evening rain.

[1: A NAMELESS MAN]

MALCOLM KHALAJI LICKED THE TASTE of sweat from taut, pale skin, gathering the salt of maleness on his tongue, languishing in that particular scent, flavor, ineffable *something* that came at just that perfect moment of satiation when the body beneath him went limp—and there was only the mingled rush of shared, gasping breaths and the heat of flesh slowly relaxing around the ache of his cock.

The lean, pretty young man beneath him laughed huskily, quiet vibratos shaking them both. His death-grip on Malcolm's shoulders peeled away, relieving crescent moons of stinging pain one at a time. The man tossed his head back against Malcolm's pillows, nestled against a damp tangle of hair. His smile was sly, his lips swollen and pink and kiss-bitten.

"Do you want to know my name *now?*" he asked, and Malcolm chuckled, sinking down against him, brushing his lips to the pointed peak of his chin.

"I might be vaguely interested." But he groaned as his phone rang on the nightstand, its trill demanding and sharp. "Though not right now."

"Who's calling you at three AM?"

"Work," Malcolm answered, then gripped the man's hips and separated their bodies with a hiss for sensitized flesh and the drag of friction. He fell against the headboard, caught up his phone, and swiped the call. "Khalaji."

"Got a body," Captain Zarate y Salazar clipped off, exhaustion ragging the edges of her voice like ripped paper. "Central District. Six hundred block of West Lexington."

Malcolm closed his eyes, rubbing his temples. "Now?"

"It's not another last call loss. I need you on scene."

"I'll be there."

He let the call drop and rolled out of bed, reaching for his pants. The nameless man sprawled against the brushed wrought bronzework of Malcolm's headboard, a sylph with a fringe of fanning lashes so light they shone nearly white, shadowing eyes a pale and laughing shade of green. Those eyes laughed at Malcolm even now, as they tracked him through dragging on his slacks and shrugging into a button-down.

"What kind of job calls you out at this time of night?"

"Homicide." Malcolm pulled his shoulder holster from its place of honor hanging from the bed post, and slid his arm into the strap. "Lock the door when you leave."

He caught up his coat and slung it on, striding for the door. The nameless man's voice drifted after him, lilting, mocking.

"You trust me alone in your flat?"

"What are you going to do?" Malcolm tossed over his shoulder. "Steal from a cop?"

The nameless man's laughter trailed him into the night, as Malcolm let his apartment door close and vaulted the stairs two at a time to the streets that waited, every night, to deliver another cold corpse in a body bag.

Another cold corpse, and a case that might never be solved if he didn't find a break within the first forty-eight.

He carried too many of those cases inside him. Too many dead ends, too many losses.

Not that a win could bring the dead back to life.

Malcolm didn't have that power, and he'd given up on saving lives long ago.

By the time he got to them now, it was already too late.

[2: A STREET CORNER IN MONOCHROME]

BY THE TIME MALCOLM ARRIVED on-scene, Captain Zarate was already stepping out of her unmarked car, the sleek black Audi throwing back the flashing red and blue of the uniformed units' bars. Malcolm slung his Camaro into a curbside slot with his bumper almost kissing her tail lights, took a moment to sweep his hair back into a messy bun and snap an elastic over it, then slid out of the car.

The night smelled like stale Jell-O shots, gasoline, and blood steaming in the lingering smolder of an autumn evening—where September chill had settled in the night air, but the pavement was unwilling to let go of the boiling heat it had absorbed throughout the day. Every crime scene had its own scent, but at the heart of each was the scent of blood. Even the ones who died without a single wound, stiff in their beds of cardiac arrest or necks purpled with the sawing marks of rope and fingers or bloated with the strange sick colors of poison…

Somehow they still smelled of that cloyingly sharp, strangely electric scent of blood.

Maybe what Malcolm called the scent of blood was really just the scent of death.

Zarate lingered by her car, her hands on her spare, angular hips, lines of exhaustion creasing beneath dark brown eyes. Even at this time of night she was sharp in flared slacks, a severely buttoned shirt, and a stylish suit coat; Malcolm had never seen her *not* perfectly on point and ready to present the picture of confident authority, even at three in the morning.

She took a few restless steps, running her fingers through her short crop of black hair. He quickened his stride and fell in at her side. Together they approached the mouth of the alley to one side of Baltimore's more prominent gay clubs. A significant cross-section of Baltimore's queer community milled in upset tangles near the club entrance, including a number of U of M College Queers™—all corralled by harried-looking officers whose raised voices tried to separate patrons from staff.

Several uniforms clustered at the very threshold of the alleyway like vampires afraid to cross onto hallowed ground, leaning in. One turned away, covering his mouth as he made heaving sounds into his palm. Malcolm arched a brow, then glanced at Zarate.

"I wasn't expecting you to be here," he said.

"This is a bit of a special case."

"Why?"

Her wide, starkly bony shoulders jerked in something that wasn't quite a shrug. She said nothing until they reached the cluster of officers, who parted before them, nearly skittering out of the way.

A body lay in the alleyway, sprawled half on the street, half slumped against the wall: a fairly well-built young man, his neck striated with angry red lines, brown hair flopping across his waxy face in a disarrayed mess. Not someone easily overpowered, Malcolm thought, already cataloguing the crime scene. He had that club queer body, hard-honed. Powerful sinew bunched in corded forearms, straining against a tight t-shirt in pale blue spattered with collateral spray in dark spots dried, by now, to near black. And he likely would have been tall.

If he still had his legs.

Rather than ragged, sawed-off stumps protruding from the shreds of his blood-soaked jeans.

Malcolm tilted his head. That was new. Sickening. Interesting. More interesting than the fact that someone must have caught him off-guard, to overpower him.

Even more interesting, though, was the man crouched over the body, hovering like a crow with the black wings of his long coat folded around him. He was tall and lean and square of shoulder, with a shag of black hair falling across a face made entirely of angles positioned in sharp opposition until he was a razor of pale golden skin. His full, sullen mouth stood out against his skin like a bruise, and that mouth tightened as he carefully lifted a red-drenched shred of denim in latex-gloved fingers, examining it closely through narrowed, slyly angled eyes.

"Him," Zarate said.

Malcolm frowned. "He's not forensics. Fed?"

"No." Zarate heaved a heavy sigh. "Transfer from LAPD. Just processed his papers yesterday."

Suspicion prickled on the back of Malcolm's neck. "What are you not telling me?"

"You're working with him on this case."

"No."

It came out before he could stop it, quick enough to more than earn the flat, expectant look Zarate fixed on him. He sighed and pinched the bridge of his nose.

"Why."

"He wanted this case," she answered. "Said it's personal."

"Personal how?"

Again that angular jerk of her shoulders. That was Zarate, all sticks bound together with steel bolts and razor wire, her movements full of kinetic tension and bristling with potential energy barely caged in the thin shell of brown skin.

"Gay kid gets murdered, gay cop takes interest," she said tersely.

Malcolm let his gaze drift back to the dark-haired man, then to the empty face of the victim. Malcolm had been young like that once—young and drunk on his own strength and raw vitality, chasing sex and some facsimile of love in dark smoky rooms, kisses that bristled with the raw burn of stubble and the taste of deep heady bourbon, clasping hands and sighs that came out like a secret.

He could see himself in the corpse's blank eyes, and it made his stomach sink.

"Yeah. I get that," he murmured. "I do." He sighed. "So it's a short-term thing for this case."

Zarate's mouth did an odd, twisty thing. She avoided his eyes. "…mnh."

"*Anjulie.*"

"We'll talk. Focus on the case. Fix it." She pinned him with a hard look. "Before any more dead gay kids show up."

He ground his teeth. But an order was an order, and Zarate had enough on her shoulders. She didn't need him throwing a tantrum about working with a partner, even if he had his doubts already. The new guy looked so *young,* so stiff. And like he was a stickler for procedure.

Malcolm wasn't particularly fond of procedure.

He eyed Zarate. "Did you show up just to make sure I'd behave?" When she said nothing, he tilted his head back, closing his eyes. "You could have told me over the phone."

"If I'd told you over the phone, you might have refused to come."

He opened his eyes and flung her a foul look. "I'm not that bad."

"Keep telling yourself that." Zarate turned away, her long, swinging strides taking her back toward her car. "I'm heading into the office early. Since I'm up, I'm up. Be good."

"When am I ever not?"

She only snorted—then paused, glancing over her shoulder. "Oh, and Malcolm?"

"Yes?"

"He outranks you. Be nice."

And while he stared, dismayed, she smirked and strutted merrily away, lifting a hand to throw a wave over her shoulder. Malcolm exhaled heavily.

For fuck's *sake*.

But there was a dead kid in the alleyway, and new guy or not it was Malcolm's job to do something about it. That kid probably had a family. Friends. *Someone* who loved him.

Malcolm never made promises to catch the one who'd taken that light out of someone's life. Not when it was too easy for people to get away, cases growing colder and colder after the first forty-eight hours.

But that didn't mean he wouldn't try.

He crossed the threshold into the alley and circled the pool of blood making a corona around the stumps of the vic's legs. Still wet, wet enough to throw back colored shimmers from the rainbow lights strobing the front of the club and spilling into the alley. He doubted the body was over an hour old.

He sank into a crouch across from the new guy. The other man glanced up, his body tensing, his expression sharp and waiting. Malcolm flipped his badge from inside his coat, held it up long enough for the man to see, then diverted his attention to the body. Up close the ligature marks on the neck were even more obvious—narrow, overlapping lines in sawed-in bands that broke the skin in multiple places, abraded raw to let blood seep out, smear, and coagulate. Malcolm fished one of a half-dozen pairs of disposable clear vinyl gloves from his coat pocket and snapped them on, then pried the victim's right eyelids apart. Red capillaries nearly swallowed the white, burst and spreading to touch the edges of darkened blue irises. Typical conjunctivitis by strangulation.

He frowned and reached behind the body, fishing for his back pocket delicately, careful not to dislodge the position of the corpse's limbs. Gingerly he slid two fingers in until he found the victim's wallet, eased it—and barely caught a phone before it fell out with the wallet, angling it into his palm with the wallet still held between two fingers. He swiped the phone screen, but it was passcode-locked; the only notification on the lock screen was a text preview from *The Moms* asking *r u planning 2 come home for Thksgvng?*

He slid the phone gingerly back into the victim's back pocket, then flipped the wallet open. Those vacant blue eyes grinned up at him, now bright with arrogance above a cheesy, cocky smile. Darian Park. Twenty-one. God, barely even old enough to be in this damned bar. A University of Maryland student ID card was tucked in behind his license. A wad of twenties sat untouched in the billfold section, a Chase Bank debit card in the card holder.

Death by strangulation, removal of the limbs for either

fetishistic or vengeful reasons, no financial motivation, no attempt to conceal the identity of the victim.

Fuck. This was going to be a hard one.

The new guy hadn't said a word, only continuing to study the body fixedly while Malcolm studied him. Pretty, but in a sort of vicious, foxlike way. No—not foxlike. He reminded Malcolm more of a feral cat that condescended to tolerate a human presence, but the moment that human came too close he'd be off with a hiss and a flick of his tail. Something about the tension of him, the intensity of his focus, the set of his jaw…

Yeah. He was going to be a hard one, too.

Malcolm propped his elbows on his knees, the victim's wallet dangling from his fingertips. "What's your take?"

The other man didn't answer, at first. He leaned in, hovering over the body, and caught the victim's jaw in gloved fingertips, carefully tipping his head to one side to get a closer view at the neck.

Then, "This was planned," he murmured. He had a voice like silk and cigarette smoke, smooth and dark with a certain husky raw edge underscored by a faint, fluid hint of an accent Malcolm couldn't quite place. "They came with tools to do this. Prepared in advance." He flicked a sharp gaze at Malcolm, eyes so black they blended with the thick fan of his lashes, before looking back to the ligature marks on the victim's throat. "Abrasions indicate steel wire used as a garrote, from the spiral pattern." He released the victim's jaw and plucked at the shredded, bloody edges of his jeans, peeling them back to expose the raw stumps. "I would gather, from the ragged edges, that the lower legs were removed with a hacksaw."

Malcolm eyed the grisly, chewed-up mess of the victim's legs. Blood had crusted and coagulated in black, gelatinous clumps, clinging to muscle and fatty tissue so shredded it looked like pulled pork. He could hardly see the sawed-off ends of the femurs past the mangled tissue, but when he leaned in close he observed what looked like flat-sawed ends demonstrating subtle ridging, grooves that might come from a saw.

"Sawtooth marks," he said, then tilted his head as something caught his eye past the smears of blood on the unbroken skin above the cuts. He squinted. Pale sky blue was visible just above where the legs cut off, fragments that looked like they'd been drawn on the skin with marker only to be half-sawn through. "Marker. The perp marked before cutting."

"Likely measuring. Based on the proportions of the remains, the cuts were made precisely six inches above the kneecap."

"Risky behavior, doing this in an alley easily visible from the street."

The other man's gaze flicked over the corpse, before he stripped one glove off with a snap of latex and pulled the sleeve of his coat back to bare his wristwatch. "I will need confirmation from forensics, but I would estimate time of death between an hour and an hour and a half ago based on coagulation. The range for time of death would either raise or minimize risk, depending on if the forensic examiner determines it was before or after last call."

"That gives the perp a narrow safe window. So we have either an opportunist or a risk-taker."

"Or both."

Malcolm lingered on the other man. Cool and calm even when looking at a legless, mutilated body. Focused. Precisely spoken, every word measured with thought and intent behind it. Either he had more experience than that smooth, unlined face indicated, or he was prone to detachment. Detachment had its own problems, but at least Malcolm wouldn't have to deal with someone soft, untested, breaking down at the sight of some of the gruesome things perps did to dead bodies on these streets.

It was hard enough for Malcolm to look at them, sometimes.

He didn't think he had it in him to coddle someone else.

Especially not someone who looked as young as this one did. He had to be early thirties at the latest, at least ten years Malcolm's junior.

He frowned, flipping the wallet open again and rifling through. "Both would indicate the victim was selected specifically, rather than the easiest available target."

"Which would lead one to believe the perpetrator was

someone who knew his habits well enough to know he would be here near last call, and would step out for a cigarette." That red blossom of a mouth settled into a frown. "Wallet, cards, and money untouched. He is still wearing an expensive bracelet. He was the motivator, not his belongings."

"So we're looking at a premeditated murder with a specific target."

"It is a possibility."

"Other possibilities?"

The man made a rough sound in the back of his throat. "Have you recently dealt with any other murders of gay or bisexual young men involving missing body parts?"

Malcolm tilted his head back, flicking through the last few months of cases, flashing crime scene photos through his mind's eye. "Yes, gay or bisexual men. Four of them. No missing body parts. They were classed as hate crimes or crimes of passion. Two, accidents."

"Where any others garroted?"

"One. Another college student, if I'm remembering the right case."

The man stood, unfolding himself and dusting off the black jeans clinging to long legs. He snapped his other glove off and bundled it with the first, then slipped both into his coat pockets along with both hands. "I would like to see the case file."

Malcolm stood as well, looking at the other man—and looking up. He blinked. That...didn't happen often. At six foot one he outstripped average height, but the new guy had a couple of inches on him.

The man was watching him, waiting expectantly. Malcolm fought back a grimace. Behave, he told himself. "I'd like to know your name."

"Yoon," he answered after an almost calculated moment of consideration.

Malcolm fished in his pocket for one of his rolling stock of evidence bags, slotted the victim's wallet in, and tucked it into his coat before peeling his own gloves off and offering his hand. "Khalaji."

Black eyes flicked down to his hand, then back up to his face. Yoon's hands remained firmly in his coat pockets. "The case file?"

Malcolm closed his eyes and breathed in deep.

Be. Nice.

"At the office," he said, letting his hand fall and retreating a step, opening his eyes again. "I want to spend a little time with the crime scene, first."

He took a few more strides back, letting himself get a wider view from deeper in the alley. Yoon obligingly stepped aside, leaving Malcolm's line of sight clear. He let his gaze unfocus, just taking in the full picture, letting it solidify before he scanned for details.

Cigarette butt in a puddle from early evening rainfall. Probably the vic's, from the position of the fall and proximity to the body. Barely burned down at all, not scuffed or stubbed.

Mental note to have forensics bag it for DNA swabbing. Dumpster off-kilter, angle indicating movement by force. Darian Park had kicked it, Malcolm thought. There'd been no one in front of him, so when he'd kicked out, when he'd struggled, he'd hit the dumpster. There were two, small ones to either side of the rear exit door. The other was unmoved.

The door itself was metal, once painted, now rusted down to peeling, jagged flakes, the topmost layer so corroded it curled back in dangerously sharp edges that could easily cut. Dark stains on those edges. Could be current or old bloodstains. Another check for forensics. Possibility of perp's blood, if they'd come up behind the vic only to be slammed back against the door as Darian struggled.

And brightly-colored scraps of thread, caught on those jagged metal edges.

"What do you see?" Yoon asked.

"He didn't feel like he was in danger," Malcolm answered, finally letting his gaze circle back to the body. "He had no reason to. Either he knew the person who killed him, or he didn't even see it coming. There's not a single other offensive mark on the body." He circled the corpse, drifting closer to Yoon. "Either they were strong enough to overpower him, or small enough that they had to use guile over strength. And there's this." He stopped next to Yoon—and next to the club's rear exit. "Look."

Yoon leaned in, peering at the threads—pastel blue, soaked in mottled reddish-black. "Not the victim's. His shirt is not torn."

"Could be a lead. What do *you* see?"

Yoon paused, his brows knitting, lips parting. He hesitated long moments, then said, "This feels…intimate. There was no hate here." He sank down into a crouch once more, the crow descending, gaze locked on the victim's legs. "I do not believe the legs were a trophy, but the killer wanted them for a reason. This is messy, but there is an aspect of…" He shook his head. "…care. That is the only word I can think of. They were careful, even if hasty."

Hm. Malcolm rubbed his fingers over his beard, tugging at the strands. "You think there's a serial sexual component to it?"

"I am not certain yet."

"We need to figure out before someone else crops up missing an arm or a leg."

Yoon flicked a cutting glance over his shoulder. "We?"

"I'm the ranking detective in the BPD homicide unit." Malcolm inclined his head. "Well. Was. But the Captain thinks we need to work together on this. I mostly work Central, but go wherever the Captain sends me. Apparently where she sent me, tonight, is with you."

Yoon studied him with a long, impenetrable look—his gaze completely unreadable, expression that closed, wary withdrawal that made Malcolm think so much of a feral cat. He wasn't sure if Yoon was assessing how best to eviscerate him, or calculating an escape route.

But in the end all Yoon did was nod, turning away with a brief, dispassionate, "Ah."

Malcolm lingered on the tight line of Yoon's shoulders as the other man moved to the mouth of the alleyway and stood, quietly looking out. He was a single captured moment, a stillness amidst the chaos and noise, a dark ghost in the world of the living. Monochrome in his paleness and dark clothing, standing poised as if the crow would take flight—or the spirit would fade away, as dead as the boy lying blank and empty on the pavement. Haunting, Malcolm thought.

No, he corrected as Yoon turned his head, gaze fixed somewhere across the street, the colored lights reflecting off the stark lines of his cheekbones, his jaw.

Haunt*ed*.

Fuck. He shouldn't be trying to figure out his cipher of a new partner when he had a case to work. He needed coffee, focus, and a lead.

The flash of a camera warned him forensics was here, and doing their thing. They'd want him out of the way. He followed Yoon to the mouth of the alley, but stopped as one of the forensic photographers—a short, bubbly blond woman he'd worked with before, Stenson, crack shot at crime scene analysis—edged past Yoon with her camera pressed to her eye. He leaned over, lightly touching her shoulder.

"Bloodied material fibers on the door. Cigarette in the puddle. If you could tag and bag and send them for priority analysis…"

"You're lucky you're pretty enough to ask me for favors, Mal." She snorted and nudged him with her elbow. "Get out of my crime scene."

"Sweet talker. Don't forget to get the phone to Sade. Back left pocket."

He pulled away and caught up with Yoon, and took a moment to just…breathe. Standing at the other man's side, he let himself *breathe*, looking up at a sky turned the flat matte black of night's darkest hour.

"This is more than a simple hate crime," Malcolm murmured. "But I'm not quite clear on what it is, either. Let's leave forensics to do their work. You wanted that case file." He glanced toward Yoon. "Did you drive?"

"Cab," Yoon answered tersely.

Malcolm tossed his head toward his Camaro. "We can take my car. Come on."

"We have yet to interview the owner or the staff."

They won't give us anything useful, Malcolm almost said. *They never do. Not when they're this rattled and confused. They're high on adrenaline, emotion, fear. They're afraid the person standing next to them might be the sick fuck who garroted a boy in a back alley, then sawed his legs off. Their memories are clouded and won't settle until morning.*

He'd rather let the uniforms take names and numbers, and follow up later.

The killer wasn't in that crowd. They'd run off with the legs. No way they'd have had time to stash the body parts and make their way back. Witness interviews right now were a waste of time.

But Yoon was still watching him. That same expectant look, that same coolly assessing stare. Malcolm had been right.

Stickler for the rules.

He sighed, then forced a smile. His mouth didn't want to move, but he felt a faint twitch. "All right. I'll take the owner if you take the bouncers. We can split the wait staff." Yoon started to open his mouth, but Malcolm held up a hand to stop him. "It's faster if we split it up."

Yoon's eyes narrowed, before he nodded. "As you say," he said, and brushed past Malcolm. Malcolm stared at his back, at the way he moved like crossed blades in motion.

God, he hoped he solved this case fast.

[3: A BRIDGE IN MADAGASCAR]

SEONG-JAE YOON WROTE DOWN ONE more name—Shane Johnson—and phone number, marked down *bartender, remembers serving rainbow vodka shooters to victim,* and starred the entry in his notebook. He would like to return to the bartender, he thought, and ask more about who had hovered around the bar when the victim had claimed his drinks. It was possible the victim had been drugged. Rohypnol in a very small amount might not have rendered the victim unconscious, but it would have left him sluggish, pliable, and quite easy to overpower.

But Seong-Jae would wait until the toxicology reports came back, before he pursued that avenue of thought.

He clipped his pen into the spiral binding of his notebook and lifted his head, searching for Khalaji. What an…*odd* man, Seong-Jae thought, as he watched Khalaji speak with a slim young man in the uniform t-shirts of the club staff. Khalaji carried himself like an old and battle-torn wolf, grave and fierce and solemn, the last one left of his pack and yet determined to defend his territory to the death, even when he could barely stand. His crisp, neat slacks, button-down, tie, and suit coat didn't match the impression he gave off; the wolf in sheep's clothing, right down to the old trench of a scar starting high on his temple and snaking in a jagged line through one severe brow, skipping over his eye, picking up at the cragged line of his cheekbone to leave an indelible mark on tanned, rugged skin.

The exhaustion of the late night was clear in the shadows beneath his eyes, in the messy tangle of a sweep of darkened silver hair that still retained a few highlights of chestnut here and there, caught up in a tie, tendrils falling into his weathered face to mingle with his grizzled beard.

Yet exhausted or not, he'd assessed the crime scene with alert sharpness—though that sharpness softened, now, something protective and soothing in the way his body language changed while interviewing the witness. He'd been clearly irritated when Seong-Jae wanted to continue according to procedure, yet not a hint of that irritation showed as he spoke to the young man as if his safety was the most important thing in Khalaji's world.

Interesting.

He would likely get in the way of wrapping up this investigation, but he was interesting nonetheless.

Khalaji raised his head, catching Seong-Jae's eye, and lifted his chin in acknowledgment before leaning down to murmur something to the young man. Khalaji squeezed his shoulder, the young man nodded, and Khalaji pulled away. As he approached Seong-Jae, he tucked a battered, chapbooksized leather-bound journal into the inside pocket of his suit coat.

"That's the last of them," he said as he drew closer. "Forensics is wrapping everything up, and they're covering the body until they can take more photos in daylight tomorrow. You ready to go?"

Seong-Jae nodded. "I am."

Khalaji looked at him strangely—as if Seong-Jae was some puzzle missing the pieces to make it into a coherent image. "You don't talk much, do you?"

"I talk when it is necessary."

"Yeah." Khalaji looked away, his dark, slate blue eyes hooded. He reached up to pull his hair loose; it came down in straggles that fell, wild, around his face and shoulders. He ran his fingers through it, gaze tracking over the crime scene, the officers escorting people to their cars, the forensics teams packing up. He looked as though he might say something, before he shook his head almost to himself and muttered, "Let's go."

He strode away, even if every stride was more of a prowling lope. Even if he was broad-shouldered and thick-set, he still had that look:

A lean and starving wolf, haggard, elegantly feral, with eyes edged by a sharp, cutting hunger.

Interesting indeed.

Seong-Jae tucked his notebook away and followed Khalaji to a sleek black car. The headlights flashed with the beep of the alarm deactivating, and Seong-Jae let himself into the passenger's seat. Khalaji slid in behind the wheel, put the car into reverse, and pulled out onto streets that were, at this time of night, nearly deserted—the only people left those straggling home from last call and one night stands, or just waking up to start the kind of morning shifts that kept cities such as Baltimore running.

Baltimore was strange, too, he thought. Los Angeles had been so *gray*, yet Baltimore—beneath the haze of street lamps in the darkest part of the night—was an odd, deeply liquid shade of gold.

Leaning his temple against the window, Seong-Jae let his eyes half-close and watched the streets slide past, buildings blending into each other with exhausting monotony broken at intervals by cross-streets as downtown faded toward Inner Harbor. He wasn't tired, though he should be; he'd not yet been to sleep by the time the call came. This was his first case with the BPD, and it looked like it would be an ugly one.

Something about the crime scene felt oddly familiar, yet he couldn't quite explain why. Not in a way that made sense. Not in a way he wanted to think about.

He was probably seeing things that weren't there.

Seeing old haunts. Old shades.

Old memories best left buried.

"LAPD?" Khalaji asked. His voice was soft, a quiet growl that blended into the rumble of the engine, touched with an Eastern accent different from the varying American

English dialects Seong-Jae was continuously surrounded by—and after nearly twenty minutes of silence, it was…jarring. As uncomfortable as an unwanted physical touch.

Seong-Jae lifted his head, glancing at him. "Yes."

One hand on the steering wheel, the other draped casually across his thigh, Khalaji kept his gaze on the road. "I've heard it's war there, day in, day out," he murmured. "Worse than Baltimore."

"I am aware," Seong-Jae said. "Do you have a question, or were you simply stating facts?"

A tell-tale jump in Khalaji's jaw, a muscle tightening and ticking, but his voice remained calm when he spoke. He had the thoughtful, slow-speaking way of someone kind who would claim he wasn't in the slightest. Someone soft.

Seong-Jae had little experience in dealing with softness, and he did not want to start now.

He should really stop psychologically profiling the people he worked with.

Nor did he want to answer, when Khalaji said, "I just want to know why here. Why Baltimore."

"Do I need a reason?"

"Most people need a reason for moving cross-country and transferring police departments, yes."

"Perhaps I am not most people."

Khalaji shot him a look, but said nothing else. Up ahead the tall, terraced, subtly curving façade of the Central District police headquarters cut against the night sky, its many and multifaceted windows reflecting back street lights and black squares of night. Seong-Jae was grateful that Khalaji held his silence, as he pulled the car into the parking garage and shut it off.

Seong-Jae didn't know his way here, not yet. So he had no choice but to let Khalaji take the lead, skipping the elevator to take the stairs up to one of the upper floors in a rattling of polished shoes against steps. They emerged into a bullpen that was a chaos of desks scattered at all angles, piled with folders and papers, whiteboards everywhere tacked with photos and scribbled with notes. The entire room was dark, but light spilled from the far end where, beyond a glass wall, a single office was lit, the distant figure of Captain Zarate y Salazar bowed over her desk.

She didn't even glance up as they entered, only lifting a hand before returning to writing in sharp, aggressively dashing strokes. Khalaji led Seong-Jae to a desk tucked away from the others, back in a recessed corner that was practically a cramped cubby. The desk was more organized than the others, the folders stacked neatly. Compulsive? And the deliberate self-isolation—

Stop profiling.

He forced himself to focus, instead, on the stack of folders that Khalaji thumbed through, pushing several aside into a second stack and lifting a few more, flicking them open and peering inside, before settling on one and extracting it from the stack.

"Here," he said, thrusting the folder at Seong-Jae. Seong-Jae arched a brow, then took the folder and thumbed it open. Khalaji settled to sit with his hip propped against the edge of the desk, shoulders bunching and rolling as he shrugged out of his suit coat and tossed it across the desk, exposing shoulder holsters strapped with a pistol under either arm.

Seong-Jae watched him from under his lashes, under the pretense of glancing down at the folder. Willing to remove his coat to be comfortable in a presumably safe environment, but not his weapons.

"Stop," Khalaji said, leaning back on one hand.

Seong-Jae lifted his head. "Stop what?"

Khalaji snorted. "I've worked with the BPD for nearly fifteen years. Done a lot of inter-agency work. You're analyzing me. I know that look."

"I was not—"

"You were. You didn't start off LAPD. What was it? CIA? FBI? NSA?"

Slate blue eyes watched Seong-Jae unerringly. Seong-Jae narrowed his eyes, teeth clenching. "I was not analyzing you."

"Don't lie to me. This partnership won't work well if you do."

"This is not a partnership."

"No. It's really not, is it?"

Khalaji draped one hand across his thigh. There was a certain casual male arrogance in his posture, quiet but still *there*, and it set Seong-Jae's teeth on edge. With a deep exhalation, Khalaji looked away, sweeping his hair back from his face with one broad, square hand.

"A partnership would require us being partners," he said. "When I don't want to work with you. You don't want to work with me, either. That's not hard to figure out. But I've got a stake in this case, and so do you. So let's stop with the looks like snakebites and just do our best here. Zahré mār. Enough."

"What is your stake in this case?"

Khalaji's shoulders moved stiffly, but that one moment seemed to release tension to flood his entire body. After long moments he muttered, low and grudging, "…you're not the only one who gets mad over dead queer kids."

As oblique as the comment was, nonetheless it slid home a piece of the profile. Seong-Jae couldn't help flicking a glance over Khalaji. He didn't look the type, but then real people never did. Real people only looked like themselves, instead of their sexuality. "Ah. You are…?"

Darkened eyes shot back to him, pinned him as fiercely as gunsights. "Yeah. What about it?"

"I only wonder if that is why the Captain decided to pair us on this case."

"She paired us on this case because this is my walk, and you asked to be on it," Khalaji growled. "It's nothing to do with us both falling off the straight and narrow."

"Ah," Seong-Jae said, and lowered his gaze to the folder once more. "As you say."

"I say I'd like your thoughts on that case. I've stared at it too long. Maybe you'll see something I overlooked."

Seong-Jae held his tongue, and focused his attention on the documents in the folder. Crime scene and autopsy reports. He scanned the text and the coroner's diagram with minimal interest; words told him little other than a name. Trevor Manson. The photographs told him more, glossy eight-by-tens in that terrible, stark light so particular to forensic photography.

The young man in the photo bore a striking resemblance to tonight's crime scene: pale blue eyes, dark brown hair, tall with a firm build. His body was sprawled half on, half off a tumbled, disarrayed bed in a bedroom with sky-blue walls. He hadn't been dismembered, but his throat was purpled and raw with ligature marks.

"Clumsy," Seong-Jae murmured. "The person who did this had never strangled anyone to death before. They were not certain of how much pressure to it required, or how much time. There was a struggle. The perpetrator almost lost control of the victim." He scanned the disarray of the room, the books flung everywhere, desk toppled over, blankets spilled onto the floor. "How long ago was this?"

"About eight months. It's been filed as cold. The leads dried up after about two weeks on the case."

"The victims look rather similar."

"They do."

Seong-Jae pressed his lips together, just letting his

brain...*stop*, for a few moments. Clearing his mind of deliberate thought and simply letting the facts drift to see how they intersected and interlocked if he tried to force them down a specific path. Disordered reasoning, some might call it; others might call it intuition; he called it less than logical, but it had helped him work through difficult problems on many occasions. And as his thoughts drifted, one single word clicked into place:

"Practice."

Khalaji's head came up sharply. "...what?"

"If the crimes are linked, this one was practice. This was the perpetrator's first kill. He did not desire anything from this one. He only wanted to test out his methodology. Practice the kill, and make any necessary adjustments before he targeted tonight's victim."

"Which would feed into your theory that it's personal. That Darian Park was someone special to the perp."

"It is possible. It is also possible that I wish my theory to be correct, and so I am creating my own confirmation bias." Seong-Jae studied the close-up of the ligature marks on the victim's neck. The same kind of sawing marks, something spiral-patterned, though he thought, perhaps, nylon twist rope this time from the difference in size and texture of the abrasions. "You kept Park's wallet, did you not?"

"Yeah."

"May I see it?"

Leaning over, Khalaji snagged his coat and fished in the

pocket. "Glove up. No prints on the evidence."

Seong-Jae restrained his retort by the thinnest thread as he fished a fresh pair of gloves from his pocket. Pride simmered, a sharp response on his lips, a reminder that the shield Khalaji had flashed belonged to a Sergeant Detective and Seong-Jae outranked him as Lieutenant Detective—and he hadn't earned that promotion with rookie mistakes like mishandling evidence.

But he bit his tongue. He was new to Baltimore, and he would make plenty of enemies soon enough without starting on his very first case.

Nonetheless, the *snap* of the gloves against his wrists brought an odd pleasure, as if the tight latex was a choking band snapping around Khalaji's neck.

Khalaji offered the evidence bag with Park's wallet, dangling from two fingers. Seong-Jae reached for the bag, but when his fingers almost brushed Khalaji's, Khalaji jerked back. Seong-Jae froze.

"What?"

Khalaji eyed his hands. "Are those latex?"

"Yes."

"Latex allergy."

Seong-Jae stared at him flatly. He had heard that one before. Khalaji tilted his head—then let out a sudden rough, sharp bark of laughter that only cemented that image of a wolf: just one quick, hoarse, coughing snap of sound, edged in a growl and flashing sharp teeth.

"Get your fucking mind out of the gutter, Yoon. I'm serious. And I use sheepskin."

Seong-Jae scowled. "I do not need to know such things about your personal life."

"Then don't look at me like you were thinking exactly what I know you were thinking." With a smirk, Khalaji offered the evidence bag again. "Take it. Don't touch me, and consider using vinyl while we're working together."

Seong-Jae only sniffed and took the evidence bag, gripping it carefully from the bottom and tugging it free without making contact with Khalaji's skin.

Jot, he thought, but clamped his teeth together so hard they hurt—and spilled the wallet into his palm.

He flicked it open, flipping past the ID to check the billfold. Past the twenties were a number of receipts, crumpled to the point of wearing the ink away. He ignored the clearly illegible ones and tugged out a few that looked more recent. One for a gas station, but two for a local hot wings franchise. He smoothed those between his fingers, eyeing them, then paused, frowned, and squinted at the sums.

Zero, both times.

"Khalaji." He held out the receipts. Khalaji leaned over and peered at them, then made a soft clicking sound with his tongue.

"Employee discount. That's one place to start looking." Sliding off the desk with a sort of brutish grace, Khalaji picked up his coat, slung it over his arm, and tossed his head toward the door. "We'll start with the restaurant, then check out the university, see if we can find his friends or anyone who knew him. Bring the wallet and the other case file."

Seong-Jae stared after him. "It is…" He paused, checked his watch. "Four o'clock in the morning."

"And I need breakfast, and at least a half-gallon of coffee. You can come with or meet me at the restaurant, but I'm going to get breakfast either way."

Seong-Jae closed his eyes, prayed for patience, and slid the receipts back into the victim's wallet before replacing the wallet inside the evidence bag and tucking the bag into his pocket.

"Fine," he muttered, and knew without a doubt he would regret the words before sunrise. "I shall come."

"Yeah?" With another of those looks that said Khalaji was likely thinking something Seong-Jae would find distasteful, he shrugged his jacket on and strode toward the exit to the stairs. "Come on if you're coming, then."

Seong-Jae started to follow—then paused as he felt the prickle of someone *watching* him. He glanced over his shoulder.

Captain Zarate rested her chin in her hand, eyeing them both through her open office door, both brows arched, her expression so bland there was no doubt she was fighting not to laugh.

"Well, Detective Yoon?" she said. "Go on if you're going, then."

Seong-Jae curled his upper lip, but spared his Captain a tight nod before turning and stalking after Khalaji.

Not on this case more than two hours, and he already had a headache.

[4: UNDER NEON LIGHTS]

MALCOLM NEVER THOUGHT HE WOULD be annoyed by silence.

He drove them to Swabbie's, a dirty all-night pub a few blocks from the university. The bar stopped serving liquor at last call, but slung greasy pub burgers twenty-four seven. Yoon didn't say a word the entire time, and while Malcolm didn't exactly want to talk to the stiff-necked bastard, the brewing tension in the silence made the hairs prickle on the back of his neck and left him uncomfortable in his own damned car.

Maybe Yoon was taking his promotion a little too seriously. Malcolm had been like that, once. Back when he'd been young and so very serious about saving everyone, before the homicide beat had taught him that wasn't what his job was about at all.

At just after four in the morning on a Sunday, Swabbie's was nearly empty. The kids had stuffed themselves with greasy food after bar-hopping and gone back to their dorms to sleep it off, so the following morning they could pretend to be respectable humans budding into upright grown-up citizens instead of horny little balls of underdeveloped neurons.

The only late hangers-on were a few older men with that empty, deflated look of someone with nothing to go home to, nursing beers they'd ordered hours ago and sucking down their cancer sticks—and the college students who wouldn't last the year when it wasn't hard to tell they were high off their asses and giggling into their sodas and onion rings. The light in the dingy room was murky, falling over stained, pitted wood and dirty floors, half the tables still covered in empty foam cups and plates and paper trays.

The place smelled like a rotting deep fryer, but they made a damned good cup of coffee.

Malcolm pushed inside, keeping the door open in his wake for Yoon, but Yoon stopped on the threshold and wrinkled his nose.

"They are smoking," he said flatly, a subtle undercurrent of offense in his voice.

Malcolm bit back a smirk. "I know."

"*Indoors.*"

"And it's illegal. But we're not here as cops. We're here for the food. Let the beat cops bust them if they're gonna get busted. This isn't our walk." He shrugged. "Let it go, Yoon."

Yoon's upper lip curled. He made a soft sound under his breath, a sort of *tch*, before he tilted his head in a way that wasn't quite agreement and brushed past Malcolm without a second glance, heading for the bar.

He sat gingerly on a cracked barstool, as if afraid it would dirty his pretty black coat. Malcolm hauled himself up onto a stool next to him and raised his hand to George—the squat, blocky, stubbled bartender who always turned surly after last call rendered him down to slinging sodas and taking down orders for the cook. George gave him a sour look, chewing on a toothpick with thick lips, his greasy bald pate shining under the lights. Heaving a sigh, he trundled himself over.

"You want a menu, or you just gonna order?"

Malcolm chuckled. "I don't suppose you have a kosher menu."

George fixed him with a venomous stare. "Not for five bucks a plate I don't."

"I'll live."

"You say that every time." George rolled his eyes. "Coffee?"

"Black. You'll have to ask my friend what he wants. He'll need a menu, as well."

Yoon drew himself up stiffly. "Coffee will do. I assume you provide cream and sugar."

George flashed Malcolm an incredulously disgusted look, as if to say *are you fucking kidding me?* before turning that same look on Yoon. "I'll bring 'em if you ask for 'em." With a snort, he bent to fetch two laminated foldout menus from under the bar and slapped them down on the wood in front of them. "I'll be back in a minute with your fuckin' coffee."

From the way Yoon peeled his menu open with just his

fingertips, Malcolm was surprised he didn't glove up before opening it. But Malcolm kept his peace; he wasn't going to make things any easier between them by ragging on his new partner. So he let things be silent, and flipped his menu open for a perfunctory look even if he ordered the same thing every time.

So he wasn't expecting Yoon to break the silence, an undercurrent of sound so quiet it almost disappeared beneath the chatter of the stoners in the back corner and the sound system murmuring that somebody who wasn't Joan Jett might have a lackluster affair with rock n' roll, from that sad, atonal cover blatting out of the speakers.

"Kosher?" Yoon asked.

Malcolm glanced at him, but Yoon was looking at his menu, his face a mask of withdrawn indifference. Malcolm couldn't help but wonder if he was genuinely interested, or only asking to put up some pretense of politeness. For a half-second Malcolm weighed whether or not he'd even answer, but finally sighed and relented.

"Mizrahim," he said. "Non-practicing. If you ask half the east coast, not even really Jewish since my mother isn't. Only my father." He shrugged. "But you get raised in certain habits. They're hard to slip."

But all Yoon said was, "Ah."

And nothing else.

Malcolm didn't know why he'd even bothered answering.

"You religious, Yoon?" he asked.

"Not really, no."

"What's the popular thing in Korea?"

Yoon stilled in the middle of turning a page of the menu, just a moment's tell-tale twitch, before he resumed as smoothly as if he'd never stopped. Yet there was a chill edge to his voice when he answered—his already formal words enunciated on a knife's edge, precise. "I would not remember. My parents fled North Korea when I was fifteen."

"Oh." Malcolm closed his eyes, swearing under his breath. Fuck. Fucking hell, he was a prick. He'd just assumed—yeah, that was his fucking problem. He'd assumed. He raked his hair back, pushed down the growl rising in his throat, and forced himself to speak. "That was a dick question. I'm sorry."

"I do not require an apology," Yoon said stiffly.

"I'm making one anyway. You don't have to take it."

"Fine."

Malcolm watched him, but Yoon wouldn't look at him. The air of pride around him was almost choking, and Malcolm wasn't enough of a prick to push at it. He let the silence be, distracting himself by watching the kids in the corner over his shoulder. He was pretty sure that was a blunt they were passing between them, held between thumb and forefinger with their other fingers splayed out like they were holding a dainty little teacup. He wasn't going to bust them for it, but fucking hell, they could at least be a little more discreet in public.

George saved him from an endless hell of bristling stillness by stomping over with two tall white coffee mugs, slinging them down almost hard enough to slosh, before plunking a carafe of creamer and a mountain of sugar packets down in front of Yoon with a sour look.

"Well? Whaddya want?"

Yoon made a face, brows knitting in something close to distress. "I do not think I want any of it."

"Look, you fucking asshole—"

Malcolm cleared his throat sharply, cutting George off before he could start on an offended tirade. "I'll have my usual," he said. "Shredded beef and Swiss toasted on rye, and the sea salt and goat cheese fries. He'll have the fries as well."

Yoon shot him a dubious, almost helpless look. Malcolm struggled not to laugh.

"You'll like them," he said. "I promise. If not, I'll eat them."

Yoon made that softly offended *tch* sound again and folded his menu, pushing it away. "Very well."

George swiped up the menus with a baleful stare, then tromped off, muttering under his breath; Malcolm couldn't catch much of it other than *I'll very your fuckin' well*. He shook his head, dragging his mug closer, and pilfered one of the sugar packets from Yoon's heap.

"You don't eat in places like this much, do you?" he asked, shaking the packet before ripping it open and spilling it

[43]

into his coffee with that particular hiss of granules dissolving into boiling-hot black. "You're not vegetarian or vegan, are you? I could have found somewhere better." He paused. "Maybe not at this time of night, but…"

"No," Yoon clipped off. "I am not. But I do not normally eat…*this*."

"Then what do you normally eat?"

"Not this."

"You like cupcakes?"

"What?" Yoon stared at him. "That is…a very bizarre question. Why do you ask?"

"No reason," Malcolm said, and hid his grin behind a sip of coffee so wonderfully, boilingly hot and bitter it practically blistered his tongue, the edge just barely taken off by that miniscule hint of sugar sweetness.

Just the way he liked it.

"*Tch*," Yoon said again, and addressed himself to his coffee quite pointedly.

Malcolm watched him with a raised eyebrow as Yoon upended the creamer into the mug, pouring until the coffee turned milky pale tan and rose up to nearly overflow the rim of the mug, the only thing keeping it in place a thin skim of surface tension. Yoon set the carafe down, then immediately gathered up ten sugar packets, arranged them precisely stacked against each other, and ripped the ends off all at once.

"…that's a lot of creamer," Malcolm said mildly.

"I am aware."

"And a lot of sugar."

"I," Yoon proclaimed firmly, "do not like coffee."

"Then why are you drinking it?"

"Necessity of the job."

Malcolm snorted. "You can say that again."

Yoon eyed him warily. "Why are you amused?"

"Nevermind." He sighed into another sip of his coffee, letting it slide down inside him and warm the deep, tired hollows of a body left cold by exhaustion, lack of sleep. "I wasn't expecting you to be such a bee namak."

"I would have to know what language that is and possess some fluency in it to even counteract that."

"It's Persian. And you don't need to know what it means." Malcolm diverted the subject before he ended up bringing that tight, stiff tension back, that hostility that bristled like a hedgehog's spines between them. "So we've been following impulse. Let's talk plan."

"I am listening."

"We'll start with the wing joint, talk to his coworkers and managers. Find out when he was last on shift, see if anyone there was close to him." He tapped his fingertips against the bartop, letting his thoughts order themselves to the drumming rhythm. "Move on from there to the university. See if he had a roommate or friends we can easily track down. After that, family."

Yoon's mouth set in a considering line, before he dipped his head in a brief nod. "It is a start."

[45]

"It's the only start we have, while we wait for forensics to do their work. DNA can't tell us everything." Malcolm shifted his weight on the barstool. "It's all surface, but we might find the right thread to unravel the entire ball of yarn."

"Do you not think we should visit his family first? Particularly his parents?"

"We haven't run his records, and I doubt he's got a criminal rap so finding information on next of kin will take a little digging. Unless we just get his school records while we're there. Get his parents' address. Path of least resistance."

"I see."

Malcolm stared down into his coffee. His reflection looked back at him, but there was something dark, judgmental in the eyes. As if it wasn't him, but some terrible, mocking doppelganger whispering, *your fault.*

It's always your fault.

Imagine the look in that boy's parents' eyes, when you have to tell them their son is dead.

Have to tell them how.

They'll hate you.

They always hate you, Malcolm.

They're always right to hate you.

He closed his eyes, as if it could silence that vile, cruel voice inside his head, and made himself speak. "We should be quick, no matter where we go first. I'd like to let the parents know before the reporters bully past the police tape and splash his mangled body all over the news. They don't need to find

[46]

out that way."

"Ah," Yoon answered softly. "I agree."

At least they could agree on something.

And it was easier, now, to just exist in the silence, sipping their coffee without words while, from the back kitchen, the sounds of sizzling food and crashing cookware filled the quiet.

Malcolm's first cup of coffee was almost gone when George returned with a bright orange tray covered with checkered wax paper and piled with paper trays and a plate. The bartender nearly threw the tray down in front of them, then topped up Malcolm's coffee with another surly look that said Malcolm was leaving a larger than normal tip tonight if he didn't want his coffee salted next time he came in. George was part-owner of Swabbie's, one of several staff members with a stake in the employee-owned business, and he could get a little...*touchy* if anyone insulted the food. Malcolm should probably warn Yoon about that before they came here again.

You won't be bringing him here again, he reminded himself. *This is temporary. Once this case is over you'll go your own ways. He'll have his cases, you'll have yours.*

He'd prefer it that way.

Something about Yoon *bothered* him.

He picked up one of the checkered paper trays of steaming, crispy slender golden fries, dotted in thick grains of sea salt and speckled with tiny green-black flecks of seaweed, half-buried in crumbles of toasted sweet goat cheese. He slid the other tray toward Yoon.

"Try it. It's not as disgusting as you'd expect from a place like this."

Yoon actually shrank back from the tray. "...they smell very greasy."

"That's part of what makes them so good." Malcolm plucked a few fries from his own tray and bit the ends off. The crispy outer shell burst with a greasy sizzle of flavor, the bits of clinging goat cheese a pleasant cool counterpoint. If fries could be gourmet, this was probably the closest he'd ever come to having anything like it—and they were why he kept coming back to Swabbie's even if he was pretty sure he was sitting in the middle of at least a half-dozen health code violations.

Yoon picked up a single fry dubiously, sniffed it, then bit the barest tip off delicately, his tongue flicking out in a little catlike pink dart to pull the morsel into his mouth. Malcolm raised a brow. Yoon grimaced, chewing carefully, then blinked.

"I...it tastes good."

"You sound so shocked."

"I am shocked."

"I get it. The first time a friend brought me here, I thought I was going to end up with food poisoning." Malcolm chuckled. "Enjoy your food, Yoon. Once we've fortified ourselves, the hard part starts."

"Mm," Yoon said.

But he didn't argue. He only settled in next to Malcolm to eat.

And Malcolm was good with not arguing.

It wasn't even half bad to have someone to eat with, while working a case.

Not bad at all.

[5: EMPTY ROOM]

WITH HIS HEAD CLEARED BY a total of five cups of coffee laced with half a pound of sugar, Seong-Jae was crawling inside his own skull.

In Khalaji's car, he'd settled in the passenger's seat, closed his eyes, tilted his head back against the seat, and counted his breaths—ignoring the faint tapping sounds of Khalaji looking up the exact address of the victim's employer on his phone. He needed something steady, something calm. If he let himself get too keyed up he would rabbit himself into tense, manic circles that would only end when he broke and did something inadvisable.

He hated this feeling.

Hated it, yet knew it as intimately as a lover.

He knew every pulse of blood in his veins, traced it from the heavy bass drumbeat of his heart pushing it outward again and again and again to spread toward the farthest reaches of his fingertips and toes. His skin didn't feel right on his body, in moments like this. Slowly his fingers curled, until his knucklebones were writhing creatures trapped under the cage of flesh, squirming and cracking to get out.

"You all right?" Khalaji asked.

Seong-Jae opened his eyes to find that grave slate blue gaze regarding him. He looked away, staring out the window. "I am fine. Do you have the address?"

"Yeah. It's only about ten minutes away."

Seong-Jae just waited—until Khalaji got the point and started the car, pulling it out into early morning traffic, sunrise glinting off the hoods of cars and throwing back flares until the fields of metal carapaces shone like morning off a glimmering sea.

Even the sunrise sky here was gold, Seong-Jae thought. Deep whiskey gold, with just enough of a soft pink tinge to make him think of blood, stained and spreading and slowly dissolving.

He was surrounded by gold, when everything inside him was bloody and tarnished.

A brief drive brought them to a bank of restaurants crammed together along a single block, the central one announcing itself with HOUSE OF WINGS in garish orange and white below a goggle-eyed cartoon chicken that appeared to be caught in the midst of some...sort of dance. Seong-Jae managed not to grimace. He just didn't understand certain matters of *taste*, sometimes. In Los Angeles that had made him a snob, according to others in the precinct.

He supposed here it would simply make him odd.

He was used to that.

The restaurant front was dark when he and Khalaji left

the car and approached the glass-fronted door, but movement was clearly visible inside—people bustling around busily, sweeping or wiping down tables or arranging condiment stations. Khalaji rapped his knuckles at the door.

No one answered.

No one even looked up.

Khalaji quirked a cynical brow, then rapped again, harder. Still nothing, not even an acknowledgement. He slammed his fist hard enough to make the door shiver in its framing, the glass panes rattling.

One person inside stopped.

Gave them both a dirty look.

Then kept wiping down tables, hardly even missing a beat.

Khalaji made a disgruntled sound under his breath. "…if they think I won't break this door down…"

"One moment, please." Seong-Jae pulled his wallet from the back pocket of his jeans and flipped it open. He thumbed past the credit card holders to an insert stitched in with a number of small, slim metal tools in little slots, each no larger than a hairpin. He eyed the lock on the door, then selected a half-diamond pick and pulled it from the slot.

"Yoon?"

"Yes?"

"Why do you have lockpicks in your wallet?"

Seong-Jae glanced at Khalaji. "You do not?" he asked, and fitted the pick to the keyhole.

Khalaji caught his wrist. "You can't pick the lock."

"I am not," Seong-Jae said, and shook that broad, rough hand off; he hadn't told Khalaji he could *touch* him. "I only want them to think I a—"

He broke off as the door jerked open, the bell over the frame jangling harshly. A smartly-dressed, stern-faced woman with a precisely articulated dip above her upper lip and a strong Italian jaw glared at him, spots of irritated color high in her cheeks. Her nametag said *MANAGER* above a smaller, less bold *Maria*.

"The fuck do you think you're doing?" Maria demanded. "We don't open until ten. Do I have to call the cops?"

Seong-Jae slipped his lockpick back into his wallet, then flipped it to his badge and held it up. "Baltimore Police Department."

"So BPD is picking locks now?"

"You would not answer when we knocked."

She worked her jaw with an irritated sound, then sighed. "What can I do for you?"

Khalaji flicked Seong-Jae a heavy look, then turned his gaze to Maria. "Have a few questions about one of your employees."

Maria leaned in the doorway, folding her arms over her chest. "Look, I stay out of their personal lives. I know some of them got a habit, but as long as they come to work sober, I don't make it my business."

"We're not with narcotics," Khalaji corrected gently.

[53]

"We're with homicide."

"Oh," Maria said. It came out blankly, and after a moment that click happened behind her eyes, a light switching on—before dimming as her face went pale. "*Oh*," she said again, more hushed, before swallowing, stepping back, removing the obstacle of her body. "Come in, then."

Malcolm held back, gesturing for Seong-Jae to enter before him with an almost mocking deference.

Were Seong-Jae a different man, he might well have bitten him.

But he stepped into the restaurant, the room shaded and lit only by sunlight through the windows. A few waiters and waitresses in logo-emblazoned, obnoxiously orange shirts and black half-aprons tidied tables, all of them college-aged or younger, their curiosity evident in their plain, open faces as they stole surreptitious glances at Seong-Jae and Khalaji. Maria led them to a table far in the back; Yoon would guess far from prying ears. She sank down to a heavy seat in one of the chairs, sighing and gesturing them to the other chairs.

Neither of them sat.

"Who was it?" she asked.

"Darian Park," Khalaji responded. "We found a few receipts in his wallet with the employee discount. Those tracked him back here."

"Shit. Shit. Seriously?" She stared at them. "He was…" She bit her lip, fretting idly with the watch on her wrist, those little motions that gave away tell-tale signs of distress. "He was a good kid. Hell, everyone liked him. Always brought home the most tips because he'd charm every damned table."

She fell silent, a lost look in her eyes that said she wasn't seeing the restaurant, wasn't seeing its black and white checkered floor or the Venetian blinds with their broken ends or the two men standing over her. But she shook herself, a sharp full-body shudder, and rubbed at her chest, focusing on them again.

"How did he die?"

"It is best if you do not know the details," Seong-Jae said. "When was the last time you saw Mr. Park?"

"Friday night. He doesn't—*didn't*—work weekends. That was the one thing we fought about all the time. He was a model employee and I needed my best server during our busiest times, but he…" Her eyes went misty, and she smiled, watery and wavering. "He wanted to be a kid as long as he could. Wanted to be…be…*bright*, I guess. He had that way about him. He was bright. That's why I never fought him too hard. I threatened to fire him, but we both knew I never wou—" She broke off with a choked sound, pressing her hands over her mouth and nose. "Sorry. Sorry. Shit, this is just—I just saw him Friday, and—"

Khalaji leaned over to pluck a napkin from the table's dispenser and offer it to her. "Take a moment if you need it," he rumbled softly. "I understand if this is sudden."

Maria took the napkin and dabbed at her eyes, her nose, before heaving in a deep breath and patting fretfully at the tight, dark knot of her silver-streaked hair. "You have any idea who did it?"

"That's why we're here," Khalaji said. "Hoping you or anyone else could point us toward a few leads. We're trying to get an idea of who he spent time with, and who might have motive."

"Like I said, I stayed out of their personal lives." She spread her hands helplessly, then paused, her brows knitting. "Though he had this boyfriend who'd come hang out here, Noah or Nathan or Noel?" She shook her head. "I don't remember. I know they broke up and he came in with his eyes all swollen like he'd been crying, and the next day Darian almost got in a fight with one of the fry cooks. Had to send him home before lock-up. That was Friday."

"Is that fry cook here right now?" Khalaji asked.

"Jake? Yeah, he's in the back doing prep. Jake…um…Jake Alberts."

Khalaji caught his eye and tossed his head toward the door to the kitchen. "Yoon?"

Seong-Jae inclined his head. "Of course."

He drew away and angled between the tables, behind the bar-style serving area, and pushed through the kitchen door into a steaming-hot space walled in pale yellow tile and thick with the scents of barbeque sauce and frying chicken fat. Two young men in aprons were busy over the fryers, scrubbing them out with scratchy Brillo pads, the noise screeching and loud.

Seong-Jae cleared his throat. The two didn't even notice. He closed his eyes, taking a deep breath. He hated raising his voice, but he projected enough to at least be heard over the clanging and scratching.

"Alberts," he said. "I am looking for a Jake Alberts."

Both young men stopped, one glancing back irritably, the other frozen stiff. He was a wiry, bony thing, small and slim with lank straggles of dishwater-blond hair falling into a sallow face. Not particularly strong.

As if he could easily need to fall back on stealth, surprise, and weapons such as a garrote to subdue a victim.

Slowly, the blond turned just enough to fix a stark, wide-eyed look over his shoulder. Seong-Jae raised his badge.

The blond bolted.

He flung the steel wool and dishrag in his hand aside and *bolted*, nearly knocking the other young man over as he shoved past and clambered toward the employee entrance in the rear of the kitchen. Dishware crashed and clattered as he slammed into it, knocking over pans and trays and knives, sending them scattering across the floor. He rounded the central prep counter, nearly vaulting it, then lunged for the door.

Darting to intercept, Seong-Jae circled the other side of the counter. He was closer to the door, and he skidded the last few steps to shove himself into the blond's path. The blond crashed into him, stumbled back, stared at him in frozen horror, then pivoted and tried to lunge away.

Seong-Jae caught him by the back of his shirt, and shoved him down against the steel countertop.

The blond struggled, wriggling, but Seong-Jae clamped his hand against the back of his neck until he could grapple for his wrists, twisting his arms behind his back and pinning his wrists together against the base of his spine. With a sobbing sound the blond arched, twisting, kicking—but Seong-Jae had leverage, and leaned down on him harder. Just enough to hold him, not enough to hurt him. He only wanted him to be *still*.

"I didn't do anything!" the blond gasped out, lips almost slobbering. "I swear I didn't do anything!"

"Then why did you run?"

"Look—look, I'm just holding for a friend—"

"I am not here to arrest you for drug possession." Seong-Jae sighed, clenching his jaw. Of course this had to get complicated. He let go of the back of the blond's neck and patted over his hips until he felt the thin tell-tale lump in his pocket, then delved two fingers inside and hooked onto the Ziploc baggie inside. He tugged it out and eyed the scattering of ground, grey-green leaves gathered in the corner. "Though perhaps I should."

"I swear it's not mine!"

Seong-Jae eyed the back of the blond's head. "It is on your person."

The young man made another weak attempt to struggle, flopping like a beached fish. "God, man, what do you *want?!*"

[58]

"Information on Darian Park," Seong-Jae said. The other man at the sink was watching them with his eyes wide and mouth hanging open, but Seong-Jae ignored him. "You are Jake Alberts?"

"Y-yeah…" Jake stopped struggling, limp, his expression blank and confused. "Yeah, that's me."

"You fought with Mr. Park on Friday night."

Jake's shoulders jerked. "He was being a dick! He told me to fuck off just because I couldn't rush his friend's order!" He huffed, his face red. "Look, tempers get hot sometimes, okay? So we fought, so what?"

"Did he make you angry?"

Something flickered in Jake's eyes. Something like fear. It wasn't hard to miss him piecing the bits together, realizing something more was going on here than an inquiry about a fight.

"Yeah," he straggled out warily. "Yeah, I guess so…"

"Angry enough to kill him?"

Jake went white. "…Darian's dead?"

Seong-Jae craned his head. The response seemed genuine, but then certain classes of the psychologically disordered were expert at feigning the expected emotional reactions to function in society—and conceal their crimes, if they took a violent bent. He wasn't yet sure which Jake was.

A psychopath with a well-crafted mask, or a very young man shocked that his coworker was dead.

It would take a psychopath to do what had been done to

Darian Park's body.

"No fucking way," Jake whimpered, his fingers curling helplessly against each other. He craned his head as much as he could, looking at Seong-Jae with wet eyes. "You're shitting me, right? Don't fuck with me like that."

"Yoon," Khalaji said. "For hell's sake, let the kid up."

Seong-Jae looked up. Khalaji watched from the kitchen doorway, brows drawn into a thick and thunderous line, slate blue eyes snapping.

"He ran," Seong-Jae pointed out, and held up the baggie. "And he has drugs."

"He has a dime bag of weed." With an irritated, impatient growl, Khalaji stalked closer, jerked the baggie from Seong-Jae's hand, and nudged him aside. Seong-Jae was taller than Khalaji, but Khalaji was bulkier, crowding him, and Seong-Jae had no choice but to let Jake go, stepping back. A spark of temper shot through him with a bolt of heat, that violent pounding starting under his skin again, but he held himself in check with a thin thread of self-control.

Not in front of a possible perpetrator.

Not against someone who would take advantage of Seong-Jae and Khalaji turning against each other.

Khalaji gripped Jake's shoulder and helped him up, hauling him to his feet. "We're not busting him over a dime bag of weed."

Seong-Jae thinned his lips. "We are not?"

"Dude!" Jake protested.

"We're not," Khalaji said firmly—then suddenly turned that cutting gaze on Jake, the wolf with prey in its sights. "Not unless you're a suspect in the murder of Darian Park, and then this dime bag will give me grounds to hold you a lot longer than forty-eight hours until we track down the evidence we need."

Jake stumbled back, pressing against the counter, staring between Khalaji and Seong-Jae with a flicking, panicked gaze, breathing shallowly as a cornered rabbit and clearly weighing which of them was the worst. "I don't know *shit* about Darian! Look, we worked together, that was it! We have, like, two classes together at school!"

"So you are not familiar with his circle of friends and acquaintances," Seong-Jae said.

"I…n-not really, no…I mean, I guess I could recognize his roomie or a couple of people, but we just…you know…" Jake made a helpless, tense gesture. "We just didn't cross. We weren't even in each other's orbit."

Seong-Jae eyed Jake. This was not a mask. He was not a suspect. His eyes were too dilated, his pulse flicking against his throat. Sweat beaded on his skin. Some psychopaths were able to coax these sorts of physical reactions at will, but it took a lifetime of practice—experience someone as young as Jake wouldn't have. Young psychopaths were still testing themselves, still learning how to fit into a social architecture that wasn't made for them, many blundering as they struggled to find their place. Many were able to skillfully integrate into society, using their mask as defensive armor, and lived as ordinarily as anyone else.

While others lost their way, and expressed themselves in ways that nearly always had violent and bloody ends.

Jake was neither.

Jake was only a college student afraid of the two police officers crowding him when he was just trying to clean the fry cooker and get ready for another minimum wage shift.

But Jake might also be a valuable source of information, and Seong-Jae prodded, "And the boyfriend who frequented this establishment?"

Jake hesitated, then said, "Nathan." His Adam's apple bobbed severely. "Nathan McAllister. Yeah, him I know."

"How?" Khalaji asked.

"He was my lab partner in freshman chem one-oh-one," Jake said. "He was like…one of those guys who attracted…you know, fag hags?"

Khalaji went still—but in that stillness was a vibrating potential that seemed to fill the room with a silent and unspoken growl more felt than heard, a thing that raised fine hairs all over the body and brought the day to a dark and clouded standstill. His eyes narrowed, and he leaned subtly closer to Jake. His gaze flicked over him as if looking for the best place to sink his jaws into vulnerable flesh.

"You," he bit off with slow deliberation, "are gonna want to avoid that word in front of two queer cops."

Seong-Jae raised both brows.

Interesting, he thought once more.

"Sorry!" Jake squeaked, shrinking back, hands up, eyes bulging. "Fuck, sorry, just—you know what I mean!"

Khalaji eyed him balefully, then snarled something under his breath and turned away. Jake stared at his back uncertainly, then flicked a confused gaze to Seong-Jae.

"The girls," Seong-Jae prompted.

"Y-yeah." Jake blew out his cheeks. "There were like, six of them. This weird fan club that were always hanging around our desk. Like what the fuck did they even think was going to happen?" He made a derisive sound. "It pissed me off. I could never get my shit done because of them, and he never did anything about it. So I didn't really like Nathan much."

"How did he behave toward Mr. Park when he was here?"

"I dunno." Plucking at a bit of peeling skin on his lower lip, Jake looked to one side, avoiding eye contact. "They weren't like, PDA everywhere, but I guess…like…you could tell? They'd like watch each other all the time and Darian would be fucking dropping trays and walking into walls with this goofy smile on his face, and Nathan would laugh like it was the cutest thing he'd ever seen. Like they were really fucking in love." He barked out a ragged, humorless laugh. "I was kind of jealous. Like, man, I'd love to have a girl love me enough to stare at me that moony fucking way, y'know?"

No. Seong-Jae did not particularly know. He eyed Jake.

"But they broke up."

"I guess so, yeah."

"Do you think Nathan McAllister is the type who could kill his ex-boyfriend?"

"Fuck, man, why are you asking me? I don't know!"

Khalaji cut in with an irritated growl. "Can you describe Nathan to us?"

"Um, sure." Jake edged away from Khalaji nervously. "He's like…your height? Maybe a little less? But skinny. Like, he's that kind of skinny that makes his arms and legs look too long? And he's got black hair. It's shaved on…um…uh…the right side? No, the left. I dunno about what color his eyes are, I don't remember, but he's got some tattoos and big black gauges in his ears. And I guess…I mean he's pretty? Sorta? I dunno, I don't look at guys like that?" By the time he was finished he was shaking, shrinking smaller and smaller. "I…I dunno what you want to hear, I…I…"

"That's enough," Khalaji interrupted curtly, and dropped the bag of marijuana on the counter. "Thank you for your time, Jake." He tossed his head at Seong-Jae. "We got what we need. Let's go."

He turned and swept from the kitchen without waiting. He trailed anger behind him like a cloak. Seong-Jae cocked his head one way, then the other. Jake stared at him, making soft little frightened sounds that shook through his teeth. Seong-Jae looked down at the bag of weed. Looked at Jake.

Then turned and followed Khalaji without looking back.

Jake Alberts was no longer his concern.

He caught up with Khalaji just as the man thrust out into the early morning sunlight, the glare of the lightening sky blinding after the dimmed lights in the restaurant. Khalaji took a few pacing steps toward the car, then turned back and fixed Seong-Jae with a steady, quietly simmering look.

"You," Khalaji said firmly, "need to learn how things work around here. This isn't Los Angeles. You can't crash in here like you're military in a hostile environment."

"The way things work is that you seem to turn a blind eye to what you deem minor infractions."

"Yeah." A spark of challenge flashed in Khalaji's eyes. "I do."

Seong-Jae met his gaze unerringly. He had zero interest in masculine posturing and dominance games, but neither did he intend to allow an officer who made illegal judgment calls override him. "That is against regulations."

"And I have my reasons."

"Do you intend to share those reasons with me?"

Tension corded Khalaji's body, until his suit seemed to sit on him wrongly, like trying to fit a four-legged beast into human clothing. "It's not your business."

"You are agitated," Seong-Jae pointed out, and Khalaji's gaze hardened.

"You just pinned a kid to a table for no good goddamned reason."

"I deliberately used suppression methods intended not to

harm him."

"That's what they said about Eric Garner, too." A rough, frustrated sound grated from the back of Khalaji's throat, guttural, and he dragged his hair back with one hand, sweeping it from his face as he stared off to the side. "Look. It's one case. Humor me. Do things my way. If you want to lock up everyone you run into for every reason you can find? Shake down scared kids over a dime bag of weed? You can do that on your own cases when we go our separate ways. But don't do it when you're with me. You can write me up for it later if you want. Flex your seniority. I don't care."

How fascinating, Seong-Jae thought. Khalaji was such a knot of furious, burning emotion underneath that quiet, grave surface. Even now he tried to conceal it, tried to cage it inside stillness, yet he gave himself away in his tension, in the set of his firm-lipped mouth, in that velvety animal snarl in the back of his throat.

This was passion, Seong-Jae realized.

And he wondered if Khalaji was passionate about his job, about the people he protected...or simply about his dislike of Seong-Jae's methods.

After considering, he bowed forward briefly. "As you say."

"Yeah. As I say." Heaving a deep sigh, Khalaji shot Seong-Jae a sidelong look. "Let's check out the roommate, then track down the ex-boyfriend."

As you say, Seong-Jae thought again, but said nothing—

and simply followed Khalaji to his car.

[6: FOR THE TEAM]

MALCOLM WONDERED IF HE NEEDED to spend more time worrying about Yoon than about a potential suspect.

If he couldn't leave Yoon alone with suspects for five minutes without him body-slamming and pinning a goddamned kid, they were going to have a problem.

Silence once more reigned in the car as he drove them to the university—but the tension in this silence was different. A promise of a confrontation building to a head. If Yoon's inability to control himself ended up causing problems on this case, Malcolm would ditch him and to hell with the Captain's orders.

He'd take a demotion before he'd work with someone who attacked kids.

Right now, though, if anyone needed to get himself under control it was Malcolm. He didn't like who he became when his temper took over. He'd worked hard to suppress that person, cage him, temper him into someone better, older, wiser, more restrained, more patient. Usually it was easy to keep himself on a leash.

Less than one day with Yoon, and that leash was on the verge of snapping.

Zarate had to be smoking something, to think putting them together was a good idea.

He found an open parking meter about a block down from the edge of campus, and eased the Camaro into the spot before stepping out. "We walk from here," he said, dropping a quarter into the meter. "Easier than finding on-campus parking. That and we don't want campus police noticing BPD plates."

Yoon exited the car, watching him oddly. "Would it not be better to cooperate with campus police?"

"You've never met them. The murder didn't happen on campus, so let's leave them out of it." He smoothed his suit coat, then flicked his fingers to Yoon. "Come on. The registrar's office is in the Health and Human Services Library building."

Yoon fell into step with him. "You know your way around campus?"

"It's familiar, yeah."

Don't ask, Malcolm thought.

Yoon didn't.

They strode across the street, then took the sidewalk up to the tall white-fronted, brown-topped building, with its high vertical columns of window panels. He didn't even pause inside, hitting the stairs to the second floor. The office of the registrar looked more like the DMV, with its bizarrely yellow wall-to-wall service desk and cordon ropes marking off lines to the workstations. Several students waited in line, while others fidgeted restlessly and leaned in to talk with the administrators and clerks tapping at their computers. Malcolm spent one hot second debating waiting in line, then completely skipped it, circled around the side, and leaned in until he spotted a familiar head of gray hair bound up in multiple coiled braids and nested behind the head of a short, curving woman with thin pince-nez spectacles perched on her nose and lipstick in a shade of fuck-me red that sharply contrasted her prim little pink floral granny cardigan.

He lifted a hand. She raised her head, her lips pursing with the short of sharp comment he was all too familiar with, a *wait your turn*—only for her eyes to light up. She leaned across to the student she was speaking to, patting his hand and murmuring "I'll be right back with you, dearie," before turning her back on his offended, frustrated look and bustling away from her station.

A moment later the side door creaked open, and she barreled out and caught Malcolm up in an effusive hug. He grunted; she'd hit him like a cannonball, rocking him back, and it took a second to right himself before he could pat her back, keeping his arms held out.

He wasn't a hugger.

"Professor Khalaji!" she trilled. "It's so good to see you again."

"Hello, Janine." He gingerly pried himself free—then

caught Yoon's eye; the man was watching him stonily, but something glinted in his gaze. Malcolm flung him a warning look. *Not one fucking word.* He turned his attention back to Janine, intercepting her hands as she reached for him again and clasping them instead. "It's Detective now. You know that."

"Not to me." She clucked her tongue at him, squeezed his hands, then let go and turned to look at Yoon inquisitively. "And who is this?"

Malcolm took a defensive step back. "Detective Yoon. We're working a case together."

"Ma'am." Yoon answered with a tight nod.

Janine's face fell. She looked between them. "So this isn't a social visit, is it?" She thinned her lips, looking at Malcolm over the rim of her glasses. "Don't ask me to do anything that would get me fired."

"I wouldn't. I just need to track down a student's records. Dorm apartment, roommate, home address, next of kin."

"Next of kin?" Janine dropped her voice and leaned in close, glancing nervously at the lines of students, then whispering, "Oh, Malcolm. Did one of ours die?"

"I can't give you case details right now, Janine." But when she only looked at him, he sighed, lowering his voice. "Yes. Can we talk about this out of the open?"

"Oh—oh, dear. Yes. Please. This way."

She led them through the door to the administrative

area—an open-plan office space fronted by the service desk window, gray carpet and desks neatly spaced among potted plants, admins working fixedly over stacks of paperwork. They didn't speak again until she'd dragged them over to a secluded corner, near a few currently empty desks.

Janine wrung her hands, her forehead a terrace of worried wrinkles. "Malcolm. People will be devastated, if a student died."

"No, Janine." He pointed at her firmly. "*No*. I know you. You cannot tell anyone. It will spread quickly enough, probably on the news by tonight, but I'm trying to halt the wildfire until I can talk to the parents. I don't want to start a panic."

"Oh—*oh*." She gasped, a hand flying to her mouth. "It's not simply a dead student, is it? It's a murdered student."

"Yes."

She made a distressed little sound. "Well, whoever was it?"

"Darian Park."

With a frown, she twisted her mouth up. "I don't know the name off the top of my head, but let me look. Just give me a moment."

She bustled over to the closest empty desk and jiggled the mouse, waking the black screen of the workstation and bringing up the university system login screen. While she tapped away, red-painted nails rattling over the keys, Yoon stared at Malcolm until Malcolm couldn't stand ignoring the tingle on the back of his neck any longer and finally met his eyes.

"Professor?" Yoon asked pointedly.

Malcolm had never been so happy to feel his phone buzzing in his pocket.

He fished it out, and swiped the new text notification. Stenson, filling his text messages with digitals of the photographs she'd taken last night, plus several more taken in the light of day, timestamps just minutes old. He thumbed through them. "Prelims from the crime scene."

"Ah," Yoon said, but asked nothing else.

Janine made a soft, triumphant sound. "I think I've got him." Her fingers wiggled at them. "Come see."

Malcolm and Yoon joined her at the desk, leaning to look over her shoulder. A clean-cut, blue-eyed photo looked back, the exact same one as the university ID in the victim's wallet.

"That's him," Malcolm said grimly.

"Oh, he was a good student." Janine sighed mournfully. "He was in the dentistry program. Scholarship, perfect four-point-oh. His parents live right here in Baltimore."

"Was he living with them?"

"No, it looks like he was assigned to one of the student apartments. In…" She tapped a few more keys. "Pascault Row. At six-fifty West Lexington."

Yoon glanced at Malcolm. "That is only a few blocks from the crime scene."

"That club's popular with the on-campus queer community. I'm not surprised." Malcolm squinted at the screen. "He have a roommate?"

"Yes. It looks like...Shane Newsome. He's only nineteen, poor baby will be devastated—"

"Janine." Malcolm cut her off gently. "Can you get me the building access code, his apartment number, and his parents' address?"

"Oh—of course, dearie." She patted his arm and offered a sad smile. "I can do that much for you. Are you going to catch the man who killed Darian?"

"I'm going to try."

"We shall try," Yoon corrected softly, and Janine beamed at him.

"Aren't you a sweet boy. And handsome, too." She turned that wide smile on Malcolm. "Isn't he handsome?"

Malcolm groaned, dragging his hand over his face. "*Janine.*"

Janine only smirked, tapped a few more buttons on the screen, and bustled away, leaving them alone. Malcolm thought Yoon would leave it alone, until that soft, fluid voice lilted mockingly at his shoulder. "Well, Khalaji? Am I handsome?"

"Don't be an ass," Malcolm said, and followed Janine to the printer.

She sorted through several printouts that had already been sitting in the print tray, then fished out a thin stack of sheets and offered them. "This should have everything you need."

"Thank you." Malcolm took the printouts and leafed through them, skimming addresses and names. Parents Laura and Matt Park. Nice wholesome suburban names. He turned away, more focused on the printouts than Janine or Yoon, and only barely remembered to throw back, "I owe you."

"I'd be happy if you simply stopped by more often," Janine called after him. "You boys drive safe now!"

"Mmhm."

Malcolm drifted out to the stairwell, elbowing the door open while he read through Darian Park's course history, extracurricular activities. Lacrosse. Might be worth hunting down the coach, a few team members. He paused, frowning at a note about a class transfer. Chem 101. The same class Jake Alberts had mentioned. The door started to swing closed while he stood there—but halted when Yoon caught it, leaning over him, that long arm halfway caging Malcolm.

"You seem very familiar with a number of people, Khalaji."

Malcolm lifted his head from the printouts. "I've lived in Baltimore my entire life and worked homicide for half my career. You get to know the locals."

"It is not what I would have expected."

"What's that supposed to mean?" Malcolm tensed, then scowled. "I told you to stop fucking psychoanalyzing me."

"As you say," Yoon said, then slipped past him, angular

body brushing against Malcolm's before he slid free and took the stairs down two at a time, his boots nearly silent on the steps. Malcolm glared after him.

As he fucking said, indeed.

[7: BY THE BOOK]

IT WAS KHALAJI'S IDEA TO walk when the student apartment buildings were only three blocks away, but Seong-Jae found himself taking his time, lingering on the sensation of chill September air warming under the strengthening morning sun. Days like this were like water, moving through currents of liquid warmth and chill as bands of heating and cooling air cycled into eddying breezes.

And as they walked, he couldn't help but watch Khalaji from the corner of his eye.

He seemed less agitated now, at least. He'd settled into that sort of quiet, world-weary patience once more, that bone-deep exhaustion that said he would be ready for one more battle if needed, but one good blow would knock the last of the fight out of him. Seong-Jae first thought him to be the lone wolf archetype, and yet the people Khalaji encountered tended to respond to him with almost familial warmth.

Even if he did not quite seem to know what to do with it, gruff and uncomfortable with the displays of affection.

"You're staring at me," Khalaji pointed out, gaze fixed straight ahead.

"I am."

"There a reason why?"

"Observing."

"Try observing your surroundings." Khalaji fished an elastic from his pocket and swept his hair up in both hands, pulling it back to knot it behind his head and secure it in place. A few errant strands drifted free nonetheless, laying against his temples and his throat. "If you're new to Baltimore, you might as well start learning your way around now."

Seong-Jae shrugged. "I will acclimate over time."

"How long ago did you move here?"

"Two days."

Khalaji's bushy eyebrows rose. "You didn't even take time to unpack and set up house before coming to work?"

"I did not bring much in the way of belongings."

"Right," Khalaji said, but nothing else.

Seong-Jae considered letting it go, then thought better of it. "You do not know what to make of me, do you?"

"I'm not worried about what to make of you. We don't have to like each other. We just have to work together. And don't—" Khalaji snapped one hand up. "Don't say 'as you say.'"

"As you say," Seong-Jae answered.

Khalaji shot him a dead-eyed, dry look, then shook his head and turned to mount the steps of a brick-faced apartment building with quick, efficient strides. He tapped the door code in, then held it for Seong-Jae before following him inside.

"Fourth floor," Khalaji said, already crossing the lobby to the stairs. Seong-Jae hung back.

"There is an elevator."

"Then take it," Khalaji called down, disappearing around the first bend in the stairs. "I like the stairs."

Seong-Jae watched him until he couldn't see him anymore, nothing but the echo of his sleek leather dress shoes hitting the steps.

Then, with a sigh, he slid his hands into his pockets and started up the stairs after him.

Set in his ways, he added to his mental catalogue of Khalaji's traits, then snorted at himself. *As if you are any better.*

He caught up with Khalaji between the second and third floors, and stayed two steps behind him until they spilled out into the fourth-floor hallway. Khalaji stopped outside apartment four-twenty-three, and rattled his knuckles against the door. "Shane Newsome?" he called. "BPD. Open up."

A clatter came from inside, followed by soft swearing. Then the door creaked open, and a single wary brown eye peered out. "...yeah?"

"You want to open the door?"

The boy pulled the door back a few more uncertain inches. He was average height with that kind of corded build that said he was still growing into himself, his sandy hair shaved in stripes on both sides and his face peaked and sharp.

An oversized tank-top half hung off him, falling almost to his knees over ratty jeans. He shuffled bare feet, brows drawing together as he eyed them.

"What's wrong? Am I in trouble for something?"

"No," Khalaji said, his voice dropping into that same quiet, soothing rumble as when he'd spoken to the boy outside the club. "Can we come inside? We need to tell you something."

Shane squinted one eye up, then bobbed his head. "Sure."

He retreated, clearly reluctant, giving them access to a rather cramped apartment that looked to be a living room cut off by a half-wall from a shared bedroom, two rumpled beds barely visible on the other side, a tall picture window looking out over the Baltimore skyline. The apartment was the typical clutter of student dorms, personal effects scattered everywhere, a pennant for the Maryland Terrapins lacrosse team over the rather utilitarian-looking sofa that had likely come as part of the pre-furnished package. A half-finished slice of pizza sat on the coffee table, next to a bottle of Mountain Dew and an open textbook.

Seong-Jae followed Khalaji inside, closing the door in his wake, then leaning against it. Shane shoved a few more books off one side of the sofa, relocating them to the coffee table, then gestured at the couch. "Sorry about the mess."

"We were both college students at one point. We get it," Khalaji said with a small smile, and circled the coffee table to sit down. "Here. Sit."

His body language tight and wary and mistrustful, Shane crept closer, then sat down on the couch as far away from Khalaji as he could get, perched barely on the edge of the cushion.

Khalaji propped his elbows on his knees, lacing his hands together, leaning forward and watching Shane gravely. "I wanted to talk to you about your roommate, Shane."

Shane shook his head slightly, confusion wrinkling his nose and lips. "Darian? What about Darian?"

Seong-Jae closed his eyes, tilting his head back against the door. He hated this part. He'd never been good at it...and he couldn't stand watching it, either.

And so there was only the sound of Khalaji's voice, soft and sympathetic and almost coaxing as he said, "He was murdered last night. Outside the club down the street."

Behind Seong-Jae's eyelids, all was dark—but the sound of Shane's shocked gasp was like a dash of pale color against his inner lids, then a darker, shimmering blot as that gasp trailed into a hitched, choked sob.

"Wh-what...? No—he can't be dead. He can't. You're lying—you're *lying!*"

"I'm not. I'm sorry. I'm so sorry," Khalaji said. "Here, son. Come here."

Seong-Jae made himself look. Made himself see this, because this was his case as much as it was Khalaji's, and he'd taken it because when he looked at that dead boy in the alleyway he saw so many faces he'd loved, hated, barely even known, but they were all gone. All washed away like cigarette butts on rain-drenched streets, leaving behind people who sobbed and asked *why* and denied with everything in them just like the boy shaking and weeping in Khalaji's arms right now.

Khalaji held Shane as if he would be the rock the boy could dash his grief against, steady and murmuring formless, soothing things without meaning. Seong-Jae felt like the outsider here, an intruder making the boy's grief run deeper for his silent witness. Yet he forced himself to stand vigil, forced himself to remain in a silence punctuated by hoarse, awful sobs, this ragged symphony of grief played on a single wheezing, scraping wind instrument.

Finally Shane's tears quieted, dimming to gasping exhalations, until he pulled back and scrubbed at his swollen, reddened eyes.

"Sorry," he rasped. "I'm sorry."

"It's all right." Khalaji pulled his phone from the inside pocket of his coat. "I'm going to show you some photos. Do you think you can handle that?"

Shane darted a glance at Seong-Jae, as if he somehow had the answer, as if he could tell this boy how to endure this when Seong-Jae didn't have any answers. But after a shaky moment, Shane nodded and squared his shoulders. "Yes."

Seong-Jae couldn't watch this anymore. He pushed away from the door. "I'll be outside."

With a significant look, Khalaji caught his eye, then

nodded.

Seong-Jae let himself out of the room, leaving the door just cracked enough to hear, and settled against the wall to wait.

There was nothing for long moments save for the faint sounds of Khalaji's phone screen responding to taps, until Shane made a faint gagging sound, then swore under his breath. Then more taps, before Shane choked out a rough, loud barking sound, then swallowed audibly, his voice thick when he spoke. "N-no. No, I don't want to see anymore. I can't."

"I'm sorry. But you can confirm that's Darian?"

"Y-yeah. Yeah, why would—I...oh my god, *why*...that's so..."

"I know. Does anything in the photos jump out at you? Anything you think I should know?"

"Other than his fucking missing legs?" Shane gulped out, his voice high and breaking.

"He was a lacrosse player, wasn't he?" Khalaji asked. "So his legs were important to him. Do you think the killer knew that? Maybe a rival player?"

"I...no, that...Darian never even played, he was always benched because he's always too busy studying to go to practice. I don't know who—I—why would anyone *cut his legs off?*"

"I don't know. Can you talk to me, Shane?"

There was a certain hypnotic quality to Khalaji's voice,

Seong-Jae realized. Calming and steady, like being lulled to sleep by the rhythm of a great guarding beast's snarling breaths.

"I want to find who did this to him," Khalaji continued. "But so far all I've got is a few names and no motive."

"No one would do that to him. *No one.*" The boy's voice came out in a fierce hiss, then trailed into a sniffle. "He…h-he was like my brother. I didn't have any friends when I came here, but he was so nice about going places with me and bringing me with his friends. Like, Mike and Kai and the others treat me like I'm their friend, too, and not just Darian's tagalong. And it was Darian's idea for us to room together, you know, because he wanted to keep me safe from some of the shitty guys on campus." There came a faint thump. "When Nathan broke up with him, I wanted…I wanted to find that guy and punch him. If someone was going to kill someone, they'd go after Nathan. Darian was fucking wrecked after that shit."

"Did he say anything about why they broke up?"

"No. He just…" A hesitant pause. "He said…I can't remember exactly, but…he said Nathan didn't need a boyfriend when he already had someone more important in his life? I think that was it."

Khalaji rumbled a thoughtful sound. "Did he tell you who?"

"No."

"Do you think Nathan was cheating on him, and that

might be connected to Darian's death?"

"I'm sorry. I don't know." Shane mumbled miserably. "I wish I could tell you more."

"It's all right, son." That growling voice was warm with approval. "You did well. I'm sorry you had to see this."

A faint hiss of cloth, movement: in his mind's eye Seong-Jae saw Khalaji standing, tucking his phone away, preparing to leave. But that movement stopped as Shane spoke again.

"Do his parents know?"

"We're on our way there next."

"Be nice to them?" There was a pathetic note of entreaty there, the boy begging. "They...you know, I don't...my family, they're not good about me being..." A self-mocking, hurtful scoff in the back of his throat. "So I'd go home with Darian for Christmas, and they were always so *nice* to me..."

"There's no easy way to tell them this, Shane." Khalaji sounded like he honestly meant the regret in his voice. There was something so different about listening to someone, reading them only through the inflections in their voice without the influence of body language and eye contact and physical appearance to distract. "But we'll try."

There came a silence, one in which Seong-Jae imagined the boy nodding, dejected, huddled, miserable. They'd come like the Grim Reaper, like haunts shrieking across the night, to leave misery in their wake and move on, leaving him alone with his grief.

"Thank you for your help," Khalaji said. "Here's my card if you think of anything. Do you have any friends you can stay with tonight, Shane?"

"Yeah," Shane mumbled. "I...I should...someone's got to tell our friends...I'll go over to Mike's."

"Good."

Then steps, polished shoes quiet against tile, and the creak of the door. Seong-Jae opened his eyes, turning his head. Khalaji ducked out of the room, those heavy lines under his eyes carved so much deeper in a matter of minutes.

"Is he all right?" Seong-Jae asked.

"No. I had to show him the crime scene photos." Khalaji drew the door closed in his wake, latching it gently. "That's going to haunt him for a while. But I have a few names to start with. Mutual friends. Nathan McAllister came up again."

"I heard."

"I could swear I've heard this name before this case." Heaviness settled over Khalaji's brows, darkening them, before he sighed. "We should go."

Seong-Jae pushed away from the wall and headed toward the stairs. Khalaji fell in at his side, muted, as quiet as though something were smothering him, a demon crouching on his shoulders and digging its talons in for purchase. Seong-Jae remained quiet until they'd descended the stairs to the lobby. Words hovered on his tongue; he wanted to say them, but he didn't. Khalaji wasn't a person, to him. He was a coworker. A profile.

He needed to stay that way.

But the taste of the question wouldn't leave his tongue, and finally he gave in. "You were good with him," he said. "Do you have children of your own?"

Khalaji had been pulling his keys from his pocket, but his fingers jerked so rapidly, so awkwardly, that the keyring slipped, jangling, through his fingers and tumbled to the sidewalk. He started to bend to catch them, but Seong-Jae was faster, plucking the keys up from the pavement. They both stilled, half-bent, looking at each other, the keys dangling from Seong-Jae's fingertips between them. This close, Seong-Jae could see strange flecks against the slate blue of Khalaji's eyes, a muted shade of green as if fallen leaves floated against a still pool of glacial runoff. He cocked his head, cataloguing the detail away, only for Khalaji to pull back abruptly. Seong-Jae straightened, keys still outstretched.

Khalaji stared glassily down the sidewalk, expression oddly fixed. "No. That...I..." He swallowed, then took the keys, gripping them tightly in a white-knuckled fist. "No. I don't want children. Ever."

Seong-Jae slipped his hands back into his pockets. "Did I ask something offensive?"

"No."

From the growl in his voice, gruff and defensive, Khalaji might as well have screamed *yes*.

If the question hadn't been offensive, it had at the very least been hurtful.

But Khalaji was already moving again, that tight energy under his lazy calm propelling him forward as if, if he stopped moving, he would have to face something he couldn't bear to see.

"Come on," he called back. "It's a bit of a drive to the parents' place."

Seong-Jae traced his gaze over the tense line of Khalaji's jaw, then strode forward to join him, catching up with him halfway down the block but hanging back, so he could watch him without that ferocious, challenging glare turning on him, hackles raised.

What are you running from, old wolf?

Are you afraid Little Red Riding Hood will catch you?

[8: SEE THIS THROUGH]

THE ADDRESS JANINE HAD GIVEN them took them to Harwood—a Baltimore neighborhood half overrun with clean, brick-faced, column-fronted condominiums and houses dotted about with just enough greenery and rustically "broken" wrought-iron fences to make the place look so very suburban in the middle of a Baltimore's busy districts.

Exactly the sort of place Malcolm would expect a Laura and Matt Park to live.

The parents' house was only three miles from the school, but congested midmorning traffic made the drive into a slow crawl. He would have turned the radio on, but he had a feeling Yoon would be as uptight about Malcolm's taste in music as he was about his taste in food. Every silence, every trip from point A to point B, was harder and harder to endure and this time, he found himself grinding his fingers into the steering wheel until the offended creak of stressed, strained leather warned him to stop.

Do you have children of your own?

So much for not getting personal.

He curbed the Camaro outside the address on the printout, sliding neatly between a BMW fore and a massive, blindingly yellow Hummer aft. The block of tall townhouses in front of him was split into three residences, each with their own private set of stairs, each with their own pretentious columns, each perfectly maintained, shared lawns and parallel walkways as precise as plastic sculptures.

Somewhere inside that house were two people who'd never wanted for anything in their lives.

Somewhere inside that house were two people who would, in a matter of minutes, want nothing more in their lives than to have their son back.

Malcolm breathed in deep, pushing down the knotting in his gut. He had to have the *next of kin* conversation at least once a week, telling wives and husbands and children and sisters and brothers and cousins and friends, but the ones he could never handle were the parents.

Those were the ones who left wounds on him, the scar tissue raw and sensitive and never quite healing over fully.

He glanced at Yoon, but there was no support there. He was just as ice-cold as ever, black eyes dark pools of night that obscured everything in their lightless dark.

Malcolm looked away, smoothed his hands over his suit, and pushed the gate open with a squeal of iron hinges that sounded like the cry of a mourning soul.

Up the steps. Ring the doorbell. Wait, try to look calm, try to look reassuring, so they wouldn't open the door and immediately know something was wrong.

Better to ease them into it, rather than shock and trauma.

"I'm coming!" a pleasant, sing-song voice called.

The clatter of dishes was audible through an open window to the right of the door, before the sound of footsteps pattered farther, then closer, circling around to the door before it opened on a short woman in khakis, with Darian's blue eyes and a bobbed crop of bottle-burgundy hair. She folded her hands in that polite, precise way that seemed bred into WASPs, looking between Malcolm and Yoon quizzically.

"Hello, is there something I can do for you?"

"Mrs. Park?" Malcolm asked.

"Yes, that's me." She blinked several times, a confused, poised little rapid flutter of her lashes. "May I help you?"

He flashed his badge. "Baltimore PD."

Her fingers curled together, worrying and fretting, clutching against her chest. "Oh. Oh, no."

"Is Mr. Park home?"

Immediate defensiveness. Tension. Say what you would about suburban upper middle class elite, but Mrs. Park was clearly a woman who'd go down before she'd betray her husband. *Ride or die* came in flavors of taupe.

"Is my Matt in trouble?" she asked sharply.

"Not your husband, ma'am," Malcolm said. "But it would be better if we were able to speak with you alone."

She stared at them, incomprehension and dread turning her pale eyes shallow and reflective. Then she leaned back, calling back into the house. "Matt? Matty?" Her voice lilted up into a shrill break on the –y. "The police are here. Something's wrong."

The creak and slam of a door. The tromp-shuffle of loafers, and then a reedy man in thick glasses, his bald head ringed in a monk's scruff of gray, came down the stairs, wiping his hands on a paper towel.

"Is it Darian?" he asked breathlessly. "Something's happened to Darian, hasn't it?"

Malcolm closed his eyes, steeling himself, then made himself look at them. Made himself meet their eyes, even if he could offer no comfort. Only honesty. "Please," he said. "Let's talk inside."

He might as well have said *yes*, and their expressions said they knew it. Both of them, their mouths hanging open with that kind of horrible, frightened slackness that said they wanted to ask but they didn't want to know. They looked at each other in that way married couples had, that silent communication, before Mrs. Park made a distressed sound and ducked behind her husband, while Mr. Park stepped back and gestured toward the inside without a word.

Malcolm stepped forward—then stopped, glancing back at Yoon, his silent shadow, the crow on his shoulder. "Do you want to wait outside again?"

"No." Yoon shook his head. "You should not have to do this alone."

Malcolm stilled. His stomach did an odd thing, like it

wasn't sure if it wanted to sink or rise or twist. He just looked at Yoon, then looked away.

"Thank you," he said, and followed the Parks inside.

The interior of the townhouse was all gleaming walnut wood and lush but tasteful decorations in bland Martha Stewart colors. A bursting bunch of fresh gladiolas sat on the coffee table in a black-and-gold lacquer kintsugi vase, filling the living room with a scent so cloying it was almost unpleasant, stifling. Maybe Malcolm was odd, but he always associated heavy floral scents with death. Wreaths and bouquets laid over caskets. Air freshener in mortuaries, clouding over the scent of embalming chemicals. Old women in floral perfume and black veils, leaning on each other and sniffling into handkerchiefs.

And quiet sunlit living rooms full of life and warmth and humanity, dotted with fresh-cut flowers whose nodding heads bore witness to the terrible tidings he brought.

He sank down into the high-backed, upholstered easy chair Mrs. Park gestured him toward. Yoon took another, while the couple settled on the loveseat together and watched them in wide-eyed, nervous, pleading silence, that vase of blooming flowers standing between them.

Malcolm met their eyes, then dropped his gaze to one of the gladiolas, its petals the color of a melting sunset. *Tell the flower*, he told himself. *Tell the flower.*

"I don't want to make this hard for you," he began, his voice struggling in his throat. "I don't want to drag it out. So

I'm just going to tell you the truth. Last night, between approximately one-thirty and two-thirty a.m., your son died outside of a bar on West Lexington." He swallowed, trying to loosen that tightness that made every word strained. "He was murdered. I'm sorry."

The Parks were just a blur in his peripheral vision, the sunset gladiola in clear, sharp focus, the movements of a grieving woman as she burst into a wail and huddled against her husband distant and muted. He had to do it this way. He had to find a way to keep his detachment, or when they broke he would break too.

They couldn't see that.

They needed to see him as resolute and firm.

They needed to see him as someone strong enough to find justice for their son, and not a man made weak by years and years and a thousand losses that didn't belong to him…but were his to carry, nonetheless.

"You're lying," Mr. Park snapped, drawing himself up; his lips moved in soundless little blubbers that made the wattle under his chin bobble, before he found his indignation again. "It wasn't our son. It wasn't Darian. You have the wrong people."

Malcolm forced himself to drag his gaze back to them. Mrs. Park was just a bundle nearly buried in her husband's armpit, while Mr. Park stared at him with the accusatory anger of a man in denial. Malcolm didn't want to do this, but he reached into his pocket for his phone. The crime scene photos.

It was better if they understood and accepted as quickly as possible, but to show them their child like that…

He started to stand—only for Yoon to rise, drifting closer, holding out his hand for Malcolm's phone. Black eyes met his, searching.

Let me, Yoon mouthed, and Malcolm understood what he was offering.

He would be the cruel one, the angel of death, this time.

So Malcolm wouldn't have to.

Thank you, Malcolm mouthed back, and unlocked his phone before passing it to Yoon.

Seong-Jae circled the coffee table and settled to sit on the far edge of the couch, just close enough to lean over and angle the screen toward the Parks.

"Is this your son?" he asked softly.

Mr. Park stared at the screen, his face going pale save for two livid blotches of red high in his cheeks. He made a garbled sound, then looked away, closing his eyes tightly.

"Yes," he said raggedly, then hitched out a broken, sobbing sound, pressing shaking fingers to his face. "Yes, that's Darian."

"I won't look," Mrs. Park protested, choked and muffled against her husband's side. "Don't make me—don't make me see him, I…I won't look…"

"Don't look, Laura," Matt Park whispered, stroking her back, burying his face into her hair, the edges of his eyelids glistening wetly. "You don't need to see our boy like that.

Don't look."

"He's not dead—he's not—he was just *here* yesterday, my b-baby's not dead!"

Mr. Park said nothing to counteract. Yoon let his hand fall to rest the phone on his knee, looking at Malcolm, holding his eyes. Malcolm couldn't quite read what was in his gaze, but something about the way Yoon was looking at him made the tight knot in his chest ease its hold just enough to let him breathe.

"I'm sorry you have to find out this way," he managed to say. "I wanted to tell you personally before you saw it on the news."

Mr. Park cleared his throat, the struggle to hold himself together in every tremor of his lips, every flare of his nostrils. He drew himself up. "Do you know who did it? Did you catch him?"

"We're still working on that. We've been following leads since before dawn. That's why we didn't come to you sooner. Warm leads are better than cold."

"N-no…no, I understand." Mr. Park's voice broke, then steadied. "He…what did they do to him? There was just…so much—"

"*Don't!*" Mrs. Park nearly shrieked. "Don't say it!"

"Strangulation," Yoon said, stepping in once more to be the cruel one, the hard one, the one who told people things they needed but didn't want to hear. "Followed by removal of his legs in what we believe may have been a ritual mutilation."

Mrs. Park's only response was a terrible, full-body sob, the kind that crawled all the way up from the belly. Mr. Park lowered his eyes, his expression blank. Malcolm had seen this so many times. The struggle to visualize it, to understand the graphic depths of the horror of what one human being could do to another. Then:

"Why?" Mr. Park asked, something pathetic in his voice, small and weak and broken, nearly childlike. Shattered. "Why would anyone do that to my son?"

When what he was really asking was *why would anyone do that at all?*

"We aren't certain what the motive was yet," Malcolm said as gently as he could. "We'll tell you as soon as we can pinpoint more concrete information. Can you think of anyone who might have had a reason to hurt him? Anyone with a grudge against him?"

"Was it those gay bashers?" Mrs. Park demanded abruptly.

She snapped her head up, glaring at Malcolm with her eyes wet and running and veined in stark, angry red. Her mouth was twisted in a hard little knot, tears gathering in the faint seamed wrinkles in her cheeks, but there was a sudden fire in the way she set her jaw, in the clutch of her fingers against Mr. Park's chest, her knuckles shaking and fierce.

"I know those types," she spat. "Skinheads and thugs! Horrible people. We were always so afraid for our baby. He—

he was such a lovely boy, but those bastards, those *bastards*—
! They're all ugliness in their hearts, and with the way the
world is now—"

"Shush, Laura," Mr. Park soothed gently. "Do you think
this could have been a hate crime?" he asked, looking at
Yoon, then Malcolm.

"It's possible. We aren't discounting that line of
questioning." Malcolm shook his head. "Was Darian your
only son?"

"Yes. You know, we only planned for one, we just…we
wanted to be responsible…" Mr. Park trailed off, a glazed
look in his eyes. Yoon leaned in, just enough to catch his eye.

"May we look at his room?" Yoon asked.

"Yes—yes, of course," Mr. Park said, then stood,
tugging at his wife with gentle coaxing. "Come on, Laura."

"I—I don't want—"

"I don't want to leave you alone, sweetheart. Come with
me, and then we can let the officers do their work."

A faint twinge of memory tugged at Malcolm, the rough
ache of nostalgia. He supposed some part of him missed that.
That devotion, those moments of tender care, the way Mr. and
Mrs. Park looked at each other as if the only way they would
get through this was together.

He'd had that, once.

But not everything was meant to last forever.

Once the Parks had gathered themselves, they led
Malcolm and Yoon up the stairs, silent as a funeral march

over a runner with familiar Persian patterns, down the hall to a room with that same Maryland Terrapins pennant on the door. Mr. Park pushed the door open, then stepped back, gesturing for them.

"We'll be downstairs if you need us," he said, still so shaky but still so clearly *trying*.

"Thank you," Malcolm said—but as the Parks started to pull away, Yoon lightly touched Mr. Park's arm, halting them.

"Was there a reason your son stayed on campus instead of at home?"

"He…" Mr. Park hesitated, then smiled faintly, with a sort of wretched and awful fondness. "He wanted to be close to his friends, and I think he wanted to stretch his wings." A choked, raw, scraping thing that wasn't quite a laugh. "You know how it is. He's always my boy, and it's hard to have a love life when your dad's up watching TCM when you bring your boyfriend home."

Yoon inclined his head. That was a *thing* he seemed to do, something that continuously caught Malcolm's attention—a way of both tilting and dipping that was more acknowledgement than the agreement of a nod.

"Did you meet his last boyfriend, Nathan?" Yoon asked.

Mr. Park sighed deeply. "I have to say I never liked that boy much."

Mrs. Park scrunched her face up, dabbing at one eye with the collar of her shirt, smearing thin streaks of mascara on starched white. "He was so sullen and rude. He would barely talk to me or Matt."

"I see."

Malcolm stepped to the threshold of the bedroom. "Thank you, Mrs. Park, Mr. Park. We'll be as quick as we can."

Both husband and wife offered strained, watery smiles, leaned into each other, and shuffled toward the stairs. Malcolm stepped into Darian's room, only waiting for Yoon to follow before he closed the door and leaned against it, blowing out an explosive breath. Yoon watched him inquisitively, silent question in parted lips.

"Thank you for that," Malcolm said.

"You seemed to be struggling."

"Yeah."

Malcolm pushed away from the door and stepped forward to take the room in. Walls covered in pinups of male soccer stars in sweaty, glistening *GQ* and *Men's Health* style covers, with that gritty look that combined a suggestion of sexuality with masculinity. Pride flag above the headboard of the bed. Bold.

Dent marks in the walls in the shape of the corners of the bedposts.

Bolder.

The room was neatly organized in that way that said his mother slipped in to tidy when Darian was away, but tried to keep everything in its place. The one bookshelf against the wall was small, but packed with what had to be hundreds of dime store detective novels, all of them old and half-faded with tattered bindings. A few of them were stacked on the nightstand atop a weathered copy of Jackie Pullinger's *Crack in the Wall*, along with a scattering of worked silver rings in delicate braid and a faded, frayed leather thong-style necklace with a silver feather hanging from it. Several quilts were folded on a wooden chest at the foot of the bed.

Overall, the room painted the image of a healthy young man wild on the thrill of life.

Not a homicide victim.

Not someone anyone would even target for murder.

Darian Park was so sweetly, quietly *ordinary*, which made this make even less sense than before.

Yoon drifted toward the bookshelf and pried out a novel fronted by a glamorous, hard-eyed woman with black hair, red lips, and an off-the-shoulder black catsuit, leaning toward the viewer with a sultry femme fatale stare. *SPICY MYSTERY STORIES: The Cat Tastes Blood*. Malcolm arched a brow at the cover. Yoon thumbed it open carefully, flicking the pages.

"This copy is in better condition than mine," he murmured. "I wonder where he found it."

Malcolm blinked. "You like to read those?"

Yoon stiffened, shot him a slit-eyed look, and slotted the book back onto the shelf. He turned his head, scanning the room, then crossed to the bed. "Laptop."

A silver, somewhat scratched Dell rested on the pillow. Yoon settled to sit on the edge of the bed and dragged it across his lap.

Malcolm followed, settling down to sit next to him. "Wonder why he left this here, instead of at school."

"Perhaps he was visiting for the weekend. Mrs. Park said she saw him last night." Yoon flipped the laptop lid open. It woke from sleep immediately, the black screen clearing right to a desktop cluttered with document and image icons.

"No password protection," Malcolm said. "Check the browser."

Yoon tapped the browser icon. It opened on multiple saved tabs—over half of them social media sites, still logged in.

"Here." Malcolm pointed at the first two tabs. "Instagram account. Facebook albums. Let's see who we see."

Yoon navigated to the Facebook tab and clicked on the album of Darian Park's most recent photos. Malcolm edged in, craning to see. His shoulder brushed Yoon's. Yoon tensed, flashing him a downright venomous sidelong look. Malcolm leaned away, but still angled to see the screen. Yoon returned his gaze to the laptop and flicked through images—Darian posing with a broad grin with many other boys, including his lacrosse team and Shane. It looked like he updated nearly every day, constantly taking selfies and checking in at the wing restaurant, at school, at his team's games, at the bar on Lexington.

None of these photos were particularly romantic, no one he could pick out and say *that one. That's the boyfriend.*

"I think he may have deleted multiple photos," Yoon murmured, brows knitting tightly together. "Something is not right here."

"Look at his most recent status update."

Yoon clicked the album closed, scrolling to the most recent text post on Darian's timeline.

dont believe anyone who says theyll love you forever.

:'(

i dont even know if love is real

Malcolm lifted his head, staring at Yoon. Yoon stared back.

"He deleted photos of McAllister," Yoon said. "After their separation."

"Here. That tab. Instagram. Maybe there are more there."

Yoon clicked over. Darian's Instagram album was much more sparse—but the pictures here were more telling. In a photo dated just two weeks and a few days before, Darian swayed in while a tall, gangly boy with swirling tattoos of black feathers on his forearms, thick black rings stretching his earlobes, and a lank shag of black hair falling to one side of a half-shaved skull tilted over to kiss the corner of his mouth, both of them caught laughing, nearly falling into each other.

"That's the boyfriend," Malcolm said, then leaned in and squinted at the tattoos. His face, thin and fey and narrow. He *knew* that kid.

But before he could focus, Yoon flicked through several more photos at rapid speed—more of Park and McAllister together, sipping from the same drink at a table in a restaurant, holding hands in a park at night, the typical photos of young love wanting to broadcast itself to the world flying by before Malcolm could really take in many details.

Until Yoon stopped on a photo of Park, McAllister, and Trevor Manson hanging on each other, clearly drunk and waving lacrosse pennants.

"And that," Yoon said softly, "is our other victim."

"I guess we know who we're talking to next." Malcolm eyed McAllister. "I remember him now. The name didn't register when the case was so cold, but his face. I spoke to him on the first case. He and the vic dated about two weeks before Manson dumped him. Wouldn't tell him why." He tangled his fingers in his beard, tugging as if the little jolts of pain could spark his memory, could pull the case files up again before his mind's eye. The interview was nearly a year old in his mind, shuffled off among things that had been unimportant at the time, but the critical details were slotted away like a bulleted checklist. "His alibi checked out for time of death. He was clocked in at work, but…"

"Alibis can be faked," Yoon finished. "And it would appear he had motive. Did the other murder take place near the university campus?"

"No. The vic's parents' house. He was found by his

mother the following morning, strangled in his bed."

Yoon tilted his head, considering. "Motive and access, then."

"Let's see how he reacts to finding out another of his ex-boyfriends is dead," Malcolm said, and stood. "If he doesn't already know."

[9: PROMISES AND POTIONS]

SEONG-JAE TOOK THE LAPTOP AS evidence, bundling it up in its cords and tucking it under his arm. They left the Park residence with Khalaji's murmured promises that they would do everything in their power to find the murderer.

Seong-Jae made the tactful choice not to point out that such promises were likely empty. He had reviewed the Baltimore Police Department's closure rate for homicide cases, and it was only approaching fifty percent by a stretch of the imagination when taking into account cases closed by exception. Actual apprehension of perpetrators and successful trial was barely at twenty-five percent.

People were not comforted by facts. People were comforted by hope, no matter how false.

Seong-Jae had little talent for hope, and so he chose silence.

As he descended to the sidewalk at Khalaji's side, however, Khalaji exhaled and shook his hair loose again, pulling the elastic free and tugging it between his fingers, stretching it until it almost snapped. His teeth bared briefly, clenched together, before relaxing as he glanced at Seong-Jae.

"You got it in you to talk to the ex-boyfriend after that?"

"Yes," Seong-Jae answered. "We should not wait."

Khalaji didn't answer until they crossed the gate and were almost to the car. "...sometimes I wish we could."

Seong-Jae studied him, then admitted, "As do I."

A troubled look drifted toward him. "How long have you been on the force, Yoon?"

"Eleven years, between LAPD and other institutions." And he felt the weight of each year, right now. Perhaps it was that weight that pushed the next words from him, crushing him down so small that there was no room for vulnerability inside of him; it could only be forced out. "I...I should be used to this by now."

"You never get used to it," Khalaji said softly. "Not if you're human, you don't." He stopped at the car, and held the passenger's side door open for Seong-Jae with a wry, weary half-smile. "Come on. I'll buy you lunch."

Seong-Jae slid into the car and leaned back to toss the laptop in the back seat, then wrinkled his nose. "Not that...*pub* again."

"No. Not Swabbie's." Khalaji chuckled and slammed the car door closed, then rounded the hood and slipped in behind the wheel, fitting the keys to the ignition. "I know a place you might actually like."

"I sincerely doubt that."

"Trust me for once, Yoon. Just trust me."

Seong-Jae also sincerely doubted Khalaji was a man to

be trusted.

But he kept that to himself, and chose not to argue.

THE PLACE KHALAJI SWORE HE would enjoy turned out to be a Greek restaurant in the heart of downtown. Even if Greek was not Seong-Jae's preferred cuisine, he understood once they claimed a table near the floor-to-ceiling windows why Khalaji had chosen this place.

In the view out over the harbor, the water glittering like chips of slate, was a quiet peace. When looking across the horizon the world had a way of expanding, broadening beyond the tight narrow confines of the little boxes of pain humans tended to wall themselves into.

Seong-Jae sank into the scents of baking daktyla, watched the boats move like toys bobbing across the harbor, and lingered over a lunch of overstuffed olives and thick, creamy cubes of feta in tangy olive oil, paired with strong, creamy Greek coffee, strong enough to keep him moving for just a little bit longer. He said nothing. Neither did Khalaji.

But the air between them breathed cleaner, clearer, and that was all right.

THEIR SECOND VISIT TO THE student apartment complex, after lunch, was a dead end. Khalaji checked the leather-bound notebook in his pocket, flipping through until he found the apartment number he'd written down for McAllister during what Seong-Jae assumed was the earlier case, and led them there by memory.

But they found no one at the apartment but McAllister's roommate, a boy named Sanjit made wholly of angles of mahogany wood, who shook his head and, propped in the doorway, eyed them sidelong.

"Nathan's in class right now," he said. "He won't be back for a few hours."

"Which class? What building?" Seong-Jae asked.

"I don't know, I don't memorize his class schedule. We're in different programs."

Khalaji only looked at the boy flatly. So did Seong-Jae. Sanjit recoiled, then pinched his nose, closing his eyes. "Fuck. Fine. Let me think. Um, I think he's in his research block. Something about…loss, or something. He goes to the HKB building on Baltimore."

"Was that so hard?" Khalaji asked.

Sanjit rolled his eyes. "This is the second time this year you showed up looking for Nathan. Sorry if I'm a little freaked out. What'd he do?"

"Nothing you need to worry about," Khalaji said, then tossed his head to Seong-Jae. "Come on."

They arrived on campus on foot just as classes broke— students flooding between buildings and out onto the sidewalks and streets of the metropolitan-style campus, clustered in groups that moved and eddied around each other in subtly patterned flows that mimicked swarm behavior in bees. Such patterns were everywhere, and Seong-Jae lingered on watching the transitions between groups, how clusters broke and reformed in different configurations, guided by unconscious and yet self-determined movement principles that—

"This way." Khalaji's voice intersected his train of thought, diverting him back on course. He turned his gaze back to Khalaji, then shook himself.

"Of course."

Khalaji led him across the street toward a tall tan building with arcing windows. Yoon searched the students exiting the building and moving away, watching for the tattooed boy from the photos, until Khalaji said, "There he is."

The front door of the building opened, and a boy made of pale willow lathes and inscribed with dark, angry ink stepped out, dressed in punk-black with ripped skinny jeans and an oversized, graffiti-marked shirt. He glanced down the street, hefting a tattered backpack over his shoulder, but only made it two steps before Khalaji raised his voice, halting him in his tracks.

"Nathan McAllister?"

McAllister started, his head lifting, scanning until he landed on Khalaji. A strange stillness settled over him, as if he'd been rooted in place until he couldn't even breathe. As they drew closer, Seong-Jae could see that his eyes were red, his face swollen and puffy and reddened in places with the marks of tears. But he managed a shaky, uncertain smile for Khalaji, raising a hand limply.

"Hey. I remember you." His voice was thick and raspy, likely from crying. "I don't remember your name."

"Detective Khalaji." Then, without even a pause for breath: "Did you know your last boyfriend is dead? Again?"

Not a single moment of shock registered on McAllister's face. Nothing registered at all. He held stock-still for a few moments longer, before his mouth tightened and he spun on his heel, legs tensing, one foot swinging forward, ready to spring off.

Seong-Jae ducked around Khalaji and stepped into McAllister's path, blocking the sidewalk.

"I would not advise this course of action," he said.

McAllister froze before even completing the step, then slumped, retreating, his head bowing.

Khalaji watched the boy steadily. "Why are you trying to run, Nathan?"

McAllister shot him a resentful look. "Because you're here to arrest me," he spat, as if it should be obvious. "You think I did it. It's not hard to figure that out. I didn't, but you don't fucking care about that, do you?"

When Khalaji and Seong-Jae remained silent, only watching him, his mouth quivered, then drew up into a furious line, his reddened eyes narrowing, glimmers of wetness gathering against his lower lashes.

"I *didn't!*" he choked. "Shane told me you talked to him. He told me about Darian and after Trevor I knew you were going to fucking pin it on me. If I did it, why the fuck would I be going to class?"

"The easiest way to divert suspicion," Seong-Jae pointed out, "is to behave as normally as possible. Making normalcy, in and of itself, rather suspicious."

McAllister swung that glare on him: bitter, recriminating. "If you think I'm feeling normal right now, you're fucked in the head," he snarled. "I'm a fucking jinx. All my boyfriends die. Would you be feeling *normal* after that, asshole?"

"Then you need to tell us where you were last night, Nathan," Khalaji interjected smoothly, that soothing note entering his voice again. That note that said *I want to believe you. I do.* "Between one AM and three AM. Can you account for that time? I need it to be solid. *You* need it to be solid."

"I was in my room." McAllister's glare remained on Seong-Jae for long moments, then snapped back to Khalaji. "Ask my roommate. I was there." A humorless, almost hateful smile trembled his lips. "Stuffing my face with Oreos and doing homework and trying not to think about why guys dump me all the time."

"Perhaps your attitude," Seong-Jae said.

"*Yoon*," Khalaji growled.

McAllister sniffled, then scrubbed the back of his wrist furiously against his nose. "Look, there are security cameras in the apartment lobby. You can get those, right? They have to give the tapes to you because you're cops?" Underneath the surliness, the defensiveness, the anger, was a soft note of entreaty. "You can see me go in after dinner. I didn't come out until this morning. I didn't go anywhere but my room last night. If you see the tapes you have to believe me, right?"

Seong-Jae flicked his gaze over McAllister. His body language was tight, his face screwed into a mask of hostility.

I never liked that boy much, Mr. Park had said.

He was so rude and sullen.

He wasn't rude or sullen, Seong-Jae realized. He was shy. Terrified of people. And ready to crack, right now. He likely had a long history of rejections, only to finally find himself in university in a community that accepted him—only for a string of breakups to haunt him and leave him miserable, resentful, anger building to a breaking point with no one to direct it at but the general vagaries of social interaction and human nature.

But was he the type to break so violently that he would murder someone who had spurned him?

McAllister faltered, his scowl easing as he eyed Seong-Jae fearfully. "…what? Why are you staring at me?"

Seong-Jae cocked his head. "You realize we have enough to bring you in for questioning."

"I'll say the same thing at the police station. You can put me in cuffs, but it's not going to change a fucking thing." McAllister wrapped his arms around himself, tucking himself into a narrow bundle. "Do I look like I could kill someone?"

"With a garrote and enough leverage?" Khalaji asked.

McAllister snapped his head up, glaring at Khalaji. Fresh tears budded on his lower lashes, then rolled forward and spilled down his cheeks. "Fuck you." He heaved in a wet-sounding breath, shoulders trembling. "I fucking loved Darian. Do you get that? I've been fucked over this breakup so bad that I can't even stand to be alone. I'm with my friends all the fucking time. So they can tell you where I've been for every hour of every day since he told me I didn't get it and ghosted me." His face twisted into a harsh mask. "Though I guess you can't fucking answer texts if you're dead."

"So he broke up with you?" Khalaji pressed. "His friends said you dumped him."

"I *begged* him!" McAllister threw back; blotches of red stood out on his pale skin. "I begged him and he said I just didn't get it!"

He broke, then—an awful transformation going over his face, a moment of pale, blank-eyed shock with the realization that he was going to crumble and couldn't stop it, then his features screwing up in an attempt anyway, before crumpling as he curled forward with a sharp, aching sob. The scent of his tears was strange and subtle, yet it was a scent Yoon knew by heart.

Homicide detectives weren't dealers in justice.

They were peddlers of grief.

"W-hy?" McAllister gasped out. "Wh-why is someone killing my ex-boyfriends? Are they g-gonna kill me?"

"No. That's what we're trying to prevent." Khalaji sighed, the hard, forbidding crags of his face softening as he reached into his coat for his pen and notebook. He flipped them open to a blank page, uncapped the pen, and offered both to McAllister. "I need you to pull yourself together, Nathan. I know it hurts. But you can help us keep other people safe if you can focus for me. I want the names of everyone you've dated since coming to the university. Everyone you've even slept with. Whether it was a one-night stand, one bad date, or the love of your life."

McAllister lifted his head, looking up at Khalaji woefully. "B-but…"

"Names," Khalaji said firmly. "Phone numbers. Addresses if you have them."

A wounded expression flickered across McAllister's tear-streaked face, before he took the pen and book hesitantly. "I…o-okay…I'm…I'm gonna need to get some of them from my phone, if that's okay?"

"That's fine."

McAllister bit his lip, tongue pushing against the black ring piercing his labret and arcing over his lower lip, then started writing slowly. While Khalaji watched the boy, Seong-Jae watched Khalaji. Something had shifted the moment the boy had started crying, something that left Khalaji bristling and strange and indecipherable, a scowl haunting his brow, a subtle stiff jerk to his movements.

Almost as if he'd had some kind of reaction to McAllister's tears, and was doing everything in his power to suppress it.

Curiouser and curiouser indeed.

[10: SEEN SO MUCH YOU COULD GET THE BLUES]

THE KINDEST THING MALCOLM COULD do for Nathan McAllister was get as far away from him as possible, as quickly as possible.

He took the list Nathan wrote down in a slanted, messy hand—a total of six names, though he could easily cross Trevor Manson and Darian Park off the list—told the boy to stay close to the university and his dorm, and left before he had to look into that mourning, confused, tear-dampened face any longer.

That face that begged *please, make it stop hurting* when Malcolm couldn't make anything stop.

And he couldn't afford to go soft on a potential suspect just because he was a kid.

That urge—to shield him, to protect him just because he was a kid—would cloud his judgment when he needed to be able to step back and look objectively at the facts, rather than empathizing with the boy as if he were Malcolm's son...or young Malcolm himself.

He was twenty-one. More than old enough to commit premeditated murder twice, then cry about it after. The tears might even be genuine. Remorse was one hell of a drug, and it wouldn't be hard to break down crying in front of the cops because you were guilty and afraid, but pass it off as grief and loss.

Wasn't he a fucking cynic.

As if he had a choice, in this line of work.

In the car, he just sat there for long moments, breathing and reminding himself to keep it together in front of Yoon. Yoon said nothing, his gaze trained out the window, eyes tracking Nathan while the boy stood on the sidewalk, motionless and staring, eyes glazed—before he kicked himself into motion with a shake of his shoulders. He dragged a hand over his face, shot Malcolm's car a recriminating look, then turned to walk down the street, glancing back every few steps at the car, probably to see if they were following.

"Where do you think he's going?" he murmured.

"Likely back to his apartment," Yoon answered. "Do you think we should shadow him?"

"For now? No. He'd recognize the car anyway. That doesn't mean we shouldn't have a detail on him, though." He retrieved his phone from his inner front pocket. "Let me make a few phone calls."

Yoon nodded, eyes lidding. "Of course."

Malcolm hit three on his speed dial, then lifted his phone to his ear. Zarate snapped it up on the first ring; she always did. "Talk."

"Yes, Captain. I'm having a lovely day."

She growled. "I said *talk*, Malcolm. Words with meaning. Not a mouthful of shit."

He smiled slightly. "I'm going to text over some info on a person of interest. Think we could get a couple of cars on him and protective details on potential victims?"

"Suspect in the queer kid's murder?"

"Could be. Ex-boyfriend. Also dated another vic from eight months ago. Also death by strangulation. Want to make sure he doesn't bolt."

"Two dead ex-boyfriends by the same method?" Zarate made a disgusted sound. "Why didn't you just bring him in?"

Malcolm hesitated. Why *hadn't* he brought Nathan in? Was his judgment already compromised?

"It's not enough to hold him when he's got an alibi for the first death," he finally said. "I don't want the paperwork."

"Is that the real reason?"

"No." Malcolm sank back against the car seat, tilting his head back against the headrest and massaging his fingers and thumb against his temples. "I've just got a feeling. He may be guilty, he may not be, but let me see how things play out before we do anything else drastic."

"All right. Send the info. I'll put a detail on him."

"Unmarked?'

"Do you think I don't know how to do my job, Malcolm?" she asked, deadly-soft.

"You haven't fired me yet. That's a significant dereliction of duty."

That disgusted sound again. "Get off my phone. I have work to do."

"Captain," Malcolm acknowledged, then hung up his phone and scrolled to her contact, fishing out his notebook and flicking through the notes on Nathan McAllister.

"Do you typically make arrest decisions based on a 'feeling'?" Yoon asked, quietly pointed.

"You read gumshoe novels." Malcolm arched a brow. "Haven't you ever heard of following a hunch?"

There it was: that briefly offended look, before it closed over again and, with a "*tch*" almost under his breath, Yoon turned away without responding, staring stonily out the window.

Malcolm's lips twitched, but he restrained himself and focused on his phone again, scrolling down to the Ms and tapping *Marcus, Sade*.

Sade took longer to answer, picking up after four rings—and launched in without even saying *hello*. "Did you know that 'Malcolm' is a derivate of a Scottish name meaning 'disciple of Saint Columba'?" they rattled off—their voice smooth coffee and cream, sometimes high, sometimes low. "And Saint Columba was the monk who converted Scotland to Christianity?"

"Not one word about irony, please."

Sade laughed. "Then tell me what I can do for you, my

dear disciple."

"If I give you a list of names, can you pull up their social media accounts? I've also got a laptop with an account logged in that can likely view many of their locked posts, though I've got to check it into evidence before I can check it out to you. I just don't have the time or the skills to comb through it all myself. You up for it?"

"Sure. What am I looking for?"

He frowned, fixing his gaze on the sun visor, idly tracing the outlines of receipts bristling out from the upper edge while he thought. "Places of employment, last check-ins, family members, any notable connections. Don't worry too much about looking for anything specific. Just crawl the data and compile it in one place. Leave it to me and Yoon to find the trends."

Sade let out an exaggerated sigh. "That's boring."

"You come up with too many wild stories. Leave the fiction to your books."

A note of hope lit Sade's voice. "Are you coming to my next signing?"

"You don't want my ugly mug scaring people off."

"What people?" Sade asked dryly, and Malcolm chuckled.

"The accounts, Sade. I won't know what I'm looking for until I see it."

"Drop the laptop by as soon as you can, and I'll get a dossier together for you." Sade hesitated, voice dropping until, in the background, Malcolm could hear the noise of the bullpen, voices calling and phones ringing and somewhere close by, a printer chuffing and clattering. "I should warn you. The Park case is on the news now. The story broke about half an hour ago. Twitter's going completely off the rails. Baltimore's trending, and the Facebook hoaxes have already started." Their voice rose to normal volume again. "That's going to narrow your window, if the perp sees that. They're going to cover their tracks."

"Not much to cover at this point." Malcolm sighed heavily. "They didn't exactly try to hide before."

"But if they do it again, they'll be more careful. So *you* be careful, Mal."

Malcolm couldn't help smiling. "Thanks. I will. See you in a bit."

"I'll be waiting."

Malcolm cut the call and settled his phone back into his pocket, then started the ignition.

Yoon glanced at him from the corner of his eye, just barely turning his head. "Sade?"

"Sade Marcus. They—" Malcolm twisted to look over his shoulder at traffic as he backed the Camaro out, stretching out one arm along the back of the passenger seat to balance; Yoon's hair brushed against his wrist and hand in a wash as soft as rabbit fur, until Yoon grimaced and leaned away. Once he had a clear trajectory, Malcolm pulled his arm back out of Yoon's space and focused on drawing the car around and finishing his sentence. "They're our resident computer geek. Half our officers can barely send a coherent email. Sade keeps us from infecting half the BPD network with malware, and does a little information sniffing when we need it."

"Ah." Yoon spoke his next words as if they were alien, and he struggled to understand them. "You speak to them with affection."

"When you've worked with people for a long time, you come to care about them." Malcolm leaned over and tapped the GPS, picking the Central HQ out of his saved list of destinations. Fuck. Forty-five minutes in this traffic. He confirmed destination, then relaxed with one hand on the steering wheel and let the Camaro cruise into traffic, sparing only a single sideways glance for Yoon before keeping his gaze on the bumper in front of him. "Didn't it work that way at LAPD?"

Yoon's answer seemed more to himself than to Malcolm, quiet and introspective. "...not for me."

Malcolm could see it. Easily. Most police forces considered themselves a brotherhood almost akin to a cult. That made a lot of problems, both for average citizens and for people who didn't follow the cult mentality. Malcolm had found his own way by getting his detective shield and working his cases alone, until the only people he had to get along with were the Captain and the support staff. Someone like Yoon—someone who didn't ignore minor infractions, someone who worked by the books and kept his spine stiff and upright and shut down anything personal?

Maybe they'd run him out of LAPD.

Cops could be nasty like that. Frat boy bullies who'd harass you in dangerous ways if you didn't toe the line.

If you didn't look the other way, either, when those infractions weren't so minor.

Malcolm considered asking, but Yoon would only shut down on him. So he only said carefully, "Could work that way here."

"I do not need it to," Yoon said, and that was that.

Malcolm let it be, and only focused on navigating through the congested midafternoon inner city traffic without causing a fender bender, tapping his fingers against the steering wheel as he turned over his thoughts in his head. Something about Nathan McAllister wasn't adding up, if he was honest with himself. Nathan wasn't telling them something. Was he lying to protect himself?

Or lying to protect someone else?

His thoughts worried themselves in circles, but hadn't managed to spiral to a conclusion by the time they pulled in at HQ and he found his marked spot in the parking garage. He slid out of the car; Yoon snagged the laptop and followed, before offering the Dell silently with a quirked brow.

Malcolm tucked it under his arm, then glanced toward the stairwell entrance. "Listen," he said. "We've put in more than a full day. I don't know about you, but I'm running on over twenty-four hours without sleep and I'm ready to drop.

We did the first stage of important legwork. If we keep pushing at this any longer, we'll start making mistakes." He dragged his gaze back to Yoon, meeting those impenetrable, strangely reflective black eyes. When they caught the light they glimmered almost blue, like moon-glow reflecting off the iridescence of a raven's wing. "Go home. Get some rest. Turn in early. We'll regroup and see where things take us in the morning."

"That is perhaps wise."

Malcolm chuckled. "I'll take 'perhaps.'" He jerked his thumb toward the stairs. "I'm going to take the laptop into Sade, but I'll be right out. You need a ride home?"

"I do not."

Malcolm raised a hand, flicking two fingers in acceptance, and turned away—but Yoon called him back with a soft call of his name.

"Khalaji."

Malcolm glanced back. "Yeah?"

"About Jake Alberts." Yoon shifted uncomfortably, then jerked his gaze to one side, looking fixedly across the parking garage. His back straightened, his voice clipped, careful and proud. "I do not believe in violence against citizens. I only intercepted and pinned him because he attempted to flee before I could question him. I swear to you that I did my utmost to restrain him without harming him." His lips remained parted, but no sound came out; his lashes lowered, before he continued more tentatively, "I...do not want you to think of me as someone who abuses his power."

"That looked like it was physically painful to say." Malcolm turned back to face Yoon fully, taking him in. He held himself like he was anticipating a blow, and determined to endure it without showing a moment's pain, without any reaction at all. "You want me to trust you, don't you?"

"You could at the very least trust my judgment," Yoon said. "And my motives."

Malcolm shrugged one shoulder. "It's possible I misjudged you."

Yoon fixed him with a flat look, but something flickered around the corners of his mouth, the faintest ghost of a smile. "Only possible?"

Malcolm grinned. "Go get some sleep, Yoon."

"As you say." Yoon dipped in that slight half-nod, half-bow, then turned away with a precise, almost militant step. "Goodnight, Khalaji."

"Night."

Yoon only walked away, stepping from the parking garage and into the sunlight without looking back.

Malcolm lingered to watch him, then shook his head and stepped into the building, leaving his thoughts of Yoon behind.

[11: A STUDY IN BLUE]

MALCOLM DROPPED THE LAPTOP WITH Sade, leaned into the Captain's office just long enough to let her know he hadn't pushed Yoon off a bridge, then took himself home to his apartment.

He'd barely kicked off his shoes and collapsed across his bed, still rumpled from last night, before sleep snapped him up in a clutching grip and crushed him into the dark.

He woke to a pounding headache, with no idea who or where he was, or what time it was.

Malcolm groaned, dragging his hands through his hair, and rolled onto his back while bits of his brain woke up one by one, enough to ground him in reality. How long had he been asleep? Fuck, he'd fallen asleep in his suit. He sat up groggily and shrugged out of the coat, loosened his tie and the top button of his shirt, then fished his phone from his coat pocket and checked the time. Seven fifty-two. He'd been out for over four hours.

A missed call alert blinked in the notifications bar. He swiped it.

Leon-Khalaji, Gabrielle. Six thirty-three PM.

His heart tried to twist, tried to ache, but he was too tired for more than a faint pang. He dropped the phone and let the screen go dark.

Right now, he was too raw to go down that path.

He dragged out of bed and shed his clothing, leaving tie and shirt and slacks in trails across the sofa, the easy chair, as he crossed the massive single-room converted warehouse apartment to the delicate intersecting perpendicular wood panels of the folding Moroccan standing screen—each square made of patterns of dark wooden geometries over translucent amber inlays—that separated the bathroom from the rest of the apartment. He leaned over the clawfoot tub and turned the water on as hot as it would go, then reached up to brush his fingers through the spray trickling from the curving steel shower head bolted directly to the concrete wall. He only waited long enough for the water to warm to a tolerable level, then pulled the tie from his hair, shook it free, stepped into the bath, braced his hands against the wall, and just *leaned*.

The water sheeted down over him, striking his scalp, running down the back of his neck, pouring over his shoulders and down his back in a deluge, each wave of droplets warmer and warmer until the heat sank into him enough to melt the tension from his body. He bowed his head, closing his eyes, and just breathed in the scent of fresh water and steam, fighting not to tremble. Fighting to let go, to just let the shower wash him clean.

Darian Park in the alley.

Those grisly stumps, those blank eyes.

Parents rushed headlong into the loss of their only son, the Parks taking that pain like a fucking car crash.

Nathan McAllister looking up at him, silently begging him not to drag the boy through this when he'd already been through enough anguish and loss.

These *fucking* queer kids. And there wasn't a damned thing Malcolm could have done to stop any of this, but he still felt the weight of it on him, crushing the breath from his lungs and telling him he should have done something more, should *be* doing something more.

As if he was a necromancer, divining the dead to bring them back to life.

When he could only make them live again in the darkest recesses of his thoughts, where their accusatory voices would whisper to him until the day he died.

He pushed away from the wall, tilting his head back into the spray and slicking his hair back, taking several ragged breaths until he no longer felt like snarling, roaring, collapsing to his knees and sobbing. If he let every day on the job get to him this way he would destroy himself. He had to let it go.

If only he could be so easily cold and withdrawn as Yoon.

Malcolm stayed under the spray until the pounding droplets at least beat him numb, then shut the water off, dragged a towel over his hair and body, and padded out to snag a pair of pajama pants before checking the fridge.

He paused, though, as he caught sight of a bright blue piece of note paper tacked to the fridge. Not anything from his desk, and the handwriting wasn't familiar, a sort of jagged up-and-down scratch like every letter was a dagger, oddly playful, whimsical.

Maybe next time I'll tell you my name.

He frowned, tugging the note down and turning it over. No signature, nothing. Who in the—

Oh.

Malcolm laughed to himself wearily. The man he'd picked up last night at a quiet piano bar down near Little Italy. Malcolm was far beyond the bass-thumping club scene, bodies writhing and youth sweating from every pore, but now and then he liked to spend an evening out among other people, have a few drinks, lose himself in the soft sound of fingers on keys and the faint murmur of intimate conversation. His favorite piano bar wasn't exactly queer-exclusive, but it wasn't the first time he'd met a man of similar tastes there. Murmured words over drinks, few personal details exchanged, just those soft and careful feints that sometimes went somewhere, sometimes didn't.

Last night the nameless man had watched Malcolm for long enough that Malcolm had taken notice. He hadn't acknowledged the man directly, but he'd kept a surreptitious eye on him as he slowly nurtured a tumbler of Johnny Walker Blue. He was accustomed to this song and dance, waited for the casual wandering stroll toward him, but instead a napkin had slid down the bar, the nameless man leaning in to a woman on a barstool between them and, with a beguiling smile, coaxing her to pass the napkin to Malcolm.

Do you want to know my name?

Scribbled on the napkin in blue pen, the thin layered paper torn at the peak of the *k*, and now Malcolm remembered that handwriting. He remembered laughing to himself, too, then meeting pale green eyes across the space between them and mouthing, *Ask me later*.

He leaned his shoulder against the fridge, glanced at the rumpled bed, and turned the note over in his fingers. If he went back to the piano bar again, would the nameless man be there? Maybe. Maybe not. Malcolm wouldn't mind a little company to ease his aching thoughts, make the grinding machine of his brain stop for five minutes, chase the images of sawed-off bone and abraded skin from his mind.

But he didn't really do second times. Attachments.

Not anymore.

And right now, the best way to scour the grisly thoughts from his mind was to find a lead, pursue it to the end, and solve this case so he could at least get some closure.

He warmed up some leftover lamb-stuffed yaprak, poured a glass of wine, and settled across his bed, propped on one arm with his laptop open in front of him. His email came up, half spam, half people who had his card and misused it in copious ways. He'd responded to a potential homicide call over on Western two years ago and ever since then the little old granny who'd called it in—and who'd mistaken "neighbors having kinky sex" for murder—had abused his email to report every kid who got too close to her lawn, every cat in a tree, every broken fire hydrant. When it was relevant, he forwarded it on to her neighborhood beat cops.

Most of the time, it wasn't relevant.

Nor were the half-dozen other similar complaints in his inbox. He sat up straighter, though, at the new email from Sade at the bottom of the list. Inside was a spreadsheet that Sade had worked up into a map of interconnections between the social media accounts of Nathan McAllister, Darian Park, Trevor Manson, and their friends—including several of the names Nathan had given Malcolm. Sade had arranged them into something that bordered on an infographic.

And Nathan was at the very center.

Everyone was connected through him. Not Darian, the popular beloved one. Sade had checked the dates that different people had friended each other on social media, and a new one added to the cluster group of what was starting to look like an Ex-Boyfriends' club every time Nathan's relationship status changed to *single*.

There was a second cluster group orbiting Nathan, a group of college girls who seemed to post on his wall more than he did. Malcolm didn't understand why until he dug deeper into Nathan's history and albums. He was bassist and songwriter in some emo-punk band, Genus Corvidae.

One of his most popular posts had gathered over eleven thousand likes and more than two thousand comments.

> *I just can't get over it. I loved him so much, and this is how I remember him.*

The column of text that followed looked to be song lyrics. The comments were all crying-face emojis, calling Nathan sensitive, his lyrics were beautiful, he was beautiful, they all loved him and were with him in this hard time, broken heart emojis.

Malcolm was missing something. All these conflicting portraits. Nathan the sullen loner that parents didn't like. Nathan the brooding, tortured musician, from real-world loner to online superstar, coming alive on the stage. Nathan the quiet, vulnerable, grieving boy. Nathan who broke social strata to date and love and memorialize popular students, athletes, perfect scholars. Nathan who had only dated Trevor Manson for two weeks before breaking up, but claimed to love him enough to write a song about him and mourn him for eight months before his next relationship connection with Darian.

Would he write a song about Darian next?

None of it made *sense*.

The timeline did, though. Trevor Manson was murdered two days after their breakup. Darian Park was murdered two days after their breakup. Both murdered at night. Both murdered by the same methods.

Things weren't looking good for Nathan McAllister.

But Malcolm couldn't shake that feeling of something *wrong*.

Frowning, biting at his thumbnail, he flicked through a few more tabs on the spreadsheet, scanning the collected data, from birthdates to employment history, looking for a connection, then sank back against the headboard with a sigh and sipped his wine, letting the full, mellow oaked chardonnay roll over his tongue, staring across the apartment.

He was getting nowhere. Just tangling himself up more.

Sleep. A nap wasn't enough. He'd be fresher and capable of tackling the problem from a different angle come morning.

But as he lingered over his yaprak and wine, he couldn't help paging through the data again, letting his eyes unfocus until he was no longer instinctively looking for something and focusing in on one thing to the exclusion of all others. It was a trick he'd learned in his old life, using principles of psychology to train himself out of self-biasing habits.

Internal bias taught viewers what to expect from photographs of particular things before they had even fully visually processed the photo, so that by the time both their minds and eyes had focused they had already zeroed in on the parts of the photo that represented what they expected to see.

The brain's habit of filtering out irrelevant data to prevent overload made anything else in the photo practically invisible, even though what was irrelevant had been decided by bias and expectation rather than actual observation.

When he unfocused his eyes, he wasn't looking at anything, not really. Nothing but a blur that his ingrained biases couldn't filter before he had a chance to really *see* what was in front of him. So when one detail or another was particularly prominent and eye-catching, it jumped out from what was essentially a muddle of color—and caught him, snapping him back like whiplash.

And he snapped back as he registered one particular photo:

Nathan caught in a deep, passionate kiss with Trevor, so intimately close that Trevor nearly had Nathan bent back over the arm around Nathan's waist. The setting seemed to be a concert, maybe one of Nathan's.

And in the background, hovering almost in shadow, the camera's reflections turning his pupils red, was a sullenly glowering Darian, that bright, cheerful smile vanished behind a resentful scowl.

So Darian had been jealous when Trevor had been dating Nathan. Had that led to the split between Nathan and Darian? Had Darian still been jealous of the emotion Nathan invested in Trevor's memory? Was that what Shane had meant, that Darian had said Nathan already had someone more important?

But how would that be enough to motivate murder?

He closed the spreadsheet. If he left it open he was just going to keep looking at it, and make things worse. Instead he pulled up his media player and set Lucas King's "Last Leaf Falls" on repeat, settled back against the headboard, and lingered over his wine while the city skyline glimmered through the wide bank of shutter-style windows and soft, melodic piano fell over him like rain and the shimmer of drifting petals.

Before another hour had passed, he was asleep again.

Until his phone started its grating trill once more, dragging him from the few moments of peace he'd managed to steal for himself.

He hated that ringtone. Every work number was set to that ringtone, high and piercing with a deeply annoying buzz, so there was no chance he would sleep through an important call.

And every time it woke him up, he wanted to smash the damned phone against the wall.

Without opening his eyes, he flung one hand toward his phone, knocked his knuckles painfully against his laptop, smashed his palm down on the bits of food left on the plate he'd left sitting on the bed, then finally managed to find his phone, silence that hideous noise, and drag it to his ear.

"I am not getting out of bed. I don't even know what time it is, but I am *not* getting out of bed."

"It's one AM, and we have another body," Zarate said.

"There's always another body. When the fuck do you

sleep?"

"This one's related to last night's case, Malcolm," she continued. "Another dead kid. Missing body parts."

He snapped his eyes open, heart thudding, and sat up straight. "The same MO?" He swore under his breath in Persian, threw in some Turkish for good measure, then dragged himself out of bed. "Let me get dressed. Can you text me Yoon's number? I'll get him."

"No need." That cool, measured voice drifted through his apartment door, muted by the barrier of aged wood. "She called me first."

Malcolm scowled at the door. "...the fuck. Hold on," he muttered into the phone, then stalked to the door and yanked it open.

Yoon stood on the other side, crisp as if he hadn't been asleep at all in a sleek black turtleneck, black jeans, and that long, stiff black coat. He tilted his head at Malcolm, gaze raking over him as if to point out every detail of his shirtless, disheveled, pajama-clad state before rising to his eyes as Yoon mockingly arched both brows.

Malcolm growled. "How long have you been standing out there?"

"Only a moment." Yoon lightly rapped his knuckles against the door. "Thin walls."

Closing his eyes, Malcolm took a slow, calming breath. "Text me the crime scene," he snapped into the phone— before hanging up, tossing his phone on the bed, and shooting

Yoon a foul look as he stalked to his wardrobe. "Who told you where I live?"

Yoon stepped past the threshold and nudged the door closed with his elbow. "It was in your personnel file," he said matter-of-factly, as if it should be perfectly obvious.

"Why were you reading my personnel file?" When Yoon didn't answer, Malcolm sighed. "Asshole."

"Jot," Yoon replied without missing a beat.

Malcolm jabbed a finger at him. "Don't translate that. If I know, I'm going to hurt you." He shoved his hair back from his face. "It is too late at night for this shit." Muttering under his breath, he pulled the wardrobe door open. "I need to get dressed."

Yoon only stood there, his head tilted in that infuriating way, a damned android that seemed to be malfunctioning when it tried to process why Malcolm was so annoyed.

Malcolm clenched his jaw, stared up at the iron cross-beams overhead, sent up a prayer up to anything that would listen, then muttered, "That means *get out*, Yoon."

Yoon tilted his head to the other side. Then, "I would not have supposed you were shy," he said, before walking out and closing the door behind him.

Malcolm stared after him, then closed his eyes and thunked his forehead against the wardrobe door, reminding himself to just *breathe*.

He was getting too old for this shit.

[12: THE BOY WHO CRIED]

SEONG-JAE LEANED OUTSIDE THE door to wait for Khalaji, folding his arms over his chest and propping himself against the wall. Half of his mind was preoccupied with the case; it was unusual for a serial killer to make such a rapid escalation. From eight months between the first and second kill to less than twenty-four hours between the second and third. Normally escalations happened over the course of several kills, closing through timelines that narrowed by months, then weeks, then days. Something must be driving a sense of urgency, something the perpetrator felt a need to complete before he was caught.

The other half of his mind was annoyingly preoccupied by the differences in Khalaji by day, and Khalaji by night.

By day, Khalaji was a contradiction in his smoothly tailored suits paired with that grizzled, wolfish beard, wild hair, wilder eyes, animalistic things that didn't belong to polished patent leather shoes and the touch of slow, lazy elegance in his movements, in his smile, in the kindness in brutal hands. He looked as though a wild man of the woods and an intellectual had merged into some hybrid breed who could arrange delicate fabrics into confections of drapery—or just as easily crush a man's throat in with his bare hands, knuckles bloodied raw.

By night, Khalaji was pure beast, eyes hot and livid.

The suit had slimmed and disguised his bulk; he was a monolith, arms burly, waist thick with hard-corded muscle, his entire body slashed over with gnarled scars that looked older than a lifetime, making fault line maps down his arms, over his chest, his stomach, his back. Several had that tight pucker that promised bullets had kissed his flesh many times, while others looked like injuries from accidents or bladed weapons. One, a snaking line that looked as if it had been cut with a serrated blade edge, slashed right through a tattoo on his bicep, one that resembled a yin-yang symbol without the counterbalancing dots, inked in dark blue above a flowing 29th in stylized black letters.

Military. Army. He'd glimpsed that in Khalaji's personnel file, before the call had come in for the case and drawn him away. Mizrahim, he'd said, yet he'd violated Torah by desecrating his body with a tattoo, although Khalaji had said he was non-practicing and—

And Seong-Jae was wasting mental energy that should be focused on figuring out the case on, instead, figuring out his temporary partner.

The door creaked open at his side. Khalaji stepped out of his apartment—what little Seong-Jae had glimpsed had been tasteful, stylish, eclectic and spacious—fully dressed, his suit a sleek dark flint gray this time, fingers busily knotting a slim black tie under his collar with a deftness that could only be born of practice.

For some reason, Seong-Jae found that tie immensely irritating.

Khalaji tossed him a sharp look, smoothed his tie, and swept his hair back in both hands. "Are you with me again, or do you have your own car?"

"I will ride with you and return for my vehicle later."

"If that's what you want."

"It is a matter of convenience."

"Of course it is." Another look that could melt steel, and Khalaji turned to lead him down the stairs. "Come on, then."

Apparently Khalaji was offended by convenience.

Or he was simply extremely grouchy upon waking.

Seong-Jae followed him to the car, and let himself into the passenger seat. The drive to the crime scene wasn't overly long, but once again they didn't speak. The address they had been given belonged to a movie theater not far from the university. Another killing in a public place. Another risk, especially considering the time of night. Mondays might perhaps have fewer clientele, but this time the kill had been earlier—more risk of people on the street.

What would drive the killer to throw caution to the wind?

The marquee lights at the theater were turned off, when they arrived—the first response officers already there, already sidelining the witnesses and roping off the crime scene. Another alley, Seong-Jae noted.

Malcolm parked the car on the curb and glanced at him. "You ready for this?"

"If I must be."

They mounted the curb and approached the mouth of the alleyway. A flash of badges to the officers there and they were past the cordon, ducking underneath the spread of yellow police tape. Seong-Jae had braced himself to face something macabre.

He wasn't prepared for the strangeness sprawled before his eyes.

Literally sprawled—because no one part of the body was connected to the other.

The victim had been so completely dismembered it was almost impossible to process him as human. His head rested in the center of a grisly flower of limbs, blood smeared over his slack face, bleach-blond hair matted to his skull by crimson mud and his eyes hanging half open. He'd been sawed off at the neck unevenly, left propped on the stump and canting to one side. A coating of blood matted the pavement beneath him, as if someone had flung and spattered thin, meaty paint everywhere and let it spread, then splashed it in streaks on the walls of the buildings framing the alley.

Surrounding the head were severed arms, legs, arranged at diagonals to each other, calves separated from thighs to create a six-pointed star. If this were a compass, then the pelvic remains would be south, placed buttocks-outward and with the flaccid phallus pointing north, toward the victim's mouth.

Seong-Jae took a step back, bringing a hand up to shield his mouth. The smell was barbaric, a butcher's-shop stench that overwhelmed, but even more overwhelming was the sheer brutality of this. There was hate in it this time, in the ragged hack-marks left on the limbs, in the derisive positioning of the body parts. Hate so deep Seong-Jae could feel it in the pit of his stomach, heavy and sinking. The perpetrator had acted out of impulse and spite, projecting resentment of the victim onto his flesh. The placement of the pelvis suggested a hatred toward the victim's desire, or lack thereof.

"Fuck," Khalaji breathed at his side.

Seong-Jae was inclined to agree.

He tore his gaze from the body and looked at Khalaji. The other man was pale beneath the swarthy bronze of his skin, washed-out and sick-looking, his eyes a little too wide and stark. He was just *staring* at the body, his fingers curling into slow fists at his side.

"I know him," Khalaji whispered.

Seong-Jae frowned. "He is an acquaintance of yours?"

"No. No, I—" With a shaky breath, Khalaji turned away. "I recognize him. I don't know him. He's one of Nathan's ex-boyfriends. I was looking at the info Sade sent over before bed, and..." He just...stopped. As if he could not manage any more, as if some part of him had shut down, he stopped, looking woodenly toward the ground—before abruptly starting up again, words spilling out of his mouth in a rough, low growl laden with choked emotion. "Zack. His name was Zack…something. I saw him on Nathan's Facebook." He turned his head over his shoulder, eyeing the crime scene, then closed his eyes, his brows tight in a pained knit. "So much for being careful next time."

Seong-Jae stole a glance back at the body…body *parts*…then shook his head and touched Khalaji's arm, before jerking back and nodding toward the mouth of the alleyway.

"Please," he asked.

Khalaji stared at him as if he didn't understand, then stared at him as if he did, then nodded and followed Seong-Jae around the corner. Out of sight. Onto the sidewalk, where as long as they didn't look toward the police tape this was an ordinary street on an ordinary night.

Seong-Jae leaned against the wall of the building to one side of the alley, against the brick framing a display window full of shoes. Khalaji leaned next to him. They watched the late-night traffic for long moments, before Seong-Jae finally found his voice again.

"My apologies. I…" Pride galled him, stuck in his throat, but pride was a smaller obstacle to pass than the hard knot of something inside him that felt like *grief.*

Grief for a stranger he didn't know.

He inhaled sharply, tried again. "I was not…expecting

that. I was not prepared. I simply needed a moment. I am sorry for drawing you away from the crime scene."

Khalaji turned his head, watching Seong-Jae, but Seong-Jae turned away. He couldn't look at Khalaji, not when the man seemed to be saying without words:

I understand.

I understand that you didn't just need to leave.

You needed to leave, and not be alone with the horror crushing its weight against your chest.

"Yeah," Khalaji said. "I needed a moment too. But we have to get back in there. Do our preliminary before forensics needs us out of the way."

"I simply…" Seong-Jae shook his head, then thunked it back against the brick, staring up at the sky. "It is…impossible to imagine how anyone could do such a thing."

"It's like someone tore a doll apart." Khalaji swore softly, the sounds coming out in a low, frustrated growl that trailed from English into some other language, sharp yet with soft undertones. "Arms, legs, head, pelvis. I didn't see a torso. Did you?"

"No. Only…everything else."

Seong-Jae fixed his gaze on the stars, as he spoke. It was hard to see them, when city lights made a haze of pink and purple and strange, cloudy orange, a mist that eclipsed the stars until he could only find one or two.

One or two were enough.

Just simple points to anchor him to this earth.

"Have you ever seen anything like that?" he asked.

"Not...like this," Khalaji answered. "Mob hits, sometimes they chop the bodies up to get rid of the evidence. This isn't like that. It feels different. Did you feel it again? The intimacy?"

Too much.

This was too personal, too close.

"Yes," Seong-Jae answered. "It felt almost fetishistic. A worship that paired obsession with hatred. It felt...unclean." He struggled to find words to describe it. Struggled for words that would explain why this felt so different, so unwholesome, so dark, so *personal*. As if he could have easily been in the victim's shoes, the target of the same loathsome fixation for very similar reasons. He gave up, shaking his head.

"And we're sure this is the same killer," Khalaji said.

"The same method and tools. The same signature, if you will," Seong-Jae said. "They took what mattered to them and left the rest behind."

"Darian's legs were important. Zack's chest was important." Khalaji shifted restlessly next to him. His arm brushed Seong-Jae's.

Seong-Jae didn't pull away.

"Why?" Khalaji continued. "Why different parts from different men? Do you think the killer is trying to preserve the body parts?"

"Are we looking at someone with knowledge of

embalming techniques?"

"Or just good Google-fu. You can figure out how to do anything on the internet now." Khalaji's laugh was a dry and ragged thing. "I don't want to go back in that alley, Yoon."

"I know."

"Are we ready for this?"

"No," Seong-Jae said, and pushed away from the wall. "But we have no other choice. Gloves."

Khalaji blinked at him, his mouth seaming in a frown. "What?"

"Do you have spare vinyl gloves?"

"…oh." With a faint but genuine smile, Khalaji fished into his pocket and retrieved a limp, crumpled pair of vinyl gloves, offering them to Seong-Jae. "Thanks."

Seong-Jae took the gloves and tugged them on, then nodded toward the mouth of the alleyway. "We do this."

"Swabbie's after?" Khalaji asked, and Seong-Jae couldn't help but smile faintly even if his mouth felt frozen and cracked.

"Swabbie's after," he agreed, and followed Khalaji once more into the dark.

THEY FOUND THE VICTIM'S CLOTHING bundled up into a wad and shoved behind a few trash cans. The wallet in his pocket said his name was Zachary Weston, twenty years old, another University of Maryland student. The movie theatre manager told them he was a part-time shift employee working the ticket booth around his class schedule at the university. He'd gone out to take the trash out after close-up and clean-up, but when he hadn't come back after twenty minutes the manager had gotten worried, gone looking for him, and found him scattered like broken toy pieces across the pavement.

No one had seen anything. No one remembered anyone in particular seeking Weston out or causing a disturbance. No one had seen anyone who even vaguely resembled McAllister's description.

Seong-Jae scrawled a few notes in his notepad. "Twenty minutes from isolation to complete dismemberment. Within yards of the protective detail."

Khalaji glanced at the knotted group of theater staff and a few late stragglers who'd still been in evening films. Working with the uniformed officers were the two plainclothes officers who had been assigned to Zachary

Weston's protective detail, and who hadn't seen a thing until the manager had found Weston's body. Khalaji's jaw tightened, muscle ticking just below his ear, and he led Seong-Jae a few feet away before speaking. "The killer has more practice now. They know their method. It's just going to get easier for them every time."

"I cannot imagine anything like that being easy for anyone."

And yet he knew better. He'd spent too much time working on criminal profiles of the most violent minds in the country. Working LAPD homicide had been ordinary in comparison to that, and yet this case took him back to places he had never wanted to go again. Pacing around those scattered body parts, skirting puddles of blood so as not to contaminate the crime scene, had reminded him of who he never wanted to be: someone cold enough to find this ordinary.

Someone cold enough to find this easy.

Someone just like the killers he had tracked, spending so much time thinking like them that his mind settled in pathways he could never break free from again.

He forced his mind off those paths now, and away from the scent of butchered meat clinging in his nostrils, away from the way ragged tongues of flesh had protruded from the stumps, flapping as if trying to tell their terrible story.

"I believe the killer rushed this time," he said, lingering on those ragged tongues even though he didn't want to. "The cuts were hastier. They worried less about damaging the flesh. Did you see…?" He tapped his own throat, just above the turtleneck.

"I did. The hacksaw marks cover most of the ligature marks, but they're still recognizable." Khalaji fell silent, stroking his beard, then pointed out, "They had a shorter window. And maybe, if all they wanted was the torso, it didn't matter if the connecting joints were mangled."

"Discarded like offal. As though his life meant nothing, and his only value was in the part the perpetrator desired."

"Isn't that how it always is, though?" Khalaji countered softly. "We only define others by the value they have to us, and once they no longer provide that value, we let them go."

Seong-Jae searched Khalaji's face, but Khalaji wasn't looking at him. Khalaji was seeing things elsewhere, elsewhen—and Seong-Jae wondered who had let Khalaji go, once they no longer saw any value in him.

"Not everyone believes that," Seong-Jae said, then stepped backward, toward the car. "Come. We have everything we can take from here. Let us go to your terrible pub."

Khalaji cracked a weary smile. "It's not that terrible."

"It is."

"You liked the fries."

"I tolerated the fries," Seong-Jae corrected, then amended, "But the coffee was not wholly objectionable."

"To coffee, then?"

Seong-Jae bowed his head. "To coffee," he replied, and gestured toward Khalaji's car. "After you."

SEONG-JAE HAD NO APPETITE.

But it seemed important to Khalaji to indulge in this ritual. To establish some sense of normalcy, and rebuild the boundaries of whatever arcane circle banished the dark from the night of his soul.

And so Seong-Jae drank coffee that was half cream, ate greasy fries covered in toasted goat cheese, and tried not to think of the faces of dead boys past and present.

His third cup of coffee was almost gone before Khalaji said, "We're going to need to get an alibi from McAllister."

"I know."

"Do you think he's the one?"

Seong-Jae tried to make that fit into the puzzle pieces. Tried to visualize Nathan McAllister, the wiry lines of his arms standing out in narrow cords as he pulled hard on a piece of steel wire looped around the victim's throat, hands gloved for leverage and traction. Tried to visualize him standing over the body, straddling the hips and sawing away, flinching away from the messy, spurting gouts of blood every time he severed an artery in a body still so warm some parts of it hadn't yet figured out that it was no longer breathing.

He could picture it perfectly, and yet he couldn't imagine it at all.

"I do not know," he finally said.

"Yeah." Khalaji's shoulders slumped forward, and he stared into his coffee mug. "Neither do I."

[13: ROARING TIDES]

FOR THE SECOND TIME, DAWN was rising as they left the pub, just the barest hint of light kissing the horizon and lighting a candle's flame at the very rim of the world—but for Malcolm this was less the start of a new day and more a countdown toward the next dead body.

If the killer was escalating, collecting body parts, they would strike again. Soon. He should double the protective detail on each of McAllister's ex-boyfriends, on top of the detail on McAllister himself.

He turned his thoughts over on the drive back to HQ. It went somehow without saying that he and Yoon needed to convene at the office, go over the evidence, strategize a plan. Contact with persons of interest would probably be better off limited, when anything they asked or any information tipped off could drift back to the killer within the targets' social circles.

He would have to find Zachary Weston's parents, too. Before the story broke, and with the bloodhounds sniffing after the last murder they likely wouldn't have much time before this one hit headlines. Reporters wanted the ink dry on the newsprint before the blood went cold in the body.

"Trevor." He thumped a hand against the steering wheel. "What if it's Trevor causing them to escalate?"

Yoon jumped, and Malcolm realized he'd been dozing against the window. Blinking, rubbing at one eye, Yoon mumbled, "What?"

"They didn't take a body part from Trevor. Trevor was the first. There must have been something important about him, something unique. They haven't found it, so they're looking for it again."

"And taking what they want from other bodies in the process?"

"Something like that." He drummed his fingers on the inner bottom curve of the steering wheel, then shook his head. "No, that's not it. That's still not it. We're missing something that would tie this all together."

"Perhaps another conversation with McAllister will provide insight."

"Yeah. Maybe."

But Malcolm wasn't sure.

Once they'd parked at Central, he took the stairs two at a time. Yoon wasn't far behind him. The lights were up in the bullpen when they reached homicide's floor, a few other early risers at their desks, muttering into their phones or poring through photos and paperwork or squinting at computer screens. Malcolm beelined for his desk, but Sade leaned out of the server room tucked off to one side through a door marked with a bright yellow BIOHAZARD: DO NOT ENTER sign.

Or at least, part of Sade leaned out. One gangly arm, a long-fingered, square hand, a dusky shoulder, then the fall of dark brown hair trailing almost to the floor and approximately one half of the top of Sade's head. They leaned their chair back on its back wheels so far it was practically balanced on two casters, peering out past the doorframe.

"Mal!" Sade called. "Come on. Bring the new guy."

Malcolm changed course. Sade wheeled away, disappearing back into their lair. Ducking beneath the tangle of Christmas lights strung over the door, Malcolm muttered "Watch your head" to Yoon and slipped into the chaos of Sade's den: computer towers everywhere, a curving desk lined with a half-dozen monitors in varying sizes, all running processes he couldn't even begin to comprehend, half playing video in various windows, one completely taken up with what looked like one of Sade's games. The room was pitch black save for the glow of the screens and more Christmas lights in bright colors clustered in fire-hazard tangles along the upper edge of the ceiling; the windows had been taped over in blackout paper.

If Malcolm had been in any mood to smile, the dismayed, puzzled look on Yoon's face would have done it.

Sade spun their chair around, fingers curled against the edge between their spread thighs, jean-clad legs swinging without touching the floor. They squinted, leaning forward to peer curiously at Yoon.

"Hi, new guy. I'm Sade."

Yoon made that *tch* sound again. "I have a name."

"Lieutenant Detective Yoon," Sade proclaimed officiously, then laughed and pointed a black-tipped finger at Yoon. "I know *all* about you."

Yoon's brows clouded to a thunderhead. Malcolm pinched the bridge of his nose. "*Focus.* Why did you call us over?"

"Oh! That. I," Sade announced, pushing their little black-framed librarian glasses up their pert nose, "have presents for you. Well, *a* present. But you're going to want to see this."

"Don't tease. I'm too tired for it."

Sade's pale brown eyes glittered. "I," they said, brandishing an iPhone toward him with a flourish, "cracked Park's phone. And you're going to want to see his text history with McAllister."

Malcolm took the phone and eyed the open text history. No new sent texts to McAllister for days, but several received:

> *its not wat u think*

> *plz d talk to me*

> *i stg ill xplain evrythng*
> *just answer or pickup smthng*

i dont want 2 hurt u

They were all frantic, sent barely minutes apart. Then the last one, sent Friday night, approximately three hours before Park's murder:

u can fucking die. u were never good enough.

Swearing softly, Malcolm tilted the phone toward Yoon. Yoon's gaze tracked back and forth, his lips thinning. "That, I believe is grounds for arrest."

God *damn* it. Everything in Malcolm was screaming this was the wrong path, but if he ignored this and didn't at least haul Nathan McAllister in for questioning, the oversight could be used in a court case later.

And if he was wrong, if he was letting his own feelings impact his decisions, he could be willfully leaving a serial murderer on the loose.

He dropped his phone in his pocket and pushed past Yoon to the door. "Come on," he said. "Let's bring him in."

IT WAS STILL DARK ENOUGH to see the light on in the upstairs window of McAllister's apartment, sunrise still a golden shadow flirting with the edges of the night, by the time they parked outside the building. Fingers tight against the Camaro's steering wheel, Malcolm looked up at that square of light, watching the faint movements of shadows on the wall through that narrow glimpse into McAllister's life. He was probably up getting ready for class, with no idea what was coming for him.

"Yoon?" he asked.

Yoon looked up from where he leaned against the car window, fingers curled lightly against his lips. "Yes?"

"Who is Nathan McAllister?"

"I am not certain I understand the question."

"Are we about to arrest a murder suspect, or a grieving boy?"

"You ask that as if they cannot be one and the same," Yoon said, then unlatched the door and stepped out of the car.

Malcolm let Yoon take the lead this time. He didn't have the heart to be the one knocking on that door. Didn't have the heart to be the one the roommate saw when he opened the door, then let out an exasperated sound and flicked Yoon over with a dirty look.

"You again?" the boy sneered.

Yoon lifted both brows briefly. "I would advise that you let us in."

"I would advise that you—"

"Don't." Malcolm cut him off, shaking his head. "Don't argue, son."

Sanjit frowned, dismay and uncertainty darkening his eyes, before he stepped back. Just as Yoon stepped inside, Malcolm on his heels, Nathan ducked around the bedroom partition.

"Sanjit? What—" He froze as he looked up, gaze landing on Malcolm, then switching to Yoon. "Oh."

Yoon stepped forward, lifting his chin. "Nathan McAllister? We are bringing you in for questioning under suspicion for the murders of Trevor Manson and Darian Park."

"Whoa," Sanjit breathed.

Nathan shook his head sharply, backing away. "You can't arrest me for something I didn't do!" he cried. "Don't you need a warrant or something?"

"Probable cause," Malcolm said. "You're in the social work program, not the law program." He pulled a pair of handcuffs from his inner coat pocket. Nathan bristled, stumbling back; he was going to run, Malcolm knew it. Malcolm stopped, holding his hands up. "Don't fight. Please.

We're taking you in for questioning. That's not a conviction. But if you fight we'll have to charge you with resisting arrest, and I don't want to have to do that."

Nathan shrank back more—then deflated, the fight going out of him as if his spine had dissolved, crushed under the weight of the sheer pressure of fear, frustration, the utter unfairness of this.

You can't do this, Malcolm told himself. *You can't let yourself be compromised because you feel sorry for him.*

Anyone capable of dismembering a body is capable of pantomiming innocence.

But "Thank you," he said, stepping forward, approaching slowly. "Now turn around. Hands behind your back."

Nathan turned, moving in a sort of weary shuffle and presenting his back, already bringing his arms together at the base of his spine to touch at the wrist. Malcolm slipped the cuffs on him and locked them into place, while Yoon spoke over the silence of the room, making this official with hard, cold words, dispassionate and flat.

"You have the right to remain silent," Yoon said. "Anything you say can and will be used against you in a court of law. You have the right to speak to an attorney, and have an attorney present during questioning."

Nathan said nothing.

Malcolm took him by the shoulder, and led him from the room.

THE BOY MADE NO STRUGGLE, as Malcolm tucked him down into the back of the Camaro and fastened his seatbelt. Nathan made not a sound as Malcolm drove them back to Central HQ.

He only stared out the window, blank, glassy, as if he already knew his cause was lost.

And Nathan was unresisting as, at HQ, Malcolm took his arm gently and guided him inside with Yoon sweeping after them like a guardian vulture, the wings of his coat flapping.

Processing didn't take long, when they weren't officially booking him. Official check-in, dot the i, cross the t, make sure everything was on the up and up with records and transparency and a clear paper trail for the legal pencil-pushers. Ten minutes or less and Malcolm was escorting Nathan into an interrogation room. He caught Zarate's eye in passing, beckoning, and she slipped out of her office and into the outer corridor where she could watch through the mirrored glass window, standing witness while Malcolm and Yoon shut the door and guided the handcuffed boy to a seat at the only table in the room. Malcolm uncuffed one wrist long enough to thread the chain on the cuffs through the spokes in the chair's back, then recuffed him.

Yoon took point near the door, hovering and watchful. Malcolm drew out a chair opposite Nathan and settled in, reaching over to start the recorder before resting his elbows on the table.

"Please state your full name and date of birth for the record."

Nathan looked lifelessly down at the table, not even lifting his head. "Nathaniel Ezekiel McAllister. January fourteenth, nineteen-ninety-eight."

"Thank you." Malcolm folded his hands together. "You know why you're here."

"You think I killed my ex-boyfriends."

"Did you?"

"*No.*" It was the first spark of life Nathan had shown since the cuffs snapped closed, an emphatic flare, a resentful glance toward Malcolm followed by a mistrustful look at the recorder. "I didn't kill anyone," he said firmly, directing it at the recorder.

"You want to talk to us about why you and Darian broke up?" Malcolm pressed. "About why you and Trevor broke up?"

Nathan went silent, his jaw a tight lump. Malcolm gave him a few moments more, then said,

"Maybe you want to talk about Zachary."

Nathan's shoulders jerked so hard his handcuffs rattled against the back of his chair. His head snapped up, his eyes widening, a garbled sound sucking in on his next breath, then exhaling in a ragged moan.

"No." He shook his head, lank hair flying across his face. "Not...not Zack." He swallowed, throat working. "Is he okay?" he begged. "Tell me he's okay. Tell me he's not dead too."

When Malcolm didn't answer, Nathan lunged forward, only for the chain on the cuffs to snap him back. "*Tell me!*" he demanded, half a snarl, half a sob when his already-red eyes were bursting, brimming with a sudden rapid overflow of tears.

"I can't tell you that, Nathan," Malcolm said, watching those tears and trying to keep his own expression calm, neutral. Trying not to react.

But this was why he hadn't told Nathan about Zachary at the point of arrest.

He wanted that reaction on tape.

He wanted that startled response on record, in case of any questions later.

But he still had to pursue every line of questioning, and he retrieved Darian's phone from his pocket, activated the screen, and then slid it across the table in front of Nathan.

"Maybe you can tell me what happened to Zack," he said.

Nathan sniffled, turning his head to wipe his nose on his shoulder, then frowned down at the iPhone with a little shake of his head. "What is this?"

"Darian's phone." Malcolm leaned across and tapped

just above the latest text. "That's a text from you."

Nathan's eyes flicked back and forth over the text, before widening, his lips going slack. He shook his head again, even harder. "I didn't send that."

Malcolm said nothing. Often that was the easiest way to uncover truth or lies, in an interrogation. Let people read what they wanted into the silences, and talk themselves in circles trying to fill it with something believable. Honest people wouldn't contradict themselves. Guilty people often did, save for certain personality types that bordered on Machiavellian in their ability to lie calmly under pressure.

Those types were more rare than television made it seem. For the most part even criminals cracked under pressure, because even criminals were human beings susceptible to their own fears and anxieties.

Playing on those fears and anxieties with silence could be cruel, but Malcolm preferred it to the more violent, abusive alternatives other police officers employed.

And Nathan begged into that silence now, desperate, straining as far forward as the cuffs would allow him. "I *didn't*! You have to believe me! I don't…even…" He trailed off with a miserable, hopeless whimper, looking down at the phone. "That's not me."

Yoon stepped forward, drifting closer to the table on slow, deliberate strides, the very coolness of his voice judgmental. "So someone took your phone and texted Darian Park that he could die, hours before he was murdered."

Nathan's wide eyes snapped to Yoon; the boy faltered, shrinking back. He seemed to be afraid of Yoon, as if he read menace into that icy, withdrawn elegance. He tried to scoot his chair a few inches away from Yoon, before looking away. "Someone had to...I...I would never say..."

"Who, then?" Malcolm asked. "If it's not you, then who?"

"I...I don't know..."

Yet he wouldn't look at them. There was something different in his voice.

He knew something.

Damn it.

"It must be someone you know," Yoon pressed. "Someone with enough access to take your phone from you and return it without you knowing. Your roommate?"

"No!" Nathan protested immediately. "Sanjit would never...we...we were together when Darian died!"

"Or you're covering for him," Malcolm countered. "Or he's covering for you. Which is it?"

Nathan slumped in his chair, hanging forward until only the cuffs binding his arms to the chair held him up. "...why won't you believe me?"

"Because there's a lot of evidence against you." Malcolm leaned back in his seat, resting his hands on his spread thighs. "And you're not telling me anything to counteract it."

"I...I can't." Nathan's tongue darted nervously over his lips. "I don't know what you want me to say. I didn't kill

Trevor. I didn't kill Darian. I didn't kill Zack. I didn't even know Zack was *dead*." His voice rose to breaking pitch, snapped, dropped back down to a whimper. "B-but it's my fault they're dead, isn't it?"

"If you didn't kill them, how would it be your fault?"

"I just...I..." Nathan shrugged. The chains on his cuffs rattled. He looked away, staring at the mirrored window that threw back their reflections in pale shadow. He sniffled, clearly struggling not to start crying again, then said more firmly, "I want to call my mom."

"You're allowed your phone call." Malcolm stood, his chair scraping far too loudly in a silence that breathed dread like smoke. "But we're keeping you in holding."

"Yeah. Sure."

Malcolm uncuffed him, nudged him to his feet, then gently cuffed him again before guiding him to the door with a hand on his shoulder.

Nathan shuffled forward, his entire body bowed, moving as if the fight had already been beaten out of him before the battle had even begun.

"HE IS HIDING SOMETHING," YOON said, the moment they had turned Nathan over to the admin officers for his phone call and to be processed into holding.

"Don't," Malcolm said, holding a hand up and leaning against the wall in the hall outside the holding pen. "We'll talk in a minute. I just need a minute on my own to think."

"As you say," Yoon said, then settled against the wall next to him in silence.

Malcolm bit down on his thumb until it hurt, trying to pull together pieces that wouldn't quite fit. There was a hole in this picture, and that hole was starting to take the shape of a person.

Nathan shuffled to stand in the doorway leading to the processing area, the administrative officer hovering at his back.

"My mom says I can't talk to you anymore without a lawyer," he mumbled.

Malcolm sighed. There went that avenue of questioning, for now. He jerked his head at the administrative officer. "Take him to the pen. And hey—"

The officer stopped, flashing an impatient look. Malcolm answered that look with a stern one he'd perfected over years of managing recalcitrant students.

"Watch him," he said. "He's a kid. They get rough in holding. Don't let anything happen to him."

The administrative officer just snorted and pulled Nathan away, but Malcolm was fairly certain he'd listen. He looked like a beat cop doing double duty, his face somewhat familiar, though Malcolm hadn't ever worked with him. He'd do his job, at least, taking one more worry off Malcolm's shoulders.

Leaving only a thousand more to contend with, one at a time.

"Come on," he told Yoon. "Let's report in to the Captain."

THEY FOUND ZARATE SITTING CROSS-LEGGED atop her desk in her office, surrounded by disarrayed stacks of paperwork. Malcolm rapped on the doorframe and leaned in.

"Got a minute?"

She looked up from the sheaf of papers in her hand. "I have a minute. I have many minutes. *You* have forty-five seconds."

Malcolm stepped inside, shifting to one side to make room for Yoon. "McAllister lawyered up before we could get an alibi for time of the third death, but he swears he didn't do it."

Zarate snorted. "They always say they didn't do it."

"He seemed to be telling the truth," Yoon interjected.

"At the very least, he believes he did not send the threatening text to Darian Park's phone."

"Believes?" the Captain repeated with a skeptical loft of her brows.

"Denial is a powerful factor," Yoon said. "Many people will convince themselves they could not possibly have committed a particular crime because it does not fit their self-image. They are so desperate to believe they are good people they will concoct an entirely new reality where they were not the criminal, complete with false memories that they convince themselves are true."

"I don't think a college kid's underdeveloped little brain is going that far," Zarate countered.

"If the act of murder was traumatic enough, it wouldn't even have to be a willful decision," Malcolm added. "He could be derealizing and completely depersonalizing himself from the situation and the emotions involved until they really do feel like they belong to another person."

Zarate fixed them both with measuring looks. "Is that what you think is happening?"

"It's a little far out there," Malcolm said, just as Yoon added,

"The probability is rather low. I would rather continue to look for more plausible alternatives."

"Well you just lost a major line of evidence until that kid's lawyer shows, so maybe get on finding that more plausible alternative," Zarate said. "And maybe get on getting

out of my office. You work better out there. I work better
when you're out of my sight."

"Captain," Malcolm said dryly, and tossed a half salute
before slipping out the door.

Yoon followed him back to his desk. Yoon was always
there, right at Malcolm's shoulder. He'd hardly known the
man for twenty-four hours and yet he was part of Malcolm's
every waking moment. When Malcolm was accustomed to
working things out on his own, it sent his brain veering off
track when the air around him vibrated with the presence of
another person so close, watching, waiting, silently expecting
to be part of his thought process.

That vibration turned into a growling-deep sense of
frustration when Yoon said, "The depersonalization theory is
potentially plausible."

"And I grew horns," Malcolm bit off.

"What?"

"Nothing." Malcolm settled to prop his hip on his desk
and thumbed through his case files, looking for the folder on
Trevor Manson. "Nevermind."

Yoon remained silent for a moment, then breathed in
softly. "Ah. You are using a Persian colloquialism in
English."

Malcolm blinked. "You picked up on that?"

"Inflection. That still does not mean I have any concept
of what you said."

Turning it over, Malcolm searched for the best way to

explain. "It's like saying 'yeah, right' in English. Shāk dar āvordam. I grew horns. I don't believe it." He couldn't help laughing. He loved Persian—the language had its own flavor, a deep and musky thing with delicate notes—but even with bilingual fluency he had to admit some things just didn't carry over into English well. "I'm saying that I don't believe that he sent that text."

"I see," Yoon said in a way that said he didn't see at all.

"I'm sure you've got Korean sayings that don't make any sense in English."

"A few, yes."

"There you go." Malcolm found the folder he wanted, but settled it on his thighs, focusing on Yoon for the moment. "Are you fluent in Korean?"

"Not as much as I was when we lived in Pyongyang, but mostly." Yoon seemed to say more in his pauses and his silences than he did with the formal, proper façade of his speech, and Malcolm was beginning to pick up on the taste of certain silences that said Yoon wasn't certain of vouchsafing the words that followed. "I...would not disgrace my parents by forgetting."

"Yeah?" Malcolm's smile lingered unbidden, and he shook his head, looking down at his hands. "I know that feeling. My bābā would disown me if I forgot Persian. Even if his own wife doesn't speak it."

"Bābā. Your father?"

"Yeah." Try as he might, Malcolm couldn't stop the way

his voice softened when he spoke about his father, like there was something in his heart that took control and refused to let it be any other way. "There's something about being the children of immigrants, isn't there?"

"Indeed. There is," Yoon agreed, just as softly. "They have long memories, and want those memories to live in us."

"Yeah. Something like that." Malcolm chuckled. "You're not that bad, Yoon."

Yoon settled to lean against the desk at Malcolm's side, propping himself against the edge and crossing his legs at the ankles. "Yes, I am."

So the bastard did have a sense of humor.

…maybe.

Malcolm only shook his head and flipped the folder open, looking down at the crime scene photos from the Manson case. He kept thinking there was something he was missing, some small thing he was overlooking. "So…Nathan. You're right. I don't think he sent that text. He's not the type. He's shy. So shy, people think he's rude and dislike him for being antisocial. That might have built into anger, but I don't think murderous, vengeful anger."

"I had come to the same conclusion earlier, but was not certain at the time." Yoon rolled his shoulders. "Then who sent the text?"

"I don't know. But until we find out, we're going to have to hold him. We can't risk the off chance that it was him."

"A text was enough to detain him," Yoon observed. "It

will not be enough to hold him for more than forty-eight hours. And he has requested a lawyer."

"We'd better work fast, then." Malcolm stood, tucking the folder under his arm. "Let's go walk the crime scenes again."

"Are we looking for commonalities in location that may offer further insight?"

"Yeah."

"As you say, then."

Malcolm bit back a retort, and just turned and walked away.

[14: AND IT GOES TICK TOCK]

SEONG-JAE CROUCHED IN THE ALLEY outside the club where Darian Park had died, staring blankly at the bits of grass prying through the thin crack between the base of the building and the pavement. Grass was tenacious, yet fragile. In a way it was a sort of tenacity Seong-Jae understood; the individual blades of grass had no meaning, no matter if they were crushed or clipped or burned or killed by dehydration and poor soil nutrition. They left their seeds, so the species survived to the next generation.

The individual was nothing.

It was the *idea* of grass that survived, even when it died. The same with rocks and earth and flowers and sky, wolves and mice and birds in the trees.

Humans were the only ones who clung to the idea that each was distinct, each a thing so separate that the human race was comprised of seven billion species, and each death was nothing more than complete and utter extinction. Some cultures built their entire identity around individual exceptionalism.

That, too, Seong-Jae understood—but in a wholly

different way.

It was that individual exceptionalism he tried to comprehend now, as he studied the smallest details of the crime scene. Not an exceptionalism of the self, but an exceptionalism of the *other* so great that the only way to enshrine it was to destroy the whole and cut out the only part that had value. He tried to see through the killer's eyes, tried to walk through the minutes leading up to the murder.

He stood, pacing the width of the alley. The body had been removed, the evidence bagged for analysis, and there was only the afterimpression, the framing, the stage setting to guide him.

The door. It opened so that anyone exiting the club through the alley would spill out facing the opposite wall and the far end of the narrow corridor, not the entrance. The killer wouldn't have come from the entrance of the alley. The lights were too bright, and at the approximate time of death a bouncer would have been stationed outside the front door, people going in and out. Too many people to notice someone hovering at the mouth of the alley, behaving suspiciously, concealing weapons and the tools necessary for dismemberment.

No. The killer had bided their time, waiting. Behind the dumpster, Seong-Jae thought. He circled the dumpster and looked to the far side, then crouching down behind. He could tilt his head up and just catch the door, enough to see and recognize someone exiting.

"Am I visible from this position?" he called.

Khalaji glanced up from his own intense scrutiny of the remnants of blood spatter soaked into the brick wall. "Your knee and calf. Part of your shoulder."

"So the perpetrator would have been smaller than me."

"Ninety-seven percent of the human population is smaller than you," Khalaji said, then rose, leaning around the dumpster. "You think this was the point of attack?"

"Yes."

Seong-Jae adjusted his position, until he found a crouch that felt easy to rise from. He took a practice lunge, one step to circle around the dumpster, one more to pass it, and he was at the door. Accounting for the perpetrator's shorter legs, perhaps three steps, quick enough that Park would not have had time to react to the sound of feet on pavement. From the positioning of Park's body, he had likely been standing a short distance from the door. Seong-Jae frowned, then beckoned to Khalaji.

"Stand here."

Khalaji eyed him, then stepped closer to stand in front of Seong-Jae. "Here?"

"Not quite." He looked down at Khalaji's feet, then caught his shoulders and turned him, shoving him around to face toward the mouth of the alley, body at an angle, back mostly to the dumpster.

"Oy!" Khalaji protested.

"Here." Seong-Jae stepped back, narrowing his eyes.

"Stand as though you are smoking a cigarette. Perhaps restless. Mildly drunk."

Khalaji gave him a *look*, but complied, shifting his posture with one thumb hooked in the belt loop of his slacks, other arm hanging at his side as though letting a cigarette dangle, the lazy slouch of his hips casual and rakish. He let his gaze drift toward the mouth of the alley.

"Like this?"

"Yes."

Retreating, Seong-Jae crouched behind the dumpster again, eyeing the angle of Khalaji's body. "The killer waited here," he said. "It was someone who knew Park's habits. They knew him well enough to know that before he left the club, he would step outside for one more cigarette before going back inside for last call. As long as no other smokers followed the same pattern, the killer was safe to remain unobserved."

He put himself in the killer's mindset: approaching from the rear of the alley where it intersected another cross-street, darting in hunched over, sinking down behind the dumpster to wait. The position likely would have been uncomfortable, particularly concealing a coil of steel wire long enough to use as a garrote, a hacksaw, and whatever storage medium the killer had brought to remove the body parts and transport them unnoticed.

Adrenaline, he thought. The night would have been crisp in stark colors through the filter of adrenaline. Everything would have tasted cool and sharp, the glare of street lights off rain-damp pavement white-hot.

Rain on his shoulders, he imagined, sinking in more. He'd been waiting for Darian Park long enough for a late-night drizzle to come and go, and the shoulders of his bulky jacket were damp, but he ignored it. Because the door was open, Park was there, and his moment was coming; he only had to restrain himself a moment longer, sucking in shallow breaths and then holding them, trying not to be heard when his heart felt so brightly, thrillingly loud with anticipation and terror.

"…Yoon?"

"*Shh.*" Seong-Jae adjusted his position, thighs tensing in readiness. Khalaji started to glance back, but Seong-Jae retreated behind the dumpster with a hiss; Khalaji grimaced and turned his gaze forward again. Only he was not Khalaji; he was Park, sweat-filmed and breathless, something melancholy in the knit of his brows, his thoughts turned inward. Distracted. This was the killer's moment. This was the moment when that tension snapped, shooting the killer forward, an arrow darting forward from a bowstring.

"The perpetrator caught Park off guard," he said—and lunged forward, keeping low on the first step, deliberately shortening his strides to match a smaller person's, rising on step two, reaching inside his coat, step three, reaching out.

Then he was against Khalaji's back, pressing into him, reaching around to either side of his throat. Khalaji went rock-still.

Seong-Jae shifted his hands into the proper position to loop an invisible garrote over Khalaji's head. "They would have hit Park square in the center of his back," he said. "Even if they were small, momentum would have bowed him forward so the wire could slip over his head." He leaned into Khalaji to bend him forward just enough. Their bodies fit together, the hiss of cloth on cloth, body heat meeting and melding like two storm fronts flirting, lightning crackling where their edges kissed. "Then back. They could not hope to overwhelm Park, and so they had to keep him off-balance."

He leaned back—and pulled Khalaji with him, in the absence of a garrote instead using his forearm, gentle across Khalaji's throat. Khalaji let out a strange soft, throaty growl, the sound vibrating against Seong-Jae's arm. Khalaji's body fell back against him, letting Seong-Jae maneuver him.

"Off-balance, then," Seong-Jae continued. The knot of Khalaji's hair teased against his cheek, tickling lightly against his skin. "Just so—momentum carrying them around, until they face the back of the alley." He swung them about carefully. "Park is losing oxygen, becoming limp. His weight is heavy, and the killer stumbles back, slamming against the door, ripping their clothing and cutting their skin, but they remain braced against the door."

He fell back against the door, the steel rattling in the frame, the peeling jagged edges of rusted metal and paint digging into his coat. Khalaji fell with him, his heavy bulk molded against Seong-Jae from shoulder to hip, pinning him to the door with the pressure of hard sinew under the sleek wool of his suit.

Seong-Jae briefly tightened his forearm against Khalaji's throat, turning his head to speak, the curve of Khalaji's ear too close to his mouth. "Minutes, then, to unconsciousness and death."

Khalaji turned his head. The rough scruff of his beard brushed Seong-Jae's lips, part tingle, part burn, part odd, pulsing sensitivity as one slate blue eye locked on his.

"At which point," Malcolm murmured, "the killer lowered the body, propped him against the wall, and went to work. Fast, but not sloppy. They probably practiced on inanimate objects beforehand."

"Yes," Seong-Jae answered, his voice sticking in the back of his throat on the word before clearing, smoothing. "As you say."

For long moments, Khalaji remained silent save for low, deep breaths that heaved his body slowly against Seong-Jae's. The longer that storm-shaded blue eye held him, the warmer Seong-Jae's skin grew. Khalaji should speak. Speaking would be optimal in this moment. And what was that *smell?* Like old leather and the aged wood of whiskey casks, retaining the mellow yet deep, heated aromas of dark rye liquor. Was that Khalaji? Was that why it was so strong?

"You're going to want to let me go now," Khalaji growled.

Mortification chilled Seong-Jae like ice cubes trailed over his skin. He stiffened, jerked his arms back, and turned away, looking firmly away from Khalaji.

"My apologies," he bit off, face hot.

Khalaji straightened, adjusting his coat. "Do you always reenact kills that way?"

"It can be helpful to put myself in the killer's mindset, to understand their motives and methods." Seong-Jae firmly focused his attention on the case, the images he had reconstructed in his head. He had let himself sink too deep into the killer's mindset, their rush of adrenaline and anticipation, the thrill they'd been riding that made them reckless and emotional. "I believe they undertook this endeavor with a sort of nervous excitement. No fear, no shame. Perhaps even pleasure. This was premeditated, but not coldly calculated. Both passion and organization. A perfect meeting of organized and disorganized killer mindsets."

"People never fit neat checkboxes when it comes to criminal psychology." Khalaji fell silent another moment, then asked, "You all right?"

Seong-Jae glanced back at him, lifting his brows.

Khalaji ducked his head toward him. "Your coat."

Twisting, Seong-Jae caught his coat and drew the heavy knit fabric around. The rusted parts of the door had caught the thick felted material and pulled at the fibers until they puffed into a fuzzy patch marring the smooth black. He shrugged and let it go.

"It will mend."

Khalaji looked away, his gaze clouding. "This feels like

a waste of time." He scanned the alley again, gaze tracking up the far wall. "We're staring at bricks while we've got a killer with a motive and a hit list."

"Sometimes the slowest path is the most productive."

"Sometimes the slowest path leads to a dead end because people are confusing, and almost never leave neat evidence trails."

"There is that, as well."

"Do you think—"

A trill came from Khalaji's pocket at the same moment Seong-Jae's phone vibrated in his. They exchanged looks, then both retrieved their phones. Seong-Jae read the text on his screen, his stomach sinking.

"West Lexington again," he said.

"That's on campus. I—" Swearing, Khalaji broke off, ripped the tie viciously from his hair, and dragged his fingers through it roughly. "Broad daylight this time. While we were here sniffing cold tracks, they were—they just—barely twelve hours after the last kill."

"If the crime scene is at the university, we should assess the scene as quickly as possible before the university demands removal of the corpse from public venues."

"Yeah." Heavy lines seamed Khalaji's face. "...yeah. Let's get moving," he said bitterly. "Chasing more scraps."

THE SCENE ON CAMPUS WAS pure and utter chaos.

They arrived before a building that looked more like a political monument than part of a school, with its wide green lawn and smooth ivory columns and peaked roof. Over a hundred students milled on the lawn, their voices an overlapping roar of panic, curiosity, disgust, horror, fear, a subtle undercurrent of greedy avarice in the few that sank their teeth into the tension brimming on the air and turned it into excitement with that same compulsive fixation that made people slow their cars when driving past a wreck just to get a glimpse of the carnage, the mangled bodies.

Several BPD and campus police officers milled on the steps and front colonnade of the building, all of them eddying and swirling around a central point, masking all but glimpses of fresh, bright red blood and a few hints of dark skin. Several men and women, likely professors and administrative staff, circled the officers, barking things at them only to recoil and look away. The officers faced outward, stoic, forming a barrier between the students, the administrators, and the kind of death no one should ever have to see in their lives.

Seong-Jae and Khalaji forced through the crowd as

[183]

quickly as they could, using Khalaji's bulk and Seong-Jae's height to their advantage to elbow their way through the crowd and dash up the wide front steps. A few steps from the top, though, Khalaji stopped, hanging back, one hand snapping out to bar Seong-Jae's path and rest against his chest while hard eyes scanned the milling confusion.

"We've got to shut this down," Khalaji said, then tossed his head at Seong-Jae. "I'll run intercept. Get in there and get what you can on the body." Khalaji leaned in closer. "I'm trusting you."

Seong-Jae very firmly caught Khalaji's wrist and pried his hand away. "I will do my best," he said, and mounted the last two steps to flash his badge to the cordon of officers.

Khalaji ducked away to intercept a very angry-looking woman with extremely tall hair and a garishly red skirt suit. As he squeezed between the wall of uniforms, Seong-Jae lost sight of Malcolm; he ducked under the police tape that had been strung between columns to mark off the crime scene.

After two of these in so many days, he should be desensitized by this by now—yet it was hard to be numb to the sight of someone barely a boy, strung up like a scarecrow on a stick. The display of the body was almost *mocking*, as if with each new kill the perpetrator grew bolder, more confident that they were untouchable, and all the more derisive of their victims.

The victim had the lean build of an athlete. Death had turned his deep brown skin ashen, yet the whites of his eyes still stood out in stark contrast where his eyes rested half-open, his head hanging down until his chin touched his chest. He'd been propped upright on what looked to be a hockey stick rack, a tall narrow frame that he dangled from with the upper end of it shoved underneath the back of his shirt to keep him upright.

His arms were missing.

Sawed off at the shoulder, the juts of ragged collarbones protruding from mutilated twists of pink and glistening flesh, massive spurts of blood spilling down to mat his shirt to his skin and darken his jeans—still gleaming wet, likely still warm.

And a trail of blood running toward the door to the building, from where he'd clearly been dragged.

He'd been killed elsewhere. Inside.

And then staged here in the open in the middle of the day, as if daring anyone to catch the killer.

The perpetrator was drunk on their own success. High on their own power. Taking too many risks.

They would slip, soon. They had to.

Before this ended in yet another death.

Seong-Jae glanced over his shoulder, rising up on his toes to scan the crowd. The killer was here. He could feel it, a sort of cold, avid interest, a breathlessness. The killer wasn't sociopathic enough to insert themselves into the investigation or make direct contact with the police, but at this point the killer had to know two detectives were on the case, and wanted to watch Seong-Jae and Khalaji interact with their handiwork with their own eyes.

That was the real purpose behind this staging, he thought.

To say *I know you're watching me.*

And now I'm watching you, too.

So many people were staring, their emotions naked on their faces, running the gamut as they processed the scene, that it was impossible to narrow down the source of that attention—especially when he wasn't sure who he was looking for. Their only suspect was Nathan McAllister.

And Nathan McAllister was in a holding cell.

Seong-Jae turned back to the body. Ligature marks on the neck again. All the signature signs were there, the particular markers of a killer with a method. He circled the body, taking in the small details. The open eyes; he had probably bled out after the killer had left. The clumsiness of the body's positioning. The killer had likely struggled with his weight, with his height, and the short time frame. The posing was hasty, and he pictured a shrouded figure counting the seconds under their breath before classes broke or someone passed by or someone looked out a window.

They must have mounted the victim on the rack inside, as well. They couldn't risk that in public.

He tracked the smeared trail of blood on the floor back to the door, pulling gloves from his pocket as he did and snapping them on before he pulled the door open and stepped inside.

The blood trail continued, a slippery mess of interconnected puddles and streaks, on the tile inside. He followed it a short distance to a doorway. A broom closet.

And that charnel smell, splattered everywhere—all over the walls, the cleaning supplies, the floor, ragged bits of meat swimming in blood.

He held his breath, taking in thin, shallow washes through his nostrils, and tugged his phone from his coat. Activating the camera app, he framed the interior of the closet and snapped several photos, then followed the blood trail back outside, catching as much of the trail as he could. The trail led him back to the body—and back to Khalaji, who intercepted him mid-stride, falling in next to him as they squeezed past the cordon of officers and tape to study the body once more.

Khalaji looked harried, exhausted, his eyes dark. He dragged a hand through his beard. "The Dean is furious, and the school president is on the way. They want the body off their front doorstep immediately, but I talked her into waiting for forensics with the promise forensics would put up screens if she'd clear and close down the building."

"Witness interviews?"

"Campus police and responding officers have been on that. There are too many to handle reasonably, but as far as we can tell no one saw *anything*." Khalaji burst into soft, vituperative curses, paced left, right, stopped, stared at the body in its grisly pantomime of a scarecrow. "Reckless and careful at the same time. They want the risk, the high, but not enough to let themselves get caught for being careless." He curled both hands against the back of his neck, gaze blanking. "I don't understand how *no one* saw a single thing. This is a staged scene. There's no sports equipment in this building. How could someone not see anyone dragging a hockey rack across campus, or a body out of the building?"

"The trail of blood leads back to a janitorial closet in the main hall of the building," Seong-Jae said. He swiped back through the photos he'd just taken, angling the phone so Khalaji could see. "There is evidence in the blood spatter and other matter left behind that the initial murder occurred there. He was likely ambushed on his way out of class."

Khalaji tilted his head down, eyeing the phone screen. "And then the killer, probably covered in blood, just walked away with no one the wiser. It's like we're dealing with a ghost. How are we supposed to set up a dragnet without even the slightest description of a suspect?"

"We know they are small, possibly thin."

"Or they could be tall and bulky and just lack upper body strength. Body type doesn't mean much." He jerked his chin at the victim. "It didn't mean much to him."

"From the obvious signature markers, I take it he was another on the list."

"DeMarcus Shay." Khalaji exhaled roughly and let his arms drop. "From the data Sade scraped, apparently he and McAllister only dated briefly during their freshman year, but remained friends afterward."

"Was he not under protective detail?"

"He should have been. Which makes me wonder how they slipped past surveillance twice. Either we're doing something wrong, or they're very good at escaping notice."

"Ah." Seong-Jae glanced over his shoulder at the milling crowds. The woman in the red suit was talking to a few of the other administrators and campus police officers, gesticulating furiously. "How long do we have?"

"Minutes. The forensics team should be here by then."

"Then we should do everything we can to differentiate this crime scene. Perhaps haste made the killer more careless with evidence." Seong-Jae stepped forward, circling the body once more. "Arms, this time. They have taken the arms, legs, and torso of three separate bodies."

"It's like this macabre, twisted checklist." Khalaji's shoulder brushed his as the other man drew closer to the body and leaned in, focused intently on the sever point of one shoulder. "It feels like they're shopping for body parts. Which might make sense if this were an organ trafficking case, but…"

"Severed limbs and torsos have no value for prosthetics or other types of transplants," Seong-Jae finished. "They are missing a pelvis and a head, if they are taking unique parts from each body."

"There are two more living ex-boyfriends on McAllister's list. The third is a one-night-stand. We can probably cross that one off as an outlier."

"Do you think the killer will target the two others next?"

"I'm almost certain of it." Khalaji pressed his lips together in a grim line, then added, "We'll have to up the protective details. Maybe even move them to a safe house. We also have to let McAllister go. There's no way it can be him. It happened while he was in holding."

"There is still the possibility of an accomplice."

"Not likely. I just don't see accomplice in this case. McAllister was the obvious suspect, not the right one. If we try to hold him, it won't go well on the legal front."

Seong-Jae shook his head. "I am not certain releasing him is wise, for his safety."

"If he doesn't want to be detained, we can't keep him. We can only keep his protective detail up." Khalaji turned his head toward him. "Do you think the killer would target McAllister next?"

"No." That answer was simpler. Explaining it, explaining the intuition sitting cold in the pit of Seong-Jae's stomach and licking its raspy, terrible tongue down his spine, was harder. He lingered on the victim, trying—struggling—to contextualize the feeling radiating almost like an aura from a boy whose aura had gone dark. "Nathan McAllister is an object of desire, but not murderous desire. The victims…the kill methodology and fetishization of the bodies indicate frustration of desire, so there may be transference. The killer may be murdering to keep their urges from contaminating or injuring McAllister as an object of worship, but there is some other component to it that we cannot yet see." He met the corpse's dead, empty eyes, then looked away. "I do not think the killer would harm him. But that does not mean he is not in danger."

Khalaji didn't answer at first, his brows set in a pensive, brooding line. But then abruptly he said, "His mouth is bloody."

Seong-Jae tilted his head. Khalaji was correct; the victim's lips were somewhat swollen, his mouth smeared in blood, red streaked down his chin as if that blood had spilled from inside his mouth.

"Do you think he was struck in a struggle with the killer?"

Rather than speak, Khalaji snapped on a pair of gloves, leaned in, and gingerly caught the victim's chin, tilting his head enough to pry his mouth open carefully with two fingers—then let out a soft *"Fuck."* Hard eyes flicked to Seong-Jae. "Yoon. Look."

Khalaji drew the lips back further, more carefully—exposing raw, ragged gums, pink and pulped and covered in clots of congealing blood.

Gums and nothing else, even if the entire interior of his mouth was mutilated, his tongue cut and swollen.

Seong-Jae's breaths hitched. "The killer extracted his teeth."

With slow precision, Khalaji let the victim go, replacing

his head in the same position it had been in before. "The other two, it was only one body part. The legs, and the torso." Khalaji stared down at his blood-streaked gloves, then growled and ripped them off with sharp, jerky movements. "Two, for this one. Teeth. Arms."

"Is this another sign of escalation?"

"I don't *know*. Like you said, we're missing something." Khalaji dragged a hand over his face. "But they may only need one more kill to finish their checklist, if they're taking more parts from each body now."

"I believe, rather than details, each of the potential targets should be assigned a visible escort. McAllister as well."

"The Captain will probably sign off on it." Khalaji glanced to one side, his gaze tracking back and forth over the street, the campus. "Let's do the best evaluation we can before forensics takes over, then head in. See if we can't convince McAllister to talk after release. We need something to bring this to a close. I can't look at another of these crime sce—"

Khalaji's voice lost all meaning, cut off to a distant, droning murmur as that sensation of being *watched* shivered from a subtle prickle to a shock of static electricity over Seong-Jae's skin. He pivoted, searching, sweeping the assembly with a sharp look—just in time for a flicker of motion to the far end of the building's colonnade to catch in his peripheral vision. He turned just as that flicker of motion vanished past the side of the building.

Seong-Jae shoved through the officers surrounding the body and darted toward the edge of the colonnade, then dropped down onto the grass flanking the building and flung himself around the side. He stared down the street. A few people milled on the sidewalk, outliers from the crowd gathered on the lawn, while other people moved about their business with that fast, preoccupied gait of someone utterly focused on their destination. No sign of someone fleeing. No one person he could pick out from the crowd to say *There, that one. That is the one who was watching me.*

His heart felt strange, his stomach sick, adrenaline making a wildness out of his pulse. Something felt…*wrong.*

And there was that sense of familiarity again, that *something* he couldn't quite put his finger on.

"Yoon?" Khalaji caught up breathlessly, standing on the raised concrete lip of the colonnade and looking down at him. "What did you see?"

"I…" Seong-Jae shook his head. "It was simply a feeling."

"Yeah?" Khalaji looked down at his feet. "Then what's that?"

Seong-Jae turned back, a *what?* on his lips, only to still as he looked down at the concrete at Khalaji's feet, that sick feeling in his stomach redoubling into a terrible heaviness.

A circle had been painted on the concrete in deep red, the beginning and ending points tapered as if it had been slashed on with a brush—quick, oblong as a cursive *O*, ending with a flourish.

Seong-Jae did not have to touch it, smell it, test it, to know it was blood.

"What does it mean?" Khalaji whispered, and Seong-Jae shook his head.

"I do not know," he answered.

Yet if he were honest with himself, he could well be lying.

He hoped to all the hells that he was not.

[15: LONG DAY AT THE CORRAL]

MALCOLM DIDN'T KNOW IF IT was frustration and burnout making him overlook things, or if the killer was getting smarter—but the crime scene gave them nothing. Gave *him* nothing; nothing he could use to pluck at that one loose thread and unravel it to make the killer's carefully crafted web fall apart.

Frustration was part of the everyday process of this job. Helplessness. Feeling useless, pointless, when cases rarely slotted together as neatly and with such a fascinating trail of evidence enticing people along for the ride with detectives in everyone's favorite cop shows. The reality was often struggling through a muddle of conflicting information, and while there were always easy catches with the careless or inexperienced, the first things he'd learned in this job was that he would never catch every murderer, and sometimes failures happened.

He didn't want to accept failure.

Not on this case.

But in the end he had to walk away—for now. Hovering at the crime scene and getting underfoot with forensics wouldn't do anything. His best legwork was done elsewhere, at the moment.

Yet it wasn't hard to tell, from his restlessness and tense silence, that Yoon was just as bothered as Malcolm, even if they both held their own brooding counsel on the drive back to the office.

It gave him little satisfaction to report in to the admissions officer that Nathan McAllister was no longer wanted under suspicion, and could be released. He'd rather have the boy here where he was surrounded by armed, uniformed officers.

When he and Yoon stepped into the room outside the holding pen, for a moment Malcolm thought the boy had been let out already—until he caught a glimpse of pale skin past the milling bodies of everything from large, tattooed bikers to a mild-looking woman who looked as if she could teach middle school in suburbia, sitting primly on a bench with perfect calm. Nathan had huddled himself into a corner, carving out a bit of space for himself away from everyone else, and hunkered down the wall with his knees curled against his chest, his face buried in his thighs.

But his head snapped up when the officer on duty rapped her keys against the cell bars. "McAllister? Up and at 'em. You're free to go."

A thin man with baggy, grayed clothing and yellowed sclera piped up, slurring, "That's me. I'm McAllister."

The officer rolled her eyes. "Sit down, Jimmy. Your

daughter's on the way. She's pissed, too. This is the second time this week." She beckoned sharply to Nathan. "Come on. Everyone else, back from the bars."

Nathan looked around warily, confusion in his features, in his movements, then unfolded himself while the others grumbled and dutifully took a few steps back. The officer unlocked the cell and pushed the bars aside just far enough for Nathan to straggle out, then slammed it closed and locked it again.

The boy stared at her. "Just like that? Without a lawyer?"

"Just like that," the officer said, then nodded toward Malcolm and Yoon. "Detectives say you're not guilty."

Nathan's eyes flew to Malcolm's from across the room, and a bitter mask of fury and pain settled over his face. He took a few steps closer, then stopped, glaring.

"Why the fuck did you even make me go through this, then?"

"Nathan." Malcolm struggled for words, his throat in knots. He couldn't bring more grief to this boy's doorstep. Not after everything he'd been through. But he couldn't lie, either. Reluctantly, he said, "Another murder happened while you were in holding. It doesn't wholly clear you, but it removes probable cause needed to legally detain you."

Nathan rocked on his feet, fury draining to leave sheer, wracking pain stamped in every line of him. "A-another one…?" His lips parted, closed again, parted again. "I…wh-who this time?"

"DeMarcus Shay. I'm sorry."

The boy stared at Malcolm with the wretchedness of someone who'd cried so many tears they had no more left to cry, that reservoir empty and dried and scraped raw. Then, "Fuck," he rasped, looking away, wrapping his arms around himself. "*Fuck*. I really am cursed, huh."

Malcolm glanced at Yoon. *Give us a moment?* he mouthed. He doubted either of them were particularly Nathan's favorite people at the moment, but Yoon seemed to outright intimidate him, and he might be more willing to talk if Yoon gave them a little space.

Yoon tilted his head, lips parting soundlessly, before he nodded, stepping back a few paces and shifting to lean against the admin desk. Malcolm lightly touched Nathan's arm, coaxing him to walk a few steps with him.

The boy followed listlessly, and didn't look up when Malcolm stopped, looking down at him, trying to figure out how to handle this. If Malcolm had married early and fathered young like his own father had wanted, he might have had a son close to Nathan's age. That son might have been Nathan's classmate, friend, lover...might have been in the same position as Nathan himself. Malcolm didn't know how to comfort the boy, but that didn't stop him from wanting to no matter what professional lines he might cross.

He couldn't.

He could only try to be as gentle as possible, as he said, "If you know anything about who could be doing this...you need to tell us."

Nathan swallowed audibly, but only shook his head, silent and a touch of mutinous rebellion in the set of his jaw. Not *no*, then, but *I won't*.

"Nathan," Malcolm urged softly. "Please."

"I don't want to talk to you." Nathan jerked back. "I don't want to talk to anyone."

"Will you let us assign you a police escort?" When Nathan stiffened, Malcolm continued quickly. "You could be in danger. It's not to threaten you or cage you. It's to protect you."

"Sure. Fine." Nathan flashed him a simmering look. "My pig bodyguard gonna give me a ride back to the dorms, then?"

"If that would make you feel safer," Malcolm said. "Do you still have my card?"

"I fucking burned it."

"That's okay." Malcolm retrieved one of his cards from his breast pocket and offered it between two fingers. "If you want to talk, Nathan."

Nathan glared at him, motionless save for the trembling of his entire body, then unwrapped the protective curl of his arms long enough to snatch the card from Malcolm before immediately tucking into himself again. "Whatever. Leave me alone. Maybe if you go away, the curse will too."

He broke away from Malcolm, then, shoving past him and toward the door. Malcolm caught himself reaching after him, then made himself stop. Stop, let the boy go. He'd flag an officer to pick him up, take him home, and stay with him. In a minute. Not now.

Let Nathan have his moment.

Yoon pushed away from the desk, drifting closer. "He does not mean such things," he said.

"I know." Malcolm sighed. "It's all right if he hates me. He needs someone to hate."

"I know," Yoon replied softly. "I was once like him."

Malcolm blinked, attention dragging back from the door left swinging in Nathan's wake—and locking firmly on Yoon. "Yoon...?"

But Yoon wasn't looking at him. Yoon wasn't looking at anything at all, withdrawn and brooding, his mouth tight.

After a moment, though, he shook himself, tossing Malcolm an inscrutable glance. "We should go," he said.

Then walked away, leaving Malcolm standing there confused and heartsore and alone, before he dragged himself into motion and followed.

AT THE LEAST, NATHAN HADN'T gone far. Malcolm detoured a moment to speak to Captain Zarate, ask for a recommendation, and then track down Officer Giancomo in the chaos of the beat cops' bullpen.

"You want me to *babysit*?" Giancomo asked.

"I want you to keep him alive," Malcolm said. "He's a potential target in a murder investigation."

"Your case. Why don't you watch him?"

Yoon circled the desk. That subtle sense of elegant menace that always seemed to simmer under his skin emanated from him like a cold front pushing forward in his wake. He looked down at Giancomo, his black eyes flat and alien.

"Are you ignoring the orders of two ranking officers?"

Giancomo froze, eyeing Yoon as if he wasn't sure if he wanted to laugh or turn tail and run. Then, swearing, he pushed his chair back and stood, jabbing an accusatory finger at Malcolm. "You tell your Captain she can explain why *my* Captain has to reassign all my shifts." He grabbed his jacket and shrugged it on. "And I'd better get overtime pay for this."

"I'll log it in," Malcolm said dryly. "Thanks."

He led Giancomo to the lobby. Nathan wouldn't look at him when Malcolm handed him off to the officer, but he at least went along when Giancomo grunted, "Come on, kid. Give me your address and let's get gone."

Malcolm watched until Nathan and Giancomo disappeared through the front doors and became nothing but indistinct shapes against the bright glare of day—before he eyed Yoon, holding back a smile.

"That was a dick move. And won't make you any friends around here, pulling rank."

"I have no idea what you mean," Yoon replied blandly.

"Yes, you do."

Yoon's mouth twitched at the corners. "Perhaps."

Malcolm chuckled. "Thanks. I didn't have time to waste placating him."

"So you admit that sometimes my methods are effective."

"I admit nothing." Malcolm leaned against the wall, folding his arms. "So where to now?"

"I admit to being at something of an impasse."

"We're just going from crime scene to crime scene assembling a profile without a face." Malcolm studied Yoon. "That's what you've been doing, isn't it? Creating an official profile workup."

Something flickered in Yoon's eyes, before they shifted to look just past Malcolm without quite making contact. "...yes. But so have you."

"What did you *do* before LAPD, Yoon?"

Yoon remained stonily silent, and Malcolm thought he would once again get the cold shoulder until Yoon muttered, "FBI. Behavioral Analysis Unit."

Malcolm whistled under his breath. "Thought so. What made you quit for homicide?"

A terse jerk of angular shoulders. "I was bored."

"You were—" Malcolm buried his face in one hand, struggling not to laugh. "Of course you were."

Yoon tossed him a borderline sullen look, then looked away again with that soft *tch* sound under his breath. "…what of you?"

"University professor," Malcolm admitted grudgingly. "At U of M. Criminal psych. Army before that, just to pay for college. GI bill landed me in Afghanistan for a full tour right at the start of the war."

A quizzical tilt of Yoon's head. "Why teach criminal psychology?"

"I wanted to know how they think." He shrugged. "Now I just want to get them off the streets."

"Is there a particular reason—"

The sharp clamor of Malcolm's phone interrupted, and he let out his breath. He knew the question Yoon had been poised to ask, and that was an answer he didn't want to give.

He glanced at his phone, instead. Sade. He swiped the call and lifted the phone to his ear. "What have you got?"

"Mal?" Sade spilled out breathlessly. "Are you almost back to the office?"

"I'm downstairs. What is it?"

"I was doing cross-checks on our victim profiles, and I ran across another crime report on the first vic, Trevor Manson."

"Did he have a record?"

"No. This happened after he died."

After he died? Malcolm frowned. "What do you mean?"

"Grave desecration." Sade trailed off into a disgusted gurgle. "Oh, this is *grody*. They...ugh. Ew. Ew. I'm going to vom."

"*What*, Sade?"

"They cut off his head." Sade spoke in an exaggerated stage whisper, and Malcolm could practically see their widened eyes. "It's really fucking gross, Mal. Really gross. Someone dug him up about three months after he was buried and cut off his head. The responding officers did a sloppy report, and it didn't get linked to the right case file for the murder. I only found it by a name search." The sound of Sade's fingers rattling on the keyboard came over the line, then, "I've got hard glossies, no digital. Come into my parlor, said the spider to the fly."

Malcolm sighed with fond exasperation. "I bite back, little spider. Don't forget that."

"Promise?"

"Stop that, brat. I'll be there in a minute." Ending the call, he started for the stairs, flinging back to Yoon, "Come on. Sade's got something for us upstairs."

Yoon's soft footsteps trailed in his wake. "Do I want to know?"

"No. You really don't."

They were halfway up the stairs before Yoon spoke again, a low, taunting lilt at Malcolm's back.

"So you bite back?"

"…god damn it, Yoon," Malcolm groaned, then spilled onto their floor and into the homicide unit bullpen.

Sade's hand stuck out of their den once more, beckoning them closer, before disappearing in a flick of dark hair. Malcolm and Yoon ducked under the Christmas lights and into the server room. Sade had spread photographs and reports over their entire desk, covering the multiple keyboards.

"Here." They flicked their fingertips.

Malcolm and Yoon leaned over Sade's shoulders—only for Malcolm to jerk back, while Yoon turned away with a hiss, covering his mouth with one hand and breathing "…jen jang hai."

Malcolm didn't have to understand the word to understand the disgust and shock behind it, when they mirrored the roiling in his gut and the tightness in his throat. The photos depicted were somehow worse than the original crime scene photos; a fresh body was grisly, but nothing compared to the decay and degrading horror of a decomposing body that had been desecrated with tools that made a monstrosity out of the pulpy, yielding masses of rotting soft tissue.

He couldn't even make an accurate assessment from those pictures. It wouldn't have mattered if the killer worked with precision or went at the body in a crazed frenzy. The second a hacksaw would have touched the body's throat, the flesh would have degraded into mush.

Malcolm couldn't look at it any longer. Grim loathing

was a cloak settling around him, wrapping him up. Desecrating the dead was beyond vile. Whomever they were dealing with surpassed loathsome. He couldn't let himself sink into this feeling or loathing would become hatred, and hatred would cloud his judgment just as much as empathy, making this personal.

He focused his attention on Yoon, instead. Whether he wanted Yoon as a partner or not, the man had a talent for bouncing counter-points off Malcolm in a way that set his brain turning in new directions.

He took a calming breath, then said, "So we're dealing with someone willing to touch a decomposing corpse. High tolerance for bodily fluids, decay, things that would nauseate other people." He let his thoughts cycle, biting down on the inside of his cheek. "...Yoon, University of Maryland is a medical and natural sciences school."

"Which raises the significant possibility that this is a student."

"Or faculty. What do you place the odds for either?"

Yoon still stared at the wall, but then glanced back at the photos only to look away again. "I…"

Malcolm glanced back as well, then shuddered and stepped closer to Yoon. "...is it too much?" he asked, dropping his voice, even if little escaped Sade's curious ears.

Yoon's eyes slipped closed. "Please do not assume I am incapable of dealing with the graphic nature of the photographs," he said, but his words were rough, tight.

And it wasn't hard to read between the lines of what he wasn't saying, once again.

It wasn't the gore, the rotting flesh.

It was the act of desecration, deeply unsettling and inhuman in a way that Malcolm grasped on an innate level, a gut-deep understanding.

"It's okay," he said, then glanced back at Sade, whose dark eyes glimmered bright with unspoken questions. "You can put all that away. We'll read the report notes in the system, but as far as I'm concerned you can shred those damned photos."

"I've done enough illegal things not to get tossed for destroying evidence, thanks," Sade tripped off merrily, swinging their chair around and shuffling the glossies together into a stack before tucking them into a case folder—though they paused, scrunching their nose up as they stared at the topmost, before snapping the folder closed over it. "That is so *fucked*."

"Yeah," Malcolm said faintly. "Thanks, little spider."

Sade only grinned brightly and flashed two fingers in a peace sign. Malcolm smiled slightly, but lightly touched Yoon's arm, nudging him to leave. "Out."

They stepped from Sade's lair and crossed through the busy bullpen to Malcolm's desk. A few heads turned as they passed, and it wasn't hard to tell they were watching Yoon, wondering, but there was little time in the life of a homicide detective to rubberneck over new people. Eventually people would wander over to Yoon when they needed something on his walk or had a case connected to his, and the intersecting and diverging paths of work would build either familiarity or animosity, establishing his place one way or another as part of the department. That had been the way it was for Malcolm, how it had been for most people.

While he didn't want a partner…he wondered if Yoon would allow him to at least be his colleague, if not his friend. As stiff and cold as Yoon had been over the past few days, he wouldn't be winning any allies any time soon.

He'd need at least one person on his side.

Malcolm settled at his desk, pulling out of his suit jacket and draping it over the back of his chair before dropping into the seat. Flicking his mouse and waking up his desktop PC, he beckoned to Yoon. "I'll get the report on the desecration. We're still at a dead end and chasing our tails, but we can at least guess that the killer is going to strike at one of the last two on the list next. They're only missing one body part. We should split up. One of us on each, along with the escort detail. Try to catch them in the act."

Yoon propped his hip against the desk, folding his arms over his chest. "That may be the best course of action. If the pattern is a precedent, they will strike within hours."

"I know. But I still feel like there's something we're overlooking." Malcolm worried at the edge of his thumbnail with his teeth, leaning forward to peer at the screen while he tapped in a report search with his other hand. "You didn't tell me your thoughts on student versus faculty."

"Ah." Yoon braced his hands on the desk, leaning back, his long, tapered body cast into a lazily graceful slouch, legs stretched out before him. "From the brutal nature of the murders, I would suspect a student. An adult would be more controlled. While there is an element of premeditation and control, the reckless staging and rapid escalation suggest a more underdeveloped mind still under the influence of excessive emotion caused by late-stage developmental hormones."

"So you're saying we've got someone on the far cusp of a horny teenager discovering they gain sexual gratification from the kill, and growing more and more reckless as they look for the thrill again."

"I believe so," Yoon said, turning his head to regard Malcolm. "There is also the methodology. Steel wire and a hacksaw are inexpensive items easily procured on a student's budget, but considering that they seem to value the body parts they excise, power tools such as a bandsaw would be better for precision if not for stealth and portability. Such an expenditure would be more difficult on a student's income, even if they were supported by wealthy parents who might monitor their expenses." His lips thinned. "On-site kills also suggest someone lacking enough control over their environment to kill in private. An adult would be more likely to abduct their victims, take them to a prepared location, and use precision tools to conduct the dismemberment."

"If they're a medical or biological sciences student, there's also the labs and lab dissection and autopsy tools— no." Malcolm cut himself off, shaking his head. "Everything has to be checked out. And there's almost no privacy there, even in the dead of night. There's no way they'd be able to use lab tools or clean up the labs to leave no evidence on such an accelerating timeline, whether they're a student or faculty."

"So in the absence of a controlled kill environment, it is most likely we are looking for a student."

"A student connected to Nathan McAllister." Malcolm slumped back against the chair. "Except most of the students connected to Nathan McAllister are dead."

"Of the two former romantic entanglements," Yoon said, "it is possible one is the perpetrator, particularly if McAllister is the object of desire."

"That's looking most likely. So it's great that we have a detail on both of them, but we should try to figure out which one it is before he tries to kill the other one. If another murder happens, we'll have no choice but to get the FBI in on it if we can't close it."

"I would prefer to avoid that if at all possible."

"Somehow I guessed that." Malcolm gestured toward the empty desk across the aisle from his. "Pull up a chair. We'll get you your own desk soon."

Yoon pushed off from Malcolm's desk, snagged a rolling chair, and slung it around, spinning it next to Malcolm's and then settling down to straddle it with the back facing him, arms folded over the top, thighs spread rakishly. He rested his chin on his crossed wrists, lazy eyes watching Malcolm like a snake in the grass.

"Yours is fine for now," he said.

Malcolm just looked at him, then let out an exasperated sigh, turning back to the computer and digging for Sade's social media data dump file. "Why do you have to do that?"

"Do what?" Yoon asked mildly.

"Nevermind. Just…nevermind," Malcolm muttered. "Let's just get to work."

[16: BREAK AND SHOUT]

POLICE REPORTS MEANT NOTHING TO Seong-Jae.

Not at this juncture.

He understood procedure. Understood that when they had no leads on a suspect, everything was in the data. So he remained silent while Khalaji called the officers shadowing the last two potential victims—two more college students named Matthew Iverson and Douglas Emery—and warned them that the two might be engaged in a game of cat and mouse with only the cat the wiser. He leaned in to peer at the screen as Khalaji browsed through photo albums, until something about the scents of leather and aged wood emanating from the man annoyed him enough to make him pull away.

But this all felt increasingly pointless, and if the restless tension emanating off Khalaji was any indication, the other man felt the same way.

Especially when Khalaji swore, leaning back in his seat and dragging restless hands through his hair, gripping up handfuls of silver and chestnut, before pulling at his tie, his suspenders, finally settling on roughly snapping the cufflinks of his shirt loose and rolling the sleeves up over burly forearms bristling with dark hair salted in a few silver threads.

"There's nothing here." He shook his head, then burst to his feet, his chair rolling back loudly. He snatched up his jacket. "Let's go. I'll take Iverson, you take Emery. If one of them has a rotting head in a freezer somewhere, that's their point of urgency. They're going to strike some time today or tonight."

"I thought you would never ask," Seong-Jae muttered.

Khalaji's upper lip. "If you had a problem with my methods, you could have ordered me to try something different, *sir*."

An uncomfortable throbbing started in Seong-Jae's temple. Breathe. Do not snap back. "Would you have listened?"

"No."

"Which is why I did not waste my breath." He dismounted the chair he'd stolen, standing. "But I would say that the time for waiting is over."

"Agreed." Khalaji hooked his jacket over his shoulder, already heading for the door on firm, authoritarian strides— only to stop mid-step as a familiar-looking short blond woman in a lab coat leaned around the door, peered in, and then beelined straight for him, a folder tucked against her chest.

"There you are," she said. "Don't you ever check your email?"

"I've been out staring at dead bodies, Sten," Khalaji said,

and then her face clicked for Seong-Jae—the forensic photographer Khalaji had spoken to at the scene of Park's murder. Stenson.

Stenson only snorted and thrust the folder at him. "Got your results. DNA analysis came back on that blood from the Park scene. Came from a woman. Young, between sixteen and twenty-four. No one comes up when we run it in the system, so it might be a dead end. Might not even be connected with the crime scene."

A woman.

Or a girl, one small enough that the most efficient method of murder for tall, athletic young men would be stealth and a weapon requiring leverage and tenacity, rather than blunt force.

"Khalaji," he said, only for Khalaji to lock eyes with him, slate blue slightly wide.

"Those girls," Khalaji said. "The ones Park's roommate mentioned. The ones who surround Nathan McAllister."

"I believe," Yoon said, "we may have been overlooking the obvious."

"It makes sense," Khalaji said, then let out a rough gasp that was almost a laugh, taking a step back. "Fuck. We were so focused on the serial sexual component for these fucking queer kids that we didn't even think—oh, fuck."

"It does not fit the profile. Serial sexual predatory behavior leading to violence and murder is a very unique province of male perpetrators, and is rarely exhibited in women."

"It doesn't fit the profile, but it fits the evidence."

"Agreed."

Stenson was still standing there, watching them with an air of puzzlement, but Seong-Jae was focused on Khalaji. On the blanks that suddenly had someone to occupy them, that empty spot now a shadow offering teasing glimpses of an identity, and the answer to *who* lay somewhere in the synchronicity between them, the lines of logic and reasoning threading between his thoughts and Khalaji's until he could almost *feel* the seismic ripples radiating out from every shock of realization to intersect with the aftershocks of Seong-Jae's own.

"I don't think Trevor Manson was a test kill," Khalaji said breathlessly. "She wanted his head, but the murder didn't go the way she wanted. Either the head wasn't salvageable, or she just didn't have time and had to leave the scene. But she came back later. Dug up the grave and took the head."

"We still do not know what the body parts are for. Yet it all centers around McAllister." Seong-Jae grimaced as a grisly thought surfaced. "Is she trying to reconstruct a surrogate of him?"

"I don't think so. The parts she took don't match Nathan's body type or features."

"Perhaps attempting to protect him, then, from men she feels are preying on him."

"That would explain the deaths. Not the serial sexual

component. That element of desire." Khalaji tilted his head back, staring at the ceiling, then growled. "We don't have *time* for this."

"Then will you take the damned file so I can go back to *my* work?" Stenson asked.

Khalaji blinked blankly. "Huh? Oh. Yeah." He took the folder. "Thanks."

Stenson's only answer was another snort, and an offhand wave as she walked away. Khalaji flicked the folder open, flipping swiftly through printouts, a few of the crime scene photographs—

Seong-Jae stilled. A hard shot of adrenaline tightened his gut, and a *click* of rightness.

Photographs.

"The photo albums," he said, pivoting and darting back to Khalaji's desk. He slung himself into Khalaji's chair and brought up the data file on Nathan McAllister's Facebook and Instagram photos, browsing through in rapid clicks until he found the images from McAllister's performances with his band. "Come here."

Khalaji was already closing the distance. He hovered behind Seong-Jae, leaning over his shoulder. "What do you see?"

"The girls you spoke of. If they are so attached to McAllister, then they would be at these performances. It would be part of his allure. If she is fixated on him enough to kill over him, then she would not miss a performance." He scrolled faster, searching for that something, that *click* that would tell him this was right.

"*Her*," Khalaji said, his hand appearing in Seong-Jae's peripheral vision, stabbing at the screen.

Seong-Jae stopped. The photo Khalaji had pointed at was one of Nathan and his band-mates on stage, a close-up of Nathan bowed over his guitar. Right up against the stage, a thin, anemically pale girl huddled, looking up at him with the light shining in her eyes to turn them into adoring pools. Dyed-black hair straggled around her bare shoulders and face in a Bettie Page cut gone limp and wavy. She had the exact same labret piercing as McAllister, and down one arm were tattoos of feathers mimicking his.

"It's her," Khalaji breathed. "It's her. Look. In every photo. When she's looking at Nathan, she's happy. Anyone else, and she's angry."

Seong-Jae flicked back a few pictures and found another of Nathan wrapped up in Trevor Manson. Almost invisible in the background was that same girl, watching them lividly, her face transfixed in a mask of hate. Another photo, Nathan sitting on the edge of a darkened stage and doing something with his guitar case, while the girl sat at his side, swinging her stocking-striped legs and looking at him as if she could see nothing else. The next photo was another of Nathan performing, and leaning into the microphone next to the male vocalist until their lips almost touched, and the girl watched with rage bright in her eyes.

"She is furious," Seong-Jae said. His heart raced, the rush of his blood dizzying. This. This felt *right*. This felt true, intuition promising there was a light at the end of this tunnel, a bottom to the rabbit hole. "She feels as though she is being deprived of something. That someone is taking something away from her."

"The tags. Check who's tagged in the photos. A name. I need a name."

Seong-Jae clicked through from the saved files and to the live online profile, pulling up Facebook. When he hovered over her face, a clickable highlight came up, and he followed through to pull up her sullen features glowering from below a header with a photo of Nathan McAllister front and center.

"Sarah Sutterly," he said, staring at the name, and everything slid home like clicking tumblers falling into place to release a lock. He read the tagline in her bio. "'Number one Genus Corvidae fangirl and Nathan McAllister Fan Club President.' There is no address on her profile."

Khalaji dropped the folder on the desk and turned on his heel. "We'll work that out on the way there."

"On the way where?" Seong-Jae asked, but he was already talking to Khalaji's back. He pushed to his feet, following after him. "Khalaji, on the way *where?*"

"I'll explain in the car," Khalaji said tightly. "Let's go."

NATHAN COULDN'T BELIEVE HE HAD to deal with a fucking pig cop in his room.

He curled on his bed with his guitar in his lap, but couldn't really find it in him to play. Not when that cop—he'd said Nathan could call him Officer Giancomo, but Nathan was fine with calling him Officer Fuckface—was standing against the wall in the apartment, right at the central point where the half-wall divider bisected the room, at attention with his hands folded in front of him like he was about to say hallelujah, hey, salute the fucking flag.

Sanjit was doing homework in the living room, but he kept lifting his head, staring at Nathan significantly over the divider, looking nervously at the cop, then ducking his head over his books again. The air was so thick in the room Nathan could practically chew it.

This fucking sucked.

This fucking *sucked,* and everyone he'd ever loved was dying and he wanted to be mad at the cops for not stopping it, but everything in him told him it was his fault.

He was cursed, and wasn't allowed to love anyone or they'd die.

He'd write that into one of his songs if it didn't make him want to curl up and cry until he withered to pieces and just died.

It wasn't fair.

It wasn't fucking fair, and he hated cops like that fucking pig in his space for not doing anything to stop it. Especially the detective, Khalaji or whatever his name was, the one who acted like he got it when he wasn't any different from the rest and he was just a fucking liar.

Fuck. Nathan wasn't going to cry again. He'd cried so much if he did one more time he'd just...

He'd break.

He'd break, and there'd be nothing left of him.

Sanjit stood, pushing the coffee table back. The cop bristled.

"Where do you think you're going?"

"Fuck, man," Sanjit said. "I'm going to take a piss. You want to watch that, too?"

Rolling his eyes, the cop waved him past. Sanjit flipped his middle finger and disappeared into the bathroom.

A light knock rapped at the door. Nathan uncurled himself, laying his guitar on the bed, and started forward—but the cop stepped forward, stretching a hand out to block Nathan's path.

"Whoa, hey. Kid. You should let me get that."

Nathan batted his hand aside, scowling. "Do you fucking live here?"

"Fine, whatever," the cop snarled, stepping back and taking up his position again, staring at the far wall and muttering, "Didn't want this fucking assignment anyway."

With a glare, Nathan sidled past him, then crossed to the door and pulled it open a crack, peering out.

Sarah stood just outside, bundled up in her threadbare, ragged black *Fuck You, Kitty* hoodie, her chunky boots giving her an extra inch of height. She offered a silly smile and wiggled her fingers in a little wave.

"Hey, you."

Relief flushed through Nathan. She held out her arms to him, and he flung himself against her. "Sarah."

"*Nathan.*"

She breathed his name almost reverently, and wrapped him up close. She'd always been there for him—from almost the first day at school. When Genus Corvidae had been playing that crappy wing joint where Darian had worked for their first gig, she was the only one in the audience. She was safe, comforting, and he hadn't wanted to dump his bullshit on her doorstep in case the killer took another person he loved away from him, but now that she was here he clung to her and sucked in a hoarse, dry sob and tried so fucking hard not to cry.

She made a soft, sympathetic sound and stroked his hair. "Are you okay?" she asked. "Did they really arrest you?"

"Hey," the cop said, raising his voice. "*Hey.* What're you doing?"

Nathan jerked upright, glaring back at the pig. "It's okay. She's my fucking friend, okay?" He pushed the door open further and stepped out into the hall. "Just give us a second to talk in private, huh?"

The cop twisted his lips, then huffed dubiously. "Fine. Leave the door cracked."

Nathan stepped out into the hall and pulled the door shut all but the tiniest sliver of a crack. Sarah gave him a wry look, arching a brow. "What's his deal?"

"These fucking pigs have been driving me crazy. Like shit isn't bad enough with everyone dying." Nathan swallowed past the lump in his throat and slumped to lean against the wall. "I just...I can't deal with much more of this. I'm about to fucking snap, and they're treating me like I did it." His eyes burned, and he turned his face away sharply. He didn't want his best friend to see him breaking down sobbing after he'd already cried in front of the cops. "They think I'm a fucking murderer, and I can't...I just, I—"

His voice stopped working.

It was a strange thing that struck him somehow a moment before the pain did: something silvery and thin flashing in his vision, and then a line like a razor cutting into his neck, red-hot and tight and growing tighter. He choked, tried to suck in a breath, but got only a shallow, straggling wheeze of air. His head spun, whirled, and he jerked, trying to yank away, grabbing at the thing around his neck, but it dragged him back like a leash. His head snapped up and he stared up at the blur of the ceiling, twitching, struggling, fear and panic a heady cocktail that left him drunk and spiraling dizzily.

I don't…I don't…understand…

"The fuck is going on out there?" the cop snarled, his voice a distant thing that blended into wordless bleating noises as a roaring filled Nathan's ears.

If the cop was coming, he was too late, wasn't he? The thought drifted down the lengthening corridors of Nathan's thoughts, trying to reach him and yet growing farther and farther away as his mental pathways stretched into some dark and awful middle distance. He couldn't stand. His legs went weak, crumpling beneath him. As he sank down, his head fell back. Back against Sarah's thighs.

He looked dully up into her face, black coming in stars and clouds along the edges of his vision, irising in until there was only her.

Her, and the glint of silver wire in her hand, the serene smile on her lips, the gleam in her eye.

You…you were supposed to be safe, he thought.

You were supposed to love me.

Then he slipped away, and the dark took hold.

[17: CUT YOUR LITTLE HEART OUT]

IN THE CAR, MALCOLM CLUNG to the steering wheel with one hand and handled his phone with the other, listening tensely to the ringtone as he tried Giancomo's number.

"Pick up. Pick *up*," he snarled, swerving a hard left to duck out of brutal traffic and into a side street that would circle the long way toward the university campus apartments but get them there faster off the congested roads. A horrible feeling in the pit of his stomach said he needed to move *now*, when the timeline between every kill had shortened so dramatically.

Giancomo's voice came on the line. "Hi."

"Giancomo? You—"

"You've reached Officer Daniel Giancomo with the—"

"Fuck." Malcolm slammed his hand against the steering wheel. At Yoon's sharp look, he muttered "voicemail" before the beep came and he rattled off, "Giancomo—if you get this, be on the alert for a Sarah Sutterly. Twenty years old, about five foot two, thin, pale eyes, long black hair with straight bangs, feather tattoo down her left arm, labret piercing. Do your best to detain her." He dropped the call, then, and pressed down harder on the gas. "*Fuck.* I think there may be trouble."

Yoon was like coiled steel in the passenger's seat, perfectly still and yet the tension in him on the verge of snapping. "The officer escorting him is not answering?"

"No."

"To McAllister's apartment, then?"

"Yeah." He tossed his phone to Yoon. "Here. Call the officers on the other two potential targets. Their names are Abramson and Gervais. Numbers in my phone."

While Yoon scrolled through Malcolm's address book and tapped numbers into his own phone, Malcolm hit the gas, and fuck the speed limit. Yoon spoke in quiet murmurs into his phone, all tight hard edges and corners on the words, identifying himself, exchanging a few words, calling again only to hang up his phone and shake his head.

"*Anything?*" Malcolm asked.

"Everything is quiet. They have seen neither the suspect nor McAllister. Both targets are safe."

"That's something." Malcolm slalomed the Camaro around the street corner onto Lexington and shoved the car into the first open parking slot he saw, barely pausing to kill the engine before he was out. "Come on."

He let them into the building and vaulted the steps to the third floor with Yoon riding his heels, slowing only as they came in sight of Nathan McAllister's door.

A door which swung subtly open, just barely cracked.

Alarm shot through him in cold, tingling chills. He unslung one of the Glock service pistols from his shoulder holster, checked the safety, and held it at the ready, pointed at the ceiling and finger held away from the trigger as he gestured for Yoon to stay behind him. Yoon nodded, silent, as a pistol melted from inside his coat with practiced movements, held in both hands and pointed defensively ready toward the floor. Yoon nodded for him to proceed, and Malcolm edged the door open with his shoulder, peering around it carefully.

Empty room. Coffee table flipped over. No sign of anyone past the partition.

Fire extinguisher tossed on the floor, the base bloody and smearing crimson against the tile.

A foot in a glossy black shoe, protruding limply past the partition wall.

"Son of a—" Malcolm shoved inside, holstering his pistol and vaulting around the wall. Giancomo lay on the floor, sprawled face-down, his hair matted red around a skin-splitting wound, his blood pooling around his head. Malcolm crouched over him, feeling against his throat—and breathing out sharply as he caught a steady, strong beat. "He's alive."

Yoon's pistol disappeared. He sank down next to Malcolm, critical eyes darting over Giancomo. "She hit him from behind with the extinguisher, then left him—likely too eager to escape to finish the job." He pressed two fingers carefully around Giancomo's jaw and neck, then delicately parted his matted hair to expose split skin. "We should not move him without medical assistance. It may worsen his condition, but we should staunch the bleeding."

He was already moving, pacing quickly to the living room's kitchen inset and snatching up a clean dish towel from the counter. Just as he turned the water on, a voice drifted from a closed door across the room.

"…h-hello?"

They both stilled, battle-ready tension rippling through Malcolm's body. Yoon looked sharply over his shoulder, hand disappearing inside his coat. Malcolm rose from his crouch and drew his gun, flicked the safety off, and aimed it at the door. "Come out," he said. "Hands on your head and come out slowly."

"…d-dude, I can't open the door with my hands on my head…"

He recognized the voice. The roommate. Still he kept his gun aimed, moving it to the left instead of pointing right at the door. "Just come out."

The door clicked open. A single brown eye peered out, and then Sanjit edged out, elbowing the door open, hands on his head. "Is…is it safe?"

He went pale as his gaze locked on the gun—then almost white as his gaze dropped to Giancomo's body. He gulped, arms dropping. "Oh, shit. Where's Nathan?"

Malcolm flicked the safety on and holstered his Glock. "You need to tell us that. Fast."

"I don't know! I heard Sarah come by when I was taking a piss, and then everything got loud and crazy and I was scared to come out!"

Fuck. Definitely Sarah, then. And Nathan could be dead already, or in a critical situation. Urgency was a thunder in Malcolm's veins, shouting at him to *go*, but running off directionless wouldn't do shit but get Nathan McAllister killed.

"Does Sarah live in this building?" he asked, and Sanjit shook his head.

"Nah, man. Nah."

Yoon returned with the wet compress and crouched down to press it gently over Giancomo's head wound. "Time. How long ago?"

Trembling, Sanjit shook his head sharply. "I dunno, like twenty minutes?"

"God fucking dammit," Malcolm snarled. Worse and worse. He transferred his attention to Yoon. "Get Sade to find out where his parents live, and find them. If she didn't want to kill him, there's a thin chance he could have escaped. He'd likely run home for protection."

Yoon nodded, phone already in one hand, holding the cold compress with the other. Malcolm grabbed his own phone and hit the speed dial for emergency services.

"Nine-one-one, what's your emergency?" chirped out.

"This is Sergeant Detective Malcolm Khalaji with the BPD. I have an officer down with severe head trauma at Pascault Row on six-fifty West Lexington, apartment three-seventeen. Need first responders on the scene."

"Of course, Detective Khalaji. One moment, please."

He waited, grinding his teeth with every second that passed while the dispatcher typed in castanet rattles and Yoon's quiet murmurs punctuated in the background, then:

"Emergency medical is en route, seven minutes away. Dispatching officers to the scene. Is there anything else, Detective?"

"No. That's it. Thanks." He dropped his phone back in his coat and jerked his chin to Yoon. Yoon beckoned to Sanjit, pulling his phone away from his lips briefly.

"Come here. Hold this."

Sanjit eyed him, wide-eyed, and edged closer, then crouched down and pressed his hand to the wet towel. "Uh. L-like this?"

"Yes." Yoon stood, meeting Malcolm's eyes, black brimming with a hidden dark fire, a quiet and restless impatience as he cut his call and dropped the phone from his ear.

"Let's go." Malcolm pointed firmly at Sanjit. "Lock the door. Don't open it until the EMTs get here."

Sanjit blanched. "You're leaving me alone with the dead dude?!"

Malcolm was already striding for the door. "He's not

dead, and if you want your roommate back alive, we have to go," he bit off. "Lock the fucking door."

He was already on the stairs by the time Yoon had the door shut, but long legs caught up to him a moment later, and a tight, urgent murmur. "His parents live in Oregon. They are not an option."

"Then we need to find out everywhere she might take him, and fast." The seconds were ticking down, and every step down the stairs, through the lobby, out onto the sidewalk felt like another drop of Nathan McAllister's life blood slipping away because they were too slow, the clues hadn't lined up fast enough, they weren't going to get there in time. "Come on," he said, yanking the car door open. "We'll make calls on the go."

He barely waited for Yoon to get both legs in the car before he was swerving out into traffic, phone pressed to his ear again, counting rings until—

"Office of the Registrar, how may I help you?"

Fuck. He didn't recognize that voice. "Janine," he snapped. "I need Janine."

"I'm sure I can help you—"

"*I do not have time for this,*" he snarled, earning a startled glance from Yoon. "This is official BPD business. Get me Janine."

"O-of course?"

Rattling. Distant voices, Janine asking *who*, the nasal-sounding young man answering *I don't know, some asshole barking at me to get you*, then the phone rattled again, why was everything taking so *long* until Janine's voice came over the line:

"….it's Malcolm, isn't it? Rude, my dear."

"Not the time, Janine. Sarah Sutterly," he ground out. "I need to know where her dorm is, and where she stays when she's not on campus. Now."

"I—I—oh do calm down—"

"If you don't want another student to die, type faster."

"Oh dear. Oh dear oh dear oh *dear*. I'm working, please give me a moment—" Janine trailed off, rapid typing clatters and breathless pants drifting over the phone, then, "Sarah Sutterly. She's a junior in the dentistry program. She doesn't live in the student apartments. She has an off-campus address listed as her parents'."

"What is it?" he demanded. She rattled off the address. "Got it," he said, then hung up the call before she could answer. "We've got an address. It's about six miles from here. If she's not there, then we're too late. Call it in to dispatch for backup."

Yoon already had his phone in hand, but he paused, fixing Malcolm with a laden, seething look. "Khalaji?"

"Yeah?"

"Drive faster."

He leaned over Yoon's thighs to dig in the glove compartment and fished out his flasher, pushing it onto the dash until it locked and then flicking it on. The reds and blues circled bright. The siren wailed, screaming an urgency that drummed on his heart.

And Malcolm hit the accelerator, surging through Baltimore's city streets with his heart a wild darkness, burning with hope and black with fear.

NATHAN WOKE TO A POUNDING headache—spinning, swimming, cloudy, thick—and a tight and straining pain in his arms. He was locked into an uncomfortable position, and when he tried to stretch out the pain he couldn't move, running up against a scraping bite of something wrapped around his wrists and snatching him back hard when he tried to lift his arms.

Bound. He was bound with his arms behind his back, hard wood biting into his inner arms, digging into the undersides of his thighs.

With a groan, he opened his eyes. His vision was blurry, his eyes hurting when he tried to see, but his knees swam slowly into focus, the edges of the chair underneath him, an unfinished concrete floor beneath his feet. He lifted his head carefully, neck aching, a burning ring around his throat, and glanced around.

He knew this room.

An unfinished basement, cluttered with shelves of old books, odds and ends, jars of canned fruit no one had touched in years, gathering dust. Exposed beams dripping cobwebs, and stark light with a yellow tinge, brightest near the back wall where he'd been deposited in a cleared space of dirt-streaked concrete. He'd been in this basement before, hanging out during summers when he'd stayed in Baltimore instead of making the trip home to Portland with his parents sniffing over his shoulder all the time. Sarah's house didn't have air conditioning, an older vinyl siding building from the sixties, so they'd hung out in the basement where it was dank and cool to escape the sweltering heat, sneaking sips of her dad's rye bourbon and talking shit about boys.

Sarah's house.

Sarah.

His gut twisted, a sick lurch of betrayal and fear. His heart gave a single hard thumping jolt, nearly exploding, then subsided to rapid-fire tiny mutters ramping his blood up hot and high. She'd...she'd snapped a wire around his throat...wasn't that how Darian and Trevor and Zack and DeMarcus had died? Strangled to death?

Had...had Sarah killed his ex-boyfriends?

Was she going to kill *him*?

His mouth dried. He wet his lips, darting his gaze about quickly as he tugged carefully at his wrists, testing the ropes.

"S-Sarah?" he whispered. Please don't let her answer, please let her have dumped him down here and left him long enough to try to wriggle fr—

"Coming!" she called gaily, and his blood iced. "I'll be right there, babe."

Fuck. *Fuck.* He jerked at his arms—then froze as she appeared around one of the shelves, announced by a rattling trundle. She maneuvered a tall cart, multiple shelves stacked with coolers of varying sizes, the secondary tray underneath rattling with what looked like various tools and a *hacksaw*, its teeth stained dark. Something large sat atop the cart, though, something covered with a sheet. The sheet was dark in wet splotches in places, some of those splotches vaguely pinkish-red. The smell that advanced before the cart was a mouthful of rot and chemicals, a solid thing that he gagged on, on his next breath; choking, he turned his face away from that fleshy, cloying, oddly sick-sweet stench, burying his mouth and nose against his shoulder, hiding against his shirt, refusing to look.

Refusing to look at where the sheet clung damply to whatever was underneath, and outlined the hints of arms, legs, shoulders, lips.

Sarah leaned around the cart, then angled around to peer at him, leaning into his line of sight. She wore a calf-length black rubber apron and a pair of elbow-high bulky black rubber gloves.

Both were splattered in darkly gleaming wetness, and gobbets of…*something.*

Red sprayed her cheeks in arching patterns.

And she *smiled*, eyes wide and sweet and completely manic.

"Are you comfortable, babe?" she asked, leaning in. "Are the ropes too tight?"

He stared at her. "What are you *doing?* Is that…is that blood? Sarah, what the fuck is *wrong* with you?"

"Wrong?" She blinked, confusing darkening her brow. "Nothing. I just wanted to surprise you. Just like last Christmas, remember?"

"Last Christmas you gave me a fucking guitar pick, not four dead boyfriends!"

"They're not your boyfriends." Her voice dropped to a deep, urgent snarl, her face twisting into a chilling mask of cold rage. She stared at him, the rings of her irises showing all around. "You broke up with them. Don't forget that."

Nathan shrank back against the chair. What was *wrong* with her? He'd never seen her like this. He'd always known she'd been a little jealous of his boyfriends; she'd always withdrawn a bit when he dated someone new until he reminded her he'd always have time for her. But this girl wasn't the one he knew. Wasn't the one who'd told him she was just afraid of being forgotten. Wasn't the one who'd shown up to all his shows, who'd told him there was never a man good enough for him but one day she hoped he'd meet the right one anyway.

He didn't know this person, staring at him with her teeth

bared in a rictus, her eyes strange and empty and livid.

He didn't know this person, but she terrified him.

And he was pretty fucking sure if he didn't do something to divert her, to bring her back to herself, he was going to fucking die.

He swallowed, struggling to speak. "Is that why you killed them? Because we broke up?" His breaths shuddered in and out, that awful smell riding every inhalation and coating his tongue until he wanted to throw up. "Sarah, tell me you didn't kill them." She said nothing, and he whimpered, choking on the taste of both vomit and tears, eyes blurring. "*Please!* Say...say it wasn't you. Say you didn't do this to me..."

"I didn't do anything *to* you," she said softly, almost offended, something deadly in her voice. "I did it *for* you. I've always done everything for you. You never appreciated that."

"I always appreciated it! You were my friend! You were my best friend!"

"*Were?*" she shrilled, bristling.

Shit. Shit. Nathan took several panting breaths, struggling to calm himself, to get himself under control. "Are," he croaked, then forced a smile, but he couldn't stop shaking, even his bones trembling with watery, quivering terror. "You *are* my best friend. Please...please just let me go, and we can forget this. We can forget about...about the d-dead guys."

"They're not *dead*," she said, then sighed heavily, rolling her eyes. "You're so dramatic. They're not really dead. Just recycled. They're better this way."

Dread tightened his heart. "…what way?"

Sarah's expression brightened, her smile coming back, wide, her pink lips dotted with drying red splatters. "Let me show you. He's a little cold, but he'll warm up soon."

He?

Sarah gripped the sheet. Nathan shook his head, recoiling as far back as he could, the legs of the chair rocking. Oh. Oh no.

She ripped the sheet off. He closed his eyes—but not before he caught a glimpse of a nightmare that would haunt him for whatever minutes of life he had left.

A glimpse was more than enough.

The monstrosity sitting atop the cart would have revolted Frankenstein himself. He knew every part of its body—knew because he'd felt those arms around him, knew because he'd been clasped against that broad chest turned waxy and blue-veined, knew because he'd lightly walked his fingers down those powerful calves and playfully tickled the soles of the feet, knew because he'd kissed lips turned withered and mushy and water-bloated by decay, bluish-purple and rimed with dirt and rot.

DeMarcus's arms, held to Zack's torso by thick metal industrial staples, flesh shredding and threatening to rip free. The torso propped on a wood block, circled by a ring of caulk at the waist. Darian's thighless legs were glued to the wooden block just above the knee, jutting straight out from the surface of the cart.

And Trevor's head, Trevor's swollen monstrous head of rotting flesh melting and sloughing from glistening skull-bone, crumpled skin sagging into empty sockets, his neck stapled to the stump protruding from Zack's torso—while his mouth was fixed open, frozen in a mockery of a smile that bared perfect white teeth unevenly crammed into his gums.

She'd made a doll of the parts of men, a truncated monstrosity that would have been clownish if it wasn't so terrible, so twisted, so macabre.

"He's beautiful, isn't he?" Sarah announced proudly.

Nathan retched, curling forward and coughing between his thighs, vomiting the bitter bile of his stomach onto the floor, the taste of horror on his tongue and boiling past his lips.

"Don't be upset, Nathan."

A pout was in her voice, but he couldn't look at her, coughing as the sick stream trailed off to leave him gasping.

She sighed. "I made him just for you, you know. I put all the best parts together to make him just right. He's not finished yet. I still need the perfect eyes." In his peripheral vision, her booted foot stomped. "Trevor's eyes are nice, but they had to go and rot. I fixed his teeth. I messed them up when I brought him back, but DeMarcus had nice ones so I fixed him all up."

"Jesus," he rasped. "Jesus, Jesus fuck, Jesus shit, Jesus

you're—oh God, oh *God*, what is wrong with you—"

She grabbed his chin, wet rubber slipping and smearing against his skin, that smell shoving its way up his nostrils, and he gagged. Sarah jerked him up to face her, leaning in close, almost nose to nose, staring at him with fixed, unwavering intensity.

"Do you like my eyes, Nathan?" she whispered. "They've looked at you for so long. If I give him my eyes, he'll be perfect."

He flinched, but she wouldn't let him go, staring at him until her gaze felt like needles piercing him deep, puncturing his heart to bleed his terror everywhere.

"Please don't do this, Sarah," he whispered. "Y-you didn't…I don't need this, I don't *want* this, p-please just…just stop…"

"But then if I give you my eyes, I can't see you." She continued as if he hadn't spoken. Then her eyes went flat, her voice dropping into a hard, cold sneer. "And you *never* saw me."

She let him go, jerking his face roughly, contemptuously. He stared up at her, silhouetted against the thin watery light of the overhead hanging bulbs.

"I…I did…I swear I saw you…"

"You *never* saw me!" she cried, fury blazing, her face reddening in an angry bloom. "I was just your fucking fag hag. I was there when you needed a shoulder to cry on, whining and moaning about those boys you fuck around with, but if you *saw* me, why did you need them? *Why did you always need them?!*" Her voice rose to a shriek, before dropping to a soft, sing-song whisper. "I kept making them go away, but you'd just find another one. Why did you always need another one?"

Realization drained the feeling from his limbs. She…all this time? This had been going on for all this time, building to a head and he…he'd never realized, never even *thought*…

"You? *You* were the reason?" The sudden breakups, the fights over things he "couldn't understand" until walking away to cool down turned into never coming back, the "it's not you, it's me" when it felt like a lie every time.

All of that had been Sarah chasing men out of his life, to have him to herself.

With that realization came the cold understanding, heavy as an anvil crushing down on him, that she'd planned to kill him all along.

Anything to keep him.

He had to…had to buy time. Keep her talking. Something. Anything to talk his way out of this, look for a moment when he could escape. She hadn't bound his feet, and if he could get up and *run* he could use the chair to batter his way out through the stairs to the house or the cellar door to the lawn. He was closer to the cellar door, he thought; he'd only been here a few times but he thought to his left. Yeah. Yeah. He could do that.

"Of *course* I was the reason," Sarah said airily, dragging

his focus back to her. "I had to protect you, didn't I?"

"Y-yeah. Yeah…you protected me." He nodded quickly, swallowing the taste of his own sick, and dragged up a fake smile, his mouth like stiff plastic. He kept his gaze fixed on her and her alone, avoiding seeing past her, seeing that grotesque and sagging dead thing. "But you don't need to give him eyes yet, do you? You're still missing his hips and thighs, right? Don't you need someone else for that?"

He hated even saying it. If she left him…if she left him to go kill Matt or Doug, he'd never be able to live with himself, but he just needed her *distracted.*

But she only laughed, shaking her head. "You don't need those dirty parts." She trailed her rubbery, slick gloved fingertip down the line of his jaw. "I don't want those dirty parts touching you. It's not right."

He flinched from her touch. He couldn't help it—but the moment he did, she went still, staring at him. A stricken expression crossed her face, her features drooping, her entire body seeming to deflate. Her lower lip trembled. Her eyes blanked, lifting to stare somewhere over his head.

"None of this is right," she whispered softly, forlornly, shaking her head. Her eyes brimmed with a line of glistening tears. "I didn't want to hurt you, Nathan."

"You killed *everyone!*"

"I thought you would *understand.*" She sniffled, then scrubbed the back of her hand beneath her nose, streaking more red on her skin. "They were in the *way.* I just wanted to make someone perfect for you, but it's all wrong." She shook her head rapidly, pulling back. The surgical instruments in the tray rattled as she bent, digging, half-whispering, half-hiccuping out words as tearful little sounds. "The heart inside his chest is still Zack's. It can't be Zack's." She straightened, a jagged-edged surgical bone chisel clutched in her hand. "Zack didn't love you."

She stepped closer. Nathan kicked back, shoving the chair back, shaking his head, struggling to breathe, to find voice to scream, someone had to hear—

But she stopped, just looking at him sadly. "It needs to be the heart of someone who loves you." She reversed the chisel, grasping the handle in both hands, stretching her arms out and aiming the point toward herself. "It needs to be mine."

Nathan strained forward. "Don't!"

She plunged the chisel toward her chest.

Until a deep, commanding voice interrupted, echoing over the basement.

"Drop the weapon."

SEONG-JAE LINGERED OUTSIDE THE sprawling ranch house on

the edge of Baltimore's suburbs just long enough to watch Khalaji creep up the back steps, leaning in to peer in darkened windows. Only one car in the drive, no one apparently home. They circled the house together, keeping low—only for Khalaji to catch movement through the half-windows peeking up from the foundation and glimpsing into the basement.

They'd crouched, watching as Sarah unveiled a flesh mannequin that left them both swearing, turning away, sickened—but they didn't have the luxury for shock, for disgust.

Not when Nathan McAllister was right there.

Alive.

But possibly not for long.

Unspoken signals, silent nods, and Khalaji slipped around to the back. Seong-Jae followed; Khalaji tested the door, only for Seong-Jae to nudge him aside, rolling out his wallet and slipping out a pick. He slid it in, felt carefully for the movement of tumblers, found just the right angle—then twisted.

The door popped loose, drifting open in silent invitation.

Khalaji nodded, drawing his pistol. *Go*, he mouthed, then slipped inside on stealthy movements. Seong-Jae retreated, backing down the steps, then raced across the grass to the side of the house and the double storm doors set into the earth, held closed by a steel bar.

Carefully he pulled the bar, working not to make a sound, then folded one door back on dank concrete stairs.

From this angle he could see the girl's back, and over her shoulder, McAllister. Tension pushed Seong-Jae's body to the screaming point; he wanted to take action, *do* something, but one hasty movement and she might hurt the boy. And so he slipped down the stairs, focusing on making himself a shadow, on not making a single sound as he slid down into the dark recesses to the side of the stairs, drew his Glock, and edged slowly closer.

"The heart inside his chest is still Zack's. It can't be Zack's," the girl said—and then she had a weapon, *Zack didn't love you*, and she wasn't aiming it at McAllister, she was aiming it at herself, *It needs to be someone who loves you*, the blade plunging down, Seong-Jae darting forward, swinging his gun around, one good calf shot would incapacitate her before she could harm herself but he was blocked off by shelves, his heart racing, sweat breaking out in chill beads, he had to move faster—

"Drop the weapon," Khalaji said.

The girl whirled. Khalaji came steadily down the stairs from the door leading into the house, his firearm pointed firmly at the girl, his steps slow. She stared at him, then shook her head frantically, lifting the blade again. Khalaji froze, watching her with the keen eyes of a hunting wolf.

"No," she gasped, the blade trembling in her grasp as she held it high. "No. I'm going to give him my heart, and then he'll be mine."

"*Stop!*" McAllister cried.

The *click* of Khalaji's safety disengaging echoed loud. "I said drop it!"

The girl retreated quickly—then darted around McAllister to stand behind his chair, pressing the blade to his throat. He cringed back. Seong-Jae swore under his breath. If he could get behind her unseen—

"I'll do it," she swore. "We can go together. It's better that way, isn't it, babe? It's better."

Flinching, McAllister only whimpered, soft broken breaths escaping. "S-Sarah…"

Seong-Jae edged forward, keeping the shelves between himself and her line of sight, his own breaths a roar in his ears. Just a few more steps, if Khalaji could only keep her talking…

"No one has to go anywhere," Khalaji said, that calm, hypnotic voice seeming to take control of the room. "You don't want him to die, Sarah. You killed four men because you wanted to protect him. Isn't that right?"

"I *did* protect him," she hissed. "I did!"

"Then you don't want to harm him," Khalaji coaxed. "You would never hurt Nathan. So drop the weapon. Let's talk."

He stepped closer. She let out a high scream of *"Don't you come near me!"* and jabbed the weapon toward Khalaji.

And Seong-Jae saw his opening.

He dropped his Glock, lunging forward. Sarah whirled toward him, blade upraised. He ducked under her arm—and

then it was momentum crashing, flesh to flesh, a blur of limbs
and cloth and black rubber filling his vision, the rushing wind
of breaths counting past agonizingly slow then much too fast,
the flash of the blade, the impact of her wrist hitting his palm
as he grabbed, gripped, pinned, and then they were falling,
whirling, and he had her. He twisted her, flipping her face-
down, bearing her down to the ground and twisting her blade
hand behind her back and squeezing until she had to let go.
He knocked it away, sending it skittering across the floor, and
grappled for her other wrist while she screamed and thrashed,
struggling against his weight as he straddled her to flank her
and keep her *still* before she hurt herself.

"Be still," he gasped, bearing down on her captured
wrists.

"Get *off* me!" she screamed. "I have to—I have to—"

"'You have to' nothing. It is over. Sarah Sutterly, you are
under arrest," he said, lifting his head to meet Khalaji's eyes.

They stared at each other for long moments—as if there
was no struggling murderer between them, as if a crying boy
wasn't tied to a chair next to a cart where a horror of undeath
sat mounted like a strange display figurine.

Relief. Relief, the lingering high of fear, tension,
adrenaline. Exhaustion. All of it in Khalaji's gaze, naked and
stark as grief, and so raw and real that it cut deep into Seong-
Jae when it echoed the rough emotions churning through him.

Khalaji looked away first, holstered his weapon, and
retrieved a pair of handcuffs, stepping closer. While Seong-

Jae held the girl safely immobilized, Khalaji snapped the cuffs on, then helped Seong-Jae maneuver her carefully to her feet with her kicking and twisting and sobbing the entire time.

While outside the sound of sirens wailed, bearing down on them like the keening call of a mourning angel.

Seong-Jae caught the girl by one elbow and kept his other hand on her cuffed wrists, gripping her just tight enough to keep her under control as he marshaled her toward the storm door steps. But he paused for a moment, watching Khalaji as the man flung the sheet back over the pathetic collection of body parts, hiding it once more, then moved quickly to McAllister's side, ripping at the ropes on his wrists. The boy collapsed forward, sobbing, and Khalaji caught him, wrapping him up gently in thick arms, rocking him.

"It's all right," he whispered, letting the boy clutch at him, his voice rough and haggard with an emotion that stirred something deep inside Seong-Jae. "You're safe. We've got you. You're safe."

Seong-Jae made himself look away and marched the girl outside, maneuvering her one fighting step at a time up the steps, overriding her shrieks and snarls with, "You have the right to remain silent. You have the right to…"

The light outside was too bright, when he stepped into the sun. As if the day had changed somehow, in the surge of fresh color that came with the lifting of a great and terrible weight. The pressure of a clock ticking down, a heartbeat slowing, a life riding on whether or not he'd been able to *think* fast enough to do the right thing, to make the right decisions, to stay one step ahead instead of one step behind when one step behind was just chasing bodies instead of saving lives.

In moments like this, somehow, he felt cleaner.

Nothing could absolve him of mistakes of the past, but at least in this moment…

No one else would die, and he had had a part in that.

Yet he didn't know how to feel about the fact that for once, he hadn't done it alone.

He might not have been *able* to do it alone, without the push and pull of his mind against Khalaji's.

The moment they stepped around the house, the fight seemed to go out of the girl as she saw the three police cars slewed across the drive, an ambulance just pulling in and screeching to a halt. Several uniformed officers surged toward them, but the girl stopped, looking over her shoulder at Seong-Jae plaintively.

"Don't you understand?" she pleaded. "They were never good enough for him. Not completely. I made them go away. I made them go away, but kept the good parts." She smiled, then, a ghastly and broken thing full of lost misery. "It's for him, don't you see? He doesn't need me, so I have to give him what he needs."

She stared at him as if he should understand. As if she *needed* him to understand, as if she saw something inside him that knew exactly what could drive someone to do the things she'd done.

As if he could understand desperation without end, and the darkness that pure and aching longing could breed.

He looked away, pushing her gently toward the uniformed officer who stepped forward to take custody of her. "Be careful with her," was all he said, then turned away to watch Khalaji shepherd McAllister from the basement, leading him up into the light, hunched and wrapped in Khalaji's jacket.

When the girl caught sight of McAllister she tried to lunge toward him, pleading, "Nathan!" before two officers caught her arms and pulled her back.

McAllister looked pointedly away from her, and let Khalaji guide him toward the waiting ambulance.

Once the EMTs had the boy, Khalaji retreated, drifting back to Seong-Jae's side. In the chaos of the scene—milling officers, sounds of disgust and shock as several descended to the basement, the girl screaming, EMTs talking over Nathan and other officers trying to get his statement—Seong-Jae and Malcolm were the only points of stillness, kinetic energy drained to leave them objects at rest while that momentum carried forward elsewhere, leaving them behind.

"It always feels strange when it's over," Khalaji murmured. "Like I don't know what to do with myself."

"Yes," Seong-Jae answered softly. "Something like that."

By some mutual agreement, they turned toward Khalaji's car together. Forensics and the uniformed officers would document the evidence, and make sure the remains were either disposed of or properly returned to the families.

There was nothing left for either of them here.

Yet as they passed the police car where the girl had been shut into the back seat, she leaned toward the partially slit window, peering out, her gaze tracking Seong-Jae like a physical touch.

"One green, one blue," she said.

His breaths knocked out of him as if he had been punched. He turned sharply, stepping back toward the car.

"Say that again," he demanded.

She watched him with a serene, knowing smile. "One green," she sing-songed. "One blue." Her smile spread, wider and wider, turning ghoulish with her face spackled and smeared in blood. "You know, don't you?"

"What is she talking about?" Khalaji asked.

Seong-Jae stared at her, heart racing. She stared back at him, still smiling, and in that smile he saw everything he had ever wanted to forget.

As if it wasn't *her* looking out from behind her eyes at all.

He jerked his gaze from hers, forcing himself to breathe, and turned away. "I don't know."

Khalaji caught his arm. "Don't lie." He pushed himself into Seong-Jae's path. "That means something to you. One green, one blue."

"Stay out of my personal life," Seong-Jae hissed, and

ripped his arm from Khalaji's grip. "It has nothing to do with the case."

Khalaji's stare was almost wounded. Seong-Jae brushed past him without looking back, stalking toward the car.

This was why he didn't need a partner.

Some things, no one needed to know.

[18: AS WE SAY OUR LONG GOODBYES]

ONE GREEN, ONE BLUE.

Malcolm didn't understand what it meant—but he was too drained to press, and the silence between them as they drove back to the Central office was less strained than exhausted, broken only by the terse thirty-second phone call Malcolm spared to brief the Captain on the arrest. Apprehending a suspect brought with it a kind of catharsis, whether it was a simple bag and tag or a high-stakes confrontation—and that catharsis left him emptied in a rush of emotion, scraped raw and in need of silence and solitude to restructure his thoughts into some kind of humanity instead of the constant high-alert animal hyper-focus and constant suspicion required of a case.

Solitude was how he came back to himself, and remembered how to be someone other than a cop.

Solitude, however, was hard to come by with a partner in the car.

Yoon looked half-asleep, sprawled in the seat with his

thighs spread and a thin white A-shirt clinging like a second skin to golden sinew, a tapered chest that narrowed sharply to a lean, slinking waist. Once the adrenaline had calmed it hadn't taken either of them long to notice his coat and turtleneck stank from where he'd tackled the girl, and he'd been quick to shed both and bundle them up inside out while Malcolm stood back and held the trunk so Yoon could toss them in. Malcolm had tried to be subtle about turning the heater on in the Camaro to keep the mid-September chill from Yoon's bare arms, but he didn't think the other man even noticed.

He hadn't moved since he'd settled against the passenger's side door, staring out the window with pensive half-lidded eyes, his fingers curled against his lips. Malcolm chose not to disturb him.

If neither of them could have solitude in the aftermath, they could at least have the quiet of their own thoughts.

That silence only broke when he pulled into the parking garage and stepped out. Yoon finally moved, the statue coming to life, and slipped out of the car. He started toward the stairs, but when Malcolm stayed at the car, folding his arms against the roof and just leaning against them, Yoon turned back.

"Khalaji…?"

Malcolm propped his chin on his folded forearms. He felt bone-weary all of a sudden. "Go up without me. I'm not ready to walk into the noise yet. I'm not ready to be around people." He smiled faintly. "I may save the paperwork for tomorrow. Call it a day."

Yoon drifted a step closer. "Home and rest do sound appealing."

"I could sleep for a week." He pushed away from the car enough to turn to face Yoon, before settling to lean his back against the Camaro again. "After closing a case...it takes me back to Afghanistan. Most people use shell-shock to describe something instant. An explosive shock in the moment. But that's not what it is. It's the combination of dull weariness and constant keyed-up tension that comes with living twenty-four seven in the middle of active warfare. And when you step out of it..." He shook his head. "You don't fit in the world anymore. You don't know *how* to fit in the world." He slid his hands into the pockets of the slacks, shrugging. "I always need a day after cases like this. Just to remind myself where my edges are."

Yoon settled to lean against the Camaro next to him, hooking his thumbs in the belt loops of his jeans. "Edges, I think, are a desirable thing to have."

"Yeah. That's one way of putting it." Malcolm chuckled. "Hey. Do me a favor, would you?"

"Ah?"

"Next time, don't drop your weapon before tackling an armed suspect." He smirked. "If I'm allowed to give a direct superior advice about recklessly endangering himself."

Yoon tilted his head, then nodded briefly. "I will take

that under consideration."

A grin managed to break through Malcolm's exhaustion, even if it left him far too soon. He said nothing else. Neither did Yoon.

And silence, for a time, was good.

But "I should feel better about this," Malcolm said after a while. "We saved him. That's not something that usually happens. There are still some things that don't make sense, but…we saved one, even if we couldn't save the others."

"There are always those moments, Khalaji."

"Malcolm," he corrected quietly.

Yoon lifted his head sharply from his distant study of his boots, looking at Malcolm strangely, before looking away, fixing his gaze across the parking garage. "Seong-Jae," he answered softly.

"Seong-Jae," Malcolm tried, and found he liked the way it felt on his tongue.

Seong-Jae made an odd, low sound in the back of his throat, and changed the subject. "It will be some time before Nathan McAllister recovers from this. If he ever does."

"I know. I wish I could do more for him…but he needs a qualified trauma specialist more than he needs one clumsy old man. It'll take time. He'll carry a lot of guilt with him that isn't his fault, but…" He bit the inside of his cheek. "At least he's got a chance."

"What about the suspect?"

"That's up to the courts. She'll have a competency

hearing, then…" Malcolm grimaced. It all settled uncomfortably with him, in ways he couldn't quite put his finger on. "The evidence is fairly tight. She'll either get the help she needs in a state institution, or end up in jail."

Seong-Jae dropped his gaze. "Do you ever think…"

"Hm?"

"We…" He exhaled sharply, started again. "We hunt these people. But many of them never would have committed crimes had they been availed of appropriate services before progressing to the point of murder. Do you ever think about that?"

"Sometimes," Malcolm admitted, that uneasy feeling solidifying into something clearer, with edges sharp enough to cut. "Most often murder is a crime of passion. Impulse without warning or premeditation. Sometimes it's just…bad people doing bad things. But sometimes…" He glanced at Seong-Jae sidelong. "Yeah. And it does feel like hunting them. I don't like that."

"Neither do I. But it is what we do."

Malcolm arched a brow. "We?"

Seong-Jae's lips twitched in a tell as obvious as poker: Seong-Jae refused to smile, but his body was trying to squeeze out a human emotion anyway. "Did you think if you were surly enough, I would transfer out?"

"I might have held on to some small hope." Tilting his head back against the car, Malcolm let himself sink down, taking some of the weight off a body groaning with bone-weary aches as the adrenaline began to settle and bleed off. "…you know the Captain never really intended this to be temporary."

"I had my suspicions. I had hoped to dissuade her."

"You don't change Anjulie's mind once she's set on something." He dragged out a laugh. "Not if you want to live."

"Duly noted."

"So if we're stuck with each other, what do we do?"

Seong-Jae inclined his head, considering, then murmured obliquely, "You are a good detective, Malcolm."

"So are you." Malcolm hesitated, then added, "We don't miss much between us."

"Do you have no intention of resisting the assignment, then?"

Did he? He didn't want a partner. That hadn't changed. Seong-Jae didn't seem overly enthused about the prospect, either. They'd managed not to kill each other on one case, but this moment of cathartic camaraderie wouldn't last. Tomorrow Seong-Jae would still be the same uptight, icy bastard, challenging Malcolm at every turn for his particular regulatory flexibility, as mocking in his silences as he was in his blandly sardonic responses.

But goddamn, they were lightning in a bottle when they put their heads together.

He shrugged, quirking his brows. "I might think about keeping you."

Seong-Jae immediately tensed, flicking Malcolm a slit-eyed look. "I am not a pet to be *kept*."

"See?" Malcolm chuckled. "Why would I want to reassign you when you get so huffy?"

"I am not staying if you intend to goad me regularly."

"Yes, you are. Leaving would mean disobeying orders. You don't want to do that, do you?"

"Malcolm?" Seong-Jae asked mildly, staring with a particular calculated blankness across the parking garage.

"Yes?"

"'Jot' means 'dick.'"

That startled a laugh from Malcolm. "I guessed." He trailed off, sighing. "Go home, Seong-Jae. We're back in the office bright and early tomorrow. I'll show you the exciting intricacies of the BPD reporting database, and introduce you to the people you need to placate if you don't want your evidence to end up mysteriously mistagged and your emails magically routed to spam."

Straightening, Seong-Jae pushed away from the car. "There is still one matter we have not discussed."

"Eh?"

Black eyes fixed on Malcolm, studying him searchingly. "You were very defensive when I questioned your sexuality and the reasoning behind this assignment."

"Ah. That." Malcolm groaned. "I just don't want any crossed lines. Just because we're both queer shouldn't mean anything. People seem to think if you just throw two guys together, we'll end up naked."

Seong-Jae's expression didn't change save for the faintest mocking lift of his brows. "I do not believe that is in our job description."

"Exactly."

"Yet you seem to have this idea that we could be attracted to each other."

Malcolm, for a moment, let himself just *look* at Seong-Jae. If he let himself admit it, Seong-Jae was a thing of beauty: the stark planes of his face arranged so strikingly that every glance arrested attention, the sharp angles guiding every look to that wild strawberry bruise of a mouth, to starless nights of angled, slyly tapered eyes that gleamed with the same blue-black crow's-feather sheen as the fall of wild black hair across a pale golden brow. His tall, leonine body was just as angular, a poetry of geometry, every cut of muscle a component of feline architecture, all precise edges—yet he moved as water flowed. He was grace cut with diamond edges, lethal and elegant.

And if he and Malcolm were to be partners, he was entirely off limits.

Malcolm looked away—yet even if he found himself suddenly fascinated by the patches of daylight spilling into the shadowed parking garage, he could feel Seong-Jae's eyes on him, questioning, penetrating.

"It's not outside the realm of possibility," he said neutrally.

"Such a thing would make working together somewhat difficult."

"There's that, too."

"Then let us settle the matter, once and for all."

Malcolm frowned. "How would we do that?"

A soft scuff of a boot was his only warning. Long, strong fingers curled in his tie, knotting up a handful of it. Malcolm's head jerked up, his heartbeat slowing as he looked up at the other man, those few small inches in height between them bringing them so close, his nose brushing the sharp peak Seong-Jae's chin. Seong-Jae jerked on his tie, pulling him closer still, into body heat and a faint scent of something like diesel and something else clean, sharp, rich.

Before Seong-Jae's mouth crashed against his, and that tall, catlike body slammed him back against the car, pinning him between the hard edges of the Camaro and the harder edges of Seong-Jae.

Seong-Jae's kiss was silk and flame and the hard, hot burn of a dram of raw whiskey setting Malcolm's mouth on fire and searing all the way down to his belly. That sweet bruise of a mouth teased, assaulted, feinted, drew him in only to batter him back as their mouths met and parted and met again until they locked just *so* and Malcolm reached his melting point—that peak where his chest tightened and his blood became thunder and every taunt of Seong-Jae's tongue tied another knot in Malcolm's stomach, while every spark of pain graced by Seong-Jae's teeth wound Malcolm's body tighter.

He curled his hands against Seong-Jae's narrow hips and jerked him closer, crushing them together, leaning into him until the onslaught of Seong-Jae's kiss became a war, rushed vicious needy push and pull between them, claiming caresses and vengeful bites and a taste on his tongue like the sharp sweet surge of battle-hunger—and the pulse of rough desire striking Malcolm's body hit again and again with rough gunshot bursts.

It ended as abruptly as a bullet to the heart; Seong-Jae separated their lips with a soft gasp between them that Malcolm wasn't sure was his or Seong-Jae's, breath hot on his aching, throbbing lips. Seong-Jae's mouth was as red as blood, glistening so enticingly, and yet his gaze was as frustratingly unreadable as ever as he cocked his head, studying Malcolm closely, fingers still fisted around a handful of his tie.

Malcolm swallowed thickly, his voice struggling out of his throat like gravel. "Anything?" he growled.

Seong-Jae tilted his head in the other direction, then released Malcolm's tie and straightened. "I felt nothing."

Malcolm let his hands fall. "Yeah," he said numbly—yet he could hardly hear his own voice for the pounding of his own heart. "Me too."

Still Seong-Jae lingered—standing so close that if Malcolm breathed too deep their chests would touch, and then it would be heartbeat to heartbeat, straining against the cages of bone and blood and sinew to reach each other.

But then Seong-Jae stepped back, the air between them a cooling barrier, a distance that Malcolm wouldn't cross. Seong-Jae inclined in that half-bow, half-nod, sardonic.

"Until tomorrow, Malcolm Khalaji."

And then he turned away, leaving Malcolm there with his mouth on fire and his palms still burning with the heat of Seong-Jae's body clasped in clutching hands.

[19: IT'S NOT THE ENDING]

HOME CLEARED MALCOLM'S HEAD IN ways the drive back couldn't. Not when somehow, over the course of a few days, he'd gotten used to Seong-Jae in the passenger's seat.

But the passenger's seat was empty, because Seong-Jae had kissed him until he was liquor in Malcolm's bloodstream, then walked out of the parking garage and disappeared into the glare of the afternoon sun.

That man was going to drive Malcolm out of his fucking mind.

In his apartment, he stripped out of his suit and into a more comfortable Henley and jeans, tossed Seong-Jae's forgotten coat and shirt in the wash so he could return them tomorrow, put a delicate Chopin piano arrangement on the house speakers, and settled in the kitchen with a mixing bowl and a glass of chardonnay on hand.

This was his ritual, after closing a case. Flour and sugar and a dash of vanilla, milk and butter and eggs and cream cheese and a sip of wine in between working the whisker. The soft crinkle of pleated paper cups fitting into the muffin tin, the aromas of chardonnay and vanilla chasing away the musk of diesel and masculinity clinging to him until it was soaked into his skin.

There was serenity in filling each cup precisely with batter, watching the golden pour rise. There was peace in sliding the pan into the oven and setting the timer. There was calm, thoughtless and blessedly quiet, in blending cream cheese and powdered sugar and butter, a dash of white wine and little slices of fresh strawberry into a bowl until it frothed into red-streaked swirls of stiff iced whips in little whitecaps—and he rediscovered the pleasure of simple laughter as he sucked icing off his fingertips and tried not to make messes of his cupcakes.

And some of the tense pain had finally eased from his shoulders, by the time his phone buzzed against the countertop with a new text alert from the Captain. He leaned over, setting the checkered panholder down on the counter while he read.

Thanks for not fighting me on Yoon.
See you both bright and early.

He smiled faintly.

She'd well and fairly maneuvered him, and he felt no shame in admitting it.

By the time the oven timer dinged, he'd gone through nearly a full glass of wine, melting the edges of the world with liquid halos. The cupcakes came out gold and soft and mounded, only to disappear beneath sculpted swirl-cones of strawberry chardonnay icing, each topped with a strawberry sliver.

He put most of them in the refrigerator to cool, but picked out one just for himself, fetched his reading glasses and a Yukio Mishima novel, and nestled himself into his favorite chair to read by the low golden light of amber stained-glass lamps and the glow of the city skyline pouring in through his windows.

And when he flicked to his bookmark and bit into soft, sweet cake and still-warm icing, he remembered what it meant to find humanity in the small things.

He read for hours, until the subtle background noise of the apartments below shifted to the rhythms of people coming home, the bustle and call of shoes kicked off at the door and dinner plans and familiarity and togetherness—while the noise of traffic outside changed to the particular cadence of evening. For the first time in days he didn't feel tense; didn't feel as if there was a timer on his contentment. There were other cases waiting for him, and new ones every day…but for right now, he wasn't Detective Khalaji.

He was just Malcolm, and just Malcolm was fine.

And when his phone rang and the screen once more shimmered *Leon-Khalaji, Gabrielle,* he set his novel down on his thigh and lingered on the screen, the ache in his chest bittersweet and warm.

He answered the call, then, and lifted it to his ear. "Hey," he said. "It's been a while."

"It has," she said with a soft, familiar laugh.

Malcolm smiled, leaned his elbow on the arm of the chair, and settled in for a long night.

NATHAN MCALLISTER LEANED AGAINST THE wall of his student apartment, staring at the shadows of window-bars falling across his bed. The apartment was dead silent. Sanjit was gone. He'd made some excuse about staying with friends, stared at Nathan like there was something wrong with him, and disappeared.

His parents would be here tomorrow.

But tonight he was alone and he wasn't okay, and he didn't want to be trapped here with the memory of Sarah's wide, stretched smile and the image of that hideous thing she'd created stamped on his brain.

He stared down at his phone. At his address book. At the entry *Iverson, Matt.* They'd been friends once, friends who happened to love each other, before he and Matt had started fighting over the time Nathan spent with Sarah. He hadn't understood, then, why Matt was making such a big deal out of things, but now…

Now he saw it. Now he saw everything, and he couldn't live with it by himself.

His fingers shook. His throat closed. And before he could talk himself out of it, he tapped Matt's contact and lifted the phone to his ear, his heart trembling to the rhythm of the ringtone.

Matt picked up after two rings. "Hello?"

"Hey," Nathan straggled out. "Hey, Matt."

"*Nathan?*" A long silence, then, "I…I didn't think I'd ever hear from you."

Nathan curled up in the corner of his bed, hugging his knees to himself. "Shit happened, I guess."

"Shit that had cops following me around. God, that was fucking weird. I'm glad it's over. Are you okay?"

"No," Nathan admitted, fighting back a sniffle. "My parents won't be here until tomorrow and my roommate left and I'm by myself in this fucking room. Every sound scares the fuck out of me, and I…I…" He swallowed, struggled, made himself say it. "Can I see you? I…I miss you."

Matt didn't answer at first—then let out a soft sound, not quite a laugh. "It's fucking weird that we live one floor apart and haven't talked in two years, isn't it?" he asked. "I'll be right there. Give me five."

"Thank you," Nathan whispered, and dropped the phone.

Even though he knew it was coming, when that knock rattled the door he jerked, shrinking back, huddling against the wall. But, breathing deep, he pulled himself up, drifting to the door and pulling it open.

Matt stood on the other side, just as lanky and dorky as he'd been when they dated, in his weird patterned shirts and chunky glasses. Nathan just looked at him, frozen. Matt looked back, his eyes slightly wide, then smiled shyly.

"I'm glad you called," he said.

"Me too." But then Nathan broke. Just the sight of Matt's face, when he could have ended up like the others….everything in Nathan crumpled, the dam breaking, and a rasping sob clawed out of his throat. "Matt…"

Then Matt was there: pulling him into his arms, into his warmth, into the familiar scent of his shampoo and body and everything that reminded Nathan that Matt was alive and so was he. Matt held him fiercely tight, and Nathan clutched at him, choking out gasping sobs and breathing him in and just clinging to the reminder that he wasn't alone.

"It's okay," Matt soothed softly, his voice warm, so reassuring, against Nathan's ear. "You're going to be okay."

And as Nathan huddled close and safe and spent himself in a catharsis of relief, he thought…he thought he just might believe that. It would take time. He would never be the same.

But he would be okay.

IN THE QUIET EMPTINESS OF his apartment, surrounded by bare and stark walls of brick set against concrete floors, Seong-Jae settled at the desk in the center of the open room and stared at the corkboard propped against the wall.

Night had descended long ago, but he hadn't moved for hours, the sandwich he'd made himself for dinner left limp on the plate at his elbow, his mind half on his circling thoughts, half on the tingle and burn of his lips, his mouth swollen and sensitive from the rasp of Malcolm Khalaji's beard, his tongue still alive with the taste of him.

Seong-Jae had deeper things to worry about.

He steepled his fingers together, scanning over the cork board again—dozens of photos, color and black and white, cityscapes and hints of profiles caught in motion and captures of crime scenes.

He must have missed something.

Finally he stood, picking up a new photo from the desk, a glossy printout in stark colors. He crossed to the board, found a free space, and pushed a thumbtack into the photo, pinning it into place. The eight-by-ten captured a square of concrete, the edge of grass just beyond.

And the splash of crimson, swirled in a flourishing handwritten circle, runework in blood.

He stepped back, studying the new photograph, how it fit with the others, a new branch in a tree of interconnected red lines, threads stretching from pushpin to pushpin in a map so complex it wound in and out of itself like neural networks. He pressed his knuckles to his mouth, staring at that circle until it burned on his brain.

Very well, then.

Let the games begin.

[THE END]

Read on for a preview from CRIMINAL INTENTIONS Season One, Episode Two: JUNK SHOP BLUES!

[DISCOVER YOUR CRIMINAL SIDE]

GET MORE OF THE THRILLING M/M romantic suspense serial everyone's talking about. Follow Baltimore homicide detectives Malcolm Khalaji and Seong-Jae Yoon as they trail a string of bizarre murders ever deeper down a rabbit hole—that, if they can't learn to work together, may cost them both their lives. **Full-length novels released once per month!**

[PREVIEW: CI S1E2, "JUNK SHOP BLUES"]

[0: MOTIVE FOR MURDER]

MARION GARVEY HAS A LONG and storied history of people trying to kill him.

It's a hazard of the business. A hazard of success, too. Scum always want to go for the heavy hitters at the top. The big dogs. And he's proud of being the kind of big dog who doesn't have to be afraid of showing underbelly, because even his underbelly is armor-plated and bulletproof. He is untouchable. When Marion Garvey looks at himself, he sees the definition of a self-made man. The phrase "too big to fail" was *made* for him.

When you're on top of the world, it's inevitable the small fry will try to take you down.

Tonight, though, he's hardly expecting an attempt on his life. Tonight is *special*. He's been waiting for tonight for weeks, and after he went to the trouble of booking a honeymoon suite at the Wellington everything had better damned well go off smoothly. He's thrown enough money at the valets, the bellboys, the fucking *maids* to make sure he'll get the VIP experience. He wants nothing but the best.

And he damned well intends to give nothing but the best, tonight.

The jewelry box in his pocket weighs heavy. That weight is a sense of satisfaction, of pride, of promise. Of wealth. He can buy the things other men only dream of.

Whoever said money didn't buy happiness was just trying to make the best out of his sad lot in life.

Money can buy anything, including happiness on demand.

But his happiness comes from a more immediate source, as he hears the door slip open, the faint beep of a keycard unlatching echoing from outside. He takes one last look around, taking in the champagne cooling in the ice bucket in perfect reach between the catering cart and the bed, wherever this might happen to take them. The roses, spread in splendor all across one wall, over three hundred fine red blooms without a single blemish, every last one hand-chosen and spilling their lush fragrance to fill the room. The petals of hundreds more roses still, turning the floor into a sea of blood.

He's bought happiness, all right.

He's bought it, and he won't let it go.

Marion turns, a smile on his lips, and smooths his hands over his perfectly tailored suit, hand-made to his specifications. Only the best, always. Only the best.

"Darling," he says, and spread his hands—only to stop as a strange wet feeling spreads in the center of his chest, dull and heavy.

He looks down. His chest is red, he thinks numbly. What an odd shade of red, thick and somehow more vivid than other reds. The smell of the roses is so strong. So strong he can hardly pick out another smell, hot and thick and strangely metallic.

Blood.

Oh.

That is his blood.

He should feel pain, he thinks. He should feel pain, but there is only a sort of heavy numbness. His body doesn't want to move. His head is a balloon detaching from his body, taking his consciousness with it until he is separate from the shell of meat and blood and bone that had formed a man for over thirty-seven years. Thirty-seven years in which he'd made himself into everything he'd wanted to be.

Only to be unmade in a single stroke.

The handle protruding from his chest is black. The metal inside his flesh is cold. That, he can feel. Every inch of the blade lying against his insides, this flat cool sheet of stainless steel icing his flesh. Still no pain.

That is a kindness, he thinks. That is a kindness money can't buy.

He stares at the face wavering in his vision. At the resolute stare. At skin spattered in blood, his blood, blood that had been cut out of his chest in splatters and still soaks warm down the front of his shirt.

Why, he tries to ask, but when his head is floating and only tethered on by the thinnest thread, his lips don't want to move.

He's going to die on a bed of roses.

He falls, and the last thing he hears is the rustle of leaves. The last thing he feels is the bite of thorns, hooking through his suit to find skin.

The last thing he sees is the shower of petals, as rich and velvety red as his blood.

He is cold, so cold.

And still those familiar eyes stare through him, watching his life ebb away.

Read the rest on Amazon Kindle and KindleUnlimited!

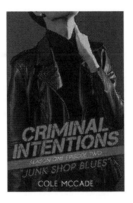

https://www.amazon.com/dp/B07CZHNDG3/

[SERIES Q&A WITH THE AUTHOR!]

HI THERE, COLE HERE. I get a lot of questions about the series, so let's answer some of the most common ones!

Q. I don't quite get the "seasons/episodes" thing.

> **A.** The general story arcs are structured less like a book series and more like a television series. Every full-length novel is akin to a TV episode in a series, where you get a single episodic story arc with a conclusion for that particular plotline while continuing the overarching storyline driving the entire season—and getting to know the characters and their developing relationships a bit at a time.

Q. So how many episodes will there be per season?

> **A.** Thirteen, just like with TV. Most TV series have either 12-13 episode seasonal arcs, or 26-episode seasonal arcs. I'm following the hour-long episode format with 13-episode seasons so that each novel has the same feel of a more in-depth hour-long show.

Q. Thirteen. Thirteen actual novels per season. Not novellas. Not chapters. 50,000-70,000 word novels. You're kidding. And you're releasing one per month?

A. Yep.

Q. *How?*

A. I have issues.

Q. So how many seasons will there be?

A. I have five loosely planned, but that's not concrete. I may realize halfway through Season Three or Season Four that we're nearing the end of any viable plot and anything else would be reaching/stretching. If that happens, no matter when, then I'll make that season the final season.

Q. Do I have to wait all the way to Season Five for Mal and Seong-Jae to get together?

A. Nah. I won't tell you exactly when in Season One that they get together, but it'll happen. That doesn't mean subsequent seasons won't bring some rocky times, but we'll get them *into* a relationship in Season One.

Q. But I thought these were kissing books!

A. They are. :) But because it's structured like a television series instead of a normal romance novel, you won't get a complete beginning-to-HEA romance arc in a single book. Instead it's like those partner shows where you watch all season as they flirt with and deny the sexual and romantic tension between them, hoping for every intimate moment until it finally happens, watching their relationship deepen (and occasionally fracture) through the work they do together. It also means now and then as long as they're not tied to each other they may get involved with other people to further complicate their romantic entanglement, but it's just part of the arc to help them realize their feelings toward each other.

Q. You write a lot of unprotected queer male sex.

A. Yes, I do. This isn't real life. There's a massive stigma in real life toward queer men in which people treat us like disease bombs waiting to go off, unclean and deadly, along with the subtle insinuation that it's our fault anyway because of societal shaming of the assumed promiscuity of the stereotyped queer male lifestyle plus a deep misunderstanding of the AIDS crisis. While it's a shitty stigma that treats us like we're disgusting and subhuman, safe sex in real life is still important regardless of gender or sexuality.

[281]

Fiction, however, provides a safe place to flip the middle finger at that stigma and very pointedly ignore condom usage. Believe me, as a queer man, with me it's entirely political, utterly deliberate, and a rather firm statement in defiance of the outrage that screams "how dare you, unclean creatures that you are, even fantasize about unprotected sex?" It's also a kink for some people—the fantasy of skin to skin and the sensations involved, and one that can often only be indulged either in fiction or with a long-term partner, allowing for a certain sense of intimacy. If you're waiting for mention of a condom, 8/10 with me you're going to be disappointed. I throw them in now and then, but more often than not I don't. Unprotected sex is always mentioned in the trigger warnings, so you can be forewarned and choose not to read it if it's something that upsets you.

Q. What's the deal with the Nameless Man?

A. ¯_(ツ)_/¯

Q. Hey, man. Glocks don't have safeties. That's not how they're designed.

A. I know. :) It's 100% dramatic license for the intense moment when the safety comes off, etc. I get why that would kind of twitch people, though. TV does stuff like this all the time (like what a gunshot actually sounds like, etc.) and sometimes it's just fun to fuck around for the sake of the tension of the moment.

Q. Will every book have super-gory, gross, extreme crimes?

A. No. Although this is a rather graphic series, I really want people more focused on the slow development of the character interrelationships and intrigue with the cases as the framing for that, and as an opportunity to find out how our leads' minds work in various situations. Besides, if every crime is super-graphic that leaves nowhere to go as overarching plots escalate to a head—so some things will end up scaled back to make the truly plot-critical ones more impactful. While I will likely always include some explicit detail of every crime scene, for the most part the details are there more to give readers clues to the evidence informing the detectives' thought processes, and less for shock value.

Q. What made you choose vinyl gloves over surgical nitrile when Mal's allergy means he can't use latex?

A. Personal preference. While I don't have a latex allergy, I do have OCD germophobia and sensitive skin; I use disposable gloves in certain situations to keep from tripping off my OCD, and the second my hands start to sweat in the gloves I'm likely to get rashes, irritation, and cracked skin on the backs of my palms and knuckles if I use latex. (Which…actually may be an allergy, I'm not sure, I just know I don't like it so I avoid it.)

So I started using both vinyl and nitrile as alternatives before dropping the nitrile unless I have no other choice. Vinyl doesn't get as sweaty as quickly, so it stays comfortable longer; vinyl gloves are also a more comfortable fit for larger hands, when nitrile gloves often feel like they're choking off my circulation at the wrists. The looser wrists on vinyl gloves also make it easier to take them off quickly without dirty portions of the gloves possibly making skin contact. Since Mal has large hands like mine and a need to keep from contaminating himself with the things he touches (such as crime scene blood), I gave him my preference just as one of those little quirks I often share with my characters. The only downside to the vinyl is that it tears more easily if it snags on something or is stretched to its limit.

Q. …why does nearly every single person in these books use some model of Android phone? Are you shilling?

iPhones are a thing, you know. (Yes, someone asked me this. I actually really love how observant y'all are with the little details like this.)

A. So. Though iPhones are hugely popular, I've never had one. Ever. I'm not really a fan of Apple interfaces or hardware as far as my particular preferences for usability and utility, or maybe I'm just holding a grudge from being forced to use really old Apple computers in art school. Point is, I don't know iPhone interfaces, what apps are or aren't supported by the platform, mobile security, user navigation flows, capabilities, etc. Which means I can't write about using them with as much confidence or ease as a more familiar Android phone. Considering the integration of mobile technology into many of these investigations, I'd rather not slip on those details. So everyone gets Androids.

Q. Why don't you always translate foreign language words, such as the Persian or Korean slang Malcolm and Seong-Jae sometimes use?

A. That's a complicated question with an even more complicated answer that involves an in-depth look at privileged expectations—and it's tied into the reason why many authors and readers who speak languages other than English are increasingly against italicizing non-English words, too. To keep it short I will say that

I translate when it's relevant to the dialogue or plot or when another character asks about things said aloud, but for minor words I don't because in a character's POV they normally wouldn't stop to define the word they just thought/said in English.

I'll also say that while the gist is often apparent from context (for example, we knew "jot" was an insult long before Seong-Jae told Malcolm what it meant), in general non-English speakers reading English language books don't have the luxury of having every word translated and explained directly to them. They have to learn the language. So. Again: ¯_(ツ)_/¯ Take from that what you will. You won't lose any of the plot by not knowing those little bits of slang.

Q. But I noticed you sneakily went back and switched "jaji" with "jot" after the first book released.

A. I did. I'm going to outright own this: my Korean is rusty and self-taught, and I messed up. Someone was kind enough to point out that I swapped the anatomical word for penis ("jaji") with the slang insult for dick ("jot"), so I went back and fixed my screw-up. (And thanked that person profusely.)

Q. Why does Sade use they/them pronouns? Are they male or female?

A. Sade doesn't identify as either male or female. They identify as two-spirit, which is a rather complex concept that differs between Indigenous nations and isn't something to be lightly discussed here. The closest analogue in non-Indigenous western culture is genderqueer, which is a nonbinary expression that may figure in masculine traits, may figure in feminine traits, or may eschew gendered traits altogether.

Not everyone identifies explicitly with the male/female gender binary, whether they're cis or trans, and identifying as genderqueer, genderfluid, agender, neutrois, genderbend, demiboy, demigirl, or many of the other identities along the nonbinary spectrum may be more comfortable. That can often mean ditching the gendered pronouns, too. While many nonbinary people default to using "they/them/their" in the singular, others use pronouns such as "xie/xer" or others depending on what suits them best. I will likely never reveal what gender Sade was assigned at birth. It's just not necessary to their story, and can cause people to start unconsciously gendering them.

Q. Why don't all the Q&As in each book have the same questions?

A. I add new questions and answers as people ask them as the series progresses and sometimes delete episode-specific questions from new episodes, but I don't always go back to update the previous books every time as it can take a while to do that with every new release each month. So newer books will have longer Q&As with more/updated questions. Eventually, though, I go back to refresh the back matter of older books, and end up adding the latest version of the Q&A.

Q. ...your avatar is wearing cat ears.

    A. Yes, yes it is.

Q. *Why?*

    A. ...

    ....

    ....

    ¯_(ツ)_/¯

[AFTERWORD]

I DON'T LIKE WRITING "BURY your gays" stories.

Honestly, that's what this felt like sometimes. Even if in the end our queer heroes survived and managed to save another queer kid, even if there's a point to be made in here about the objectification and fetishization of queer male bodies, the grisly and fetishistic deaths of queer kids it took to get there often made me uncomfortable to write.

If it made you uncomfortable to read, I'm sorry.

I had my reasons. I'm not sure how to break them down, but let me start with this.

First.

Crimes like these happen. I don't want to pretend they don't. I want to shine a light on them, and on the ugliness that still lives in our society, often masked behind self-serving allyship or the demands of socially acceptable behavior.

Second.

I was raised by cops.

Two of them, if you count my parents. Three, if you count my grandmother. Four, if you count my stepmother.

Yeah. It was a family thing.

Yet I never once even thought about becoming a cop. Never even wanted it for half a second.

Ironic, now, that I'm putting most of my energy into writing crime fiction.

Here's the thing with my family. There's always been a tug of war between blue loyalty and loyalty to our own tribes as a vast, mixed, multi-racial family with plenty of people in it quite willing to flip a middle finger at the cops. I'd like to think our POC background had an influence on my family to make them better cops, but as someone who grew up under the harsh scrutiny of police inquisition, I can say it didn't.

At all.

I think at one point my parents were actually good cops. I remember them even being kind parents, at some time in my life. But I also remember watching the years eat into them. Watching the cult mentality of police loyalty bend and break them. Watching the "us versus them" mindset erode their empathy and humanity until either you toed the line and agreed with them with wholehearted obedience, or you were guilty of something and needed to be taken down.

I remember my father keeping me trapped sitting on the kitchen counter beneath the harsh kitchen light, interrogating me as if I were a murder suspect because my sister broke a lamp and lied on me about it. He barked in my face, shouting at me, barraging me with words, putting intent in my mouth and trying to back me into a corner to force a confession. My mother had to pull him off me, remind him we were at home and I was his son.

I was five.

In another instance, I back-talked my mother. I always did have a smart mouth.

She held me down and beat me with her uniform issue belt until my arse was raw and bleeding. My father tried to stop her, and she chased him from the room and locked him in the bathroom. He stood there and counted the lashes until he couldn't take it anymore, then broke out of the bathroom and tore the belt from her hand and stopped her.

That time, I was six.

Six years old when I realized what being cops was doing to my parents. Six years old when I realized they could see the loss of humanity in each other, but not in themselves, and somehow they were trying to desperately hold each other together against the influence of an organization whose demands of solidarity weren't that far off from a cult's gaslighting methods for creating mentalities that would never question their tenets.

My parents weren't the kind of cops who would care about crimes against queer kids. They would care about crimes against people of color, sure, but they were just as likely to suspect people of color of bringing it on themselves. Even having a queer son, they just…weren't the kind of people who could give a damn. Under code blue, there was a line.

Anyone who didn't fit the standard was on the wrong

side of that line, and not worthy of what shreds of empathy they had left.

Sometimes I wonder what my parents might have been like, if the police department in my hometown hadn't gotten ahold of them. I'll never know. My father was a cop until the day he died, while my mother left the force just before my teens—but she was never the same, never capable of empathy or human connection in a safe, healthy way.

I tell myself that neither of them could have known what they would become. I tell myself that when they joined the force, they had ideals of being something better.

I tell myself a lot of things.

And then I turn those things into stories. Stories of cops who care about crimes like this. Stories of cops who don't just dismiss the escalating homicide rates against LGBTQIA+ people throughout the United States. Stories of cops who see what being on the force does to you, and fight against it to retain their humanity and empathy nonetheless. Cops who don't see "us versus them," but just people they were hired to protect.

Cops who are better police officers than my parents ever were.

But in order for them to be better about dealing with those crimes, the crimes had to happen in the first place.

That's where I was coming from, when I chose to start this series with such a grisly story. I had a purpose. An idea.

And now I have a finished novel.

I'll have to leave it to you, dear reader, to decide if I did anything of note with it.

-C

[GET VIP ACCESS]

WANT FREE STORIES AVAILABLE NOWHERE else? Subscribe to the Xen x Cole McCade newsletter:

www.blackmagicblues.com/newsletter/

Get SOMETIMES IT STORMS (previously featured in IPPY Award-winning charity anthology WINTER RAIN), Red's story in PINUPS, as well as deleted scenes from A SECOND CHANCE AT PARIS and FROM THE ASHES – and deleted scenes, bonus content, episode soundtracks, and artwork from CRIMINAL INTENTIONS.

Subscribing also gets you release announcements and

newsletter-only exclusives, including early access to new books, giveaways, and more. **Become a VIP!**

www.blackmagicblues.com/newsletter/

[FOR REVIEWERS]

XEN x COLE MCCADE
ARC REVIEWER TEAM

INTERESTED IN ADVANCE REVIEW COPIES (ARCS) of upcoming releases? Apply to join Xen x Cole McCade's arc reviewer team, A MURDER OF CROWS:

http://blackmagicblues.com/join-the-murder-of-crows-arc-team/

[ACKNOWLEDGMENTS]

I WILL ALWAYS BE GRATEFUL to the friends who've been like sisters to me. Mija, mei mei, imouto, aneki, L—you've always kept me on track and encouraged me even when I felt like I couldn't do this.

And Amanda, my intrepid editor and yet another close friend of so many years. Thank you for kicking my arse. Thank you for keeping me accountable. Thank you for being my friend.

To the Fight Club.

Well.

We won't talk about that.

But I see y'all.

I love y'all.

And I appreciate you more than you know.

[ABOUT THE AUTHOR]

COLE MCCADE IS A NEW ORLEANS-BORN Southern boy without the Southern accent, currently residing somewhere in Seattle. He spends his days as a suit-and-tie corporate consultant and business writer,  and his nights writing contemporary romance and erotica that flirts with the edge of taboo—when he's not being tackled by two hyperactive cats.

He also writes genre-bending science fiction and fantasy tinged with a touch of horror and flavored by the influences of his multiethnic, multicultural, multilingual background as Xen. He wavers between calling himself bisexual, calling himself queer, and trying to figure out where "demi" fits into the whole mess—but no matter what word he uses he's a staunch advocate of LGBTQIA and POC representation and visibility in genre fiction. And while he spends more time than is healthy hiding in his writing cave instead of hanging around social media, you can generally find him in these usual haunts:

- Email: blackmagic@blackmagicblues.com
- Twitter: @thisblackmagic

- Facebook: https://www.facebook.com/xen.cole
- Tumblr: thisblackmagic.tumblr.com
- Instagram: www.instagram.com/thisblackmagic
- Bookbub:
  https://www.bookbub.com/profile/cole-mccade
- Facebook Fan Page:
  http://www.facebook.com/ColeMcCadeBooks
- Website & Blog: http://www.blackmagicblues.com

[FIND MORE CONTEMPORARY ROMANCE & EROTICA AS COLE MCCADE]

http://blackmagicblues.com/books-by-xen-x-cole-mccade/

[DISCOVER SCIENCE FICTION, FANTASY & HORROR AS XEN]

http://blackmagicblues.com/books-by-xen-x-cole-mccade/

Manufactured by Amazon.ca
Bolton, ON